Plain Jane
A Punxsutawney Amish Novel

Karen Anna Vogel

Lamb Books

ISBN-13: 978-0692734360

ISBN-10: 0692734368

Plain Jane: A Punxsutawney Amish Novel
Bronte Inspired Tale

Contact the author on Face book at:
www.facebook.com/VogelReaders
Learn more the author at: www.karenannavogel.com
Visit her blog, Amish Crossings, at
www.karenannavogel.blogspot.com

Karen Anna Vogel Booklist

Smicksburg Tales Series
Amish Knitting Circle: Smicksburg Tales 1
Amish Knitting Circle: Smicksburg Tales 2
Amish Knit Lit Circle: Smicksburg Tales 3
Amish Knit & Stitch Circle: Smicksburg Tales 4
Amish Knit & Crochet Circle: Smicksburg Tales 5

Amish Herb Shop Series
The Herbalist's Daughter Book 1
The Herbalist's Daughter Book 2
The Herbalist's Daughter Book 3
The Herbalist's Daughter Trilogy

Standalone Novels
Knit Together: Amish Knitting Novel
The Amish Doll: Amish Knitting Novel
Amish Knitting Circle Christmas: Granny & Jeb's Love Story
Amish Pen Pals: Rachael's Confession
Christmas Union: Quaker Abolitionist of Chester County, PA
Love Came Down at Christmas: A Fancy Amish Smicksburg Tale
Nonfiction
A Simple Christmas, the Amish Way
31 Days to a Simple Life, the Amish Way

Dedication
To Charlotte Bronte and all those who keep her books
alive, especially Jane Eyre,
whose independent, sweet spirit inspired this book.

Introduction

Dear Readers,

My friend Donna told me she read Jane Eyre every year because it gave her hope and was so inspirational. It was a devotional of sorts to her. My reaction was, "Seriously? It's so gloomy." Well, I'd watched so many movie versions, but not the book; I took Donna's challenge, that it wasn't a Gothic creepy novel and from page one it was honey for the heart and soul

We first meet lonely, neglected ten-year-old Jane in a window box reading, but also hiding from her cruel cousins and aunt who is reluctantly raising her. Jane's got spunk though and speaks up about being mistreated, and that gets her placed in a boarding school, some might call the House of Horrors. But she quickly learns to "Look to God", make the best of it and eventually becomes a teacher, being part of reforming the school to make it a friendly learning environment.

But she wants more. Her independent spirit urges her to move out of her comfort zone and take a position as a governess at Thornfield Hall, where she meets an arrogant, worldly man, Mr. Rochester. Her gentle spirit pulls out hardship from his heart. He taunts her that he's not a Christian believer, like her. But after seeing Jane's goodness despite hardship, he says "Of late, Jane — only — only of late — I began to see and acknowledge the hand of God in my room. I began to experience remorse, repentance; the wish for reconcilement to my Maker. I began sometimes to pray"

After this Jane marries him, she helps him through his temporary physical blindness and helps him grown out of his spiritual blindness until he is able to agree with her to "Look to God", called Christ his redeemer.

Back to Jane's independent spirit. I wrote this novel for the Amish of Punxsutawney, some being lured away by television shows eager to exploit them. Young people naturally want independence, and the Amish provide for that need by allowing a running around time, called *rumspringa*. If you're a young Amish person reading this book, I hope you'll ponder one of your proverbs.

"If the grass looks greener on the other side, fertilize."

The Seneca Nation of Indians own 48 square miles of land near Cherry Creek, New York, where the story takes us. I hope all readers realize there is hardship everywhere, cultures that have boundaries and rules. Jane Schmucker learns this lesson on her quest for independence.

I hope you enjoy this book as much as I did writing it.

Blessings,

Karen Anna Vogel

You can contact me at

http://www.karenannavogel.com/contact.

Table of Contents

Amish-English Dictionary

How Pennsylvania Dutch overflows into Western Pennsylvanian slang.

"To be" or not to be, that is the question. Folks in Western PA, along with local Amish do not use "to be". It's not "The car needs *to be* washed." We simply say, "The car needs washed." This is only one example. This book is full of similar "grammar errors" but tries to be authentic to how people talk in our "neck of the woods."

Ach – oh

Boppli – baby

Bruder - brother

Daed - dad

Danki – thank you

Dawdyhaus – grandparent's house

Dochder -daughter

Eck table – a table set in a corner for the bride and groom

Gelassenheit. Humility and putting one's own desires aside for the good of the People.

Gmay – community or church

Grossdaddi - grandfather

Grossmammi - grandmother

Gut – good

Jah - yes

Kapp- cap; Amish women's head covering

Kinner – children

Mamm – mom

Nee- no

Okey dokey – Pittsburgese for okay, common in Western Pennsylvania

Ordnung - A set of rules for Amish, Old Order Mennonite and Conservative Mennonite living. Ordnung is the German word for order, discipline, rule, arrangement, organization, or system.

Rumspringa – running around years, starting at sixteen, when Amish youth experience the outsiders' way of life before joining the church.

Redd up – clean up

Wunderbar – wonderful

Yinz – You all or you two, slang found in Western Pennsylvania among the Amish and those who speak Pittsburghese.

Prologue

Dear Diary,

I'm only fourteen, but want to die. How could God take my family and leave me alone? Alone! And having to live here with mean old Uncle Malachi and grouchy Aunt Miriam? I've done more chores these past two months here than my whole life combined. And I don't get a break! I ran off to see Emma, who lives next door. We became fast friends like my best friend, Leah, but I don't see Leah anymore, since she lives twenty miles away, in a different church district. I used to run over the meadow to Leah's, so we could jump rope. I could jump faster than anyone down in Plum Creek. But I don't live in Plum Creek anymore.

Anyhow, I ran over to Emma's and came in late for dinner. That was enough to send Uncle Malachi into a rage. I cried in my little bedroom, but Clara came in. Sweet Clara, only ten, tries to help me stay out of trouble, but my uncle seems to hate me and find fault with everything I do. Deep down, when he yells, it's as if he's yelling at my parents, who I've learned not to talk about or else. Last time I did, Uncle shook me by the arms and left me bruised on the inside and out. Why does he get so mad when I talk about my parents? And why didn't he cry at their funeral?

My only other friend is Luke Miller. He's my age and very handsome (his brown eyes make me crave chocolate). I told him about my uncle's temper. His daed, Moses, who's a church elder, came over to talk to my uncle. That night Uncle Malachi beat me with a belt buckle and warned me never to talk to Luke ever again. Called me a flirt, too. But I like Luke and we talked at school, but then last week I was told I had enough learning and I'd be homeschooled until I got my diploma. But I do chores and there's not

1

a lick of learning going on here. Only at night, when I help Clara with grammar and drill the twins, Jeremiah and Jacob, on their multiplication. And then I have to rock little Sarah until she falls asleep. She's Uncle Malachi's little baby doll, who can do no wrong.

And after all this, tonight Uncle Malachi told me I was a lazy girl. He took all my books saved from the house fire and threw them into the woodstove. Clara cried. Jeremiah and Jacob tried to stop him, but got sent to bed with no dinner.

Uncle Malachi just came in and threw my Bible on my bed. Said he didn't burn it because I needed it to cleanse my soul. He didn't burn it most likely because he didn't want to go to hell. Now, I can only read my Bible. A book about a God who forgot about me, a speck on this spinning planet!

Six Years Later

"I desired more...than was within my reach. Who blames me? Many call me discontented. I couldn't help it: the restlessness is in my nature; it agitated me to pain sometimes."

Charlotte Bronte's *Jane Eyre*

Karen Anna Vogel

Chapter 1
Being Plain

Hanging the eleventh pair of trousers on the clothesline, Jane rubbed the crick in her neck. Being small framed and short, this chore was done on tip-toes, making it all the more demanding. At twenty, she only wished that she had some of the chores other young women had; caring for her own house and husband.

Jane's shoulders sunk under the constant weight of oppression that enveloped the isolated farm. How she'd stare at times, gazing at the magenta sunset or the morning mist, wishing she was in a distant land. A place free to fly like a sparrow, not a care in the world. She glanced over at the massive maple tree where the tire swing hung. Leaves tinged with shades of yellows and reds made her yearn for the same...*change.*

"Hurry up, Jane," her Aunt Miriam called from the barn. "Stop that daydreaming and do your chores."

She swiftly attached wooden clothes pins to several towels.

"Jane, help me with my math," eight-year-old Sarah demanded. "*Daed* said you have to."

Jane spun around and quickly nodded, picked up an empty wicker laundry basket, and followed her cousin as if she were a string along toy. Uncle Malachi had made it clear that she was the one responsible for all his *kinner's* grades. If they failed, it was Jane's lack of care.

Uncle Malachi was stormy without any sign of light on the horizon. His jet black eyes pierced her as she neared the towering white farmhouse. "Girl, how many times do I have to make myself clear? Don't wander off when the *kinner* are doing their learning."

Holding up the empty basket, she attempted to speak, but nothing came out. Her throat tightened, as usual, when around this man.

"Jane, answer me!" he shouted, hand raised to strike.

"I. The laundry."

"I. The laundry? Have you ever spoken in whole sentences? No wonder you're an old maid." He gripped her chin. "You can speak, can't you?"

Yes, she could speak. She *should* speak. *She should speak to the bishop about his behavior!* Jane wanted to scream, but didn't dare. That would mean double the chores and a strike on her face that she'd have to hide for weeks. "Aunt told me to hang laundry."

"Funny how you can talk when threatened. 'Spare the rod, spoil the child'. You're already spoiled, getting to stay here for free. At your age, you should be paying."

Child? She was a grown woman. Somehow Uncle Malachi seemed to be yelling back in time, decades ago when she was a *kinner* and not only at her. But Jane knew that money was tight feeding a large family and keeping up this big white farmhouse, quite impressive from the road, tourists stopping to take pictures. Jane was a financial burden and had offered to get a job. How she'd love to be away for a few hours a day, but was forbidden to take the carriage out. Even sixteen-year-old Clara could drive it, but not her.

Uncle Malachi pushed her face away with his hand as if disgusted to touch her. "Now go help Sarah with her schooling, and right quick." He stomped his foot as if to shoo a cat.

Jane mounted the stairway and met Sarah at the top. They made their way into the bedroom, and Sarah hugged her tight. "I didn't mean to get you in trouble. Why does *Daed* get angry with you?"

"I must upset him," was the lame response she gave the girl who was too young to understand. Not old enough to understand her *daed's* rants about Jane's parents dying in a house fire. 'The judgment of God for their sin and why he had to be 'harder on Jane, showing her the right path'. Baptism into the Amish church at sixteen, forced by her uncle to lie to the bishop about her doubts. No, she couldn't speak of doubts. Doubts were from the devil and she'd die in hell if she confessed them aloud.

Sarah released her and taking Jane's hand, led her to the pile of books on her bed. "I hate math. I'd rather be reading."

Jane picked up a clothbound green book with a quaint farm scene. *Rebecca of Sunnybrook Farm*. "What a pleasant name. *Sunnybrook*."

"I wonder why *Mamm* and *Daed* never named this farm," Sarah said, flipping her dark braids behind her.

"You can name it," Jane encouraged.

Sarah rested her chin on the eraser of her pencil. "Well, I'm happy here and we have lots of nice big windows, making it sunny. How about Sun Valley Farm?"

Jane stared hard at the patchwork quilt as sorrow flooded her soul. She'd lived on a happy Amish farm only twenty miles away, when she was Sarah's age. She'd been her *mamm's* treasure in the kitchen, and her *daed's* shadow in the farmyard where she'd tend the chickens and goats. Jane was never to speak of it though.

Sarah tugged at Jane's three-quarter length sleeve. "Why do you do that?"

"Do what?" Jane asked, astonished.

"Stare before you answer a question."

Jane rapidly blinked her eyes, trying to explain how she escaped often into her own mind to endure this most unhappy farm. "I was just thinking."

"About what?"

"About how we need to get your math done and not talk about books anymore," Jane sighed.

"Don't you like to read?"

Jane wasn't allowed to read anything but her Bible. She knew other Amish girls and women could choose from a wide variety of books, but she was forbidden. "I read my Bible."

"Do you have other books?" Sarah pressed.

"*Nee*, and I don't need any. The Bible is all I need. It instructs us for all things we need that are right and good." Over the years, Jane believed this to be true, and treasured her Bible as her means of comfort. When she read of Leah not being loved by Jacob, because she was plain, she had a friend in Leah. Her uncle called her Plain Jane in a mocking tone, saying under his breath, "Just like your *mamm*."

~*~

After dinner that night and all the chores were done, Jane sat with a lone candle, reading her Bible. The doorknob turned and she froze. What had she done? Soon she could make out Clara coming in as she held a brightly glowing oil lamp. "Jane, can we talk?"

"What is it, Clara?"

She glided across the room as if floating, her long white cotton night dress fluttering. Laying the lamp on the table near Jane's bed, she sat on the end near Jane's feet. "Do you know why *mamm's* crying?"

"Aunt is crying? Really?"

Clara hugged her knees. "I've never seen her cry before. But it started this morning after *Daed* lost his temper with you."

Jane didn't dare hope that her aunt's heart could be softening towards her, but was it? Could it be?

"*Mamm* and *Daed* argued in the barn. They thought no one was there, but I was there with Sarah. *Mamm* accused *Daed* of taking his anger out on you because..."

"Because of what?"

"You look like your *mamm*."

Jane was baffled. So what if she had the same blonde hair and blue eyes like her *mamm*? Many Amish women, being German, had the same features. "I'm sure husbands and wives quarrel at times, Clara," Jane managed to say.

"It scared me how loud *Mamm* got. And she got dizzy and *Daed* had to help her sit down. I know Old Joe got dizzy before his heart attack and died. Do you think *mamm's* alright?"

"She's not old yet," Jane said softly.

"Yes she is. She's fifty. That's old."

"Not like Old Joe. He was eighty."

"I guess you're right." Clara relaxed her legs a bit. "Jane, why do you have such a small room? I' asked *Mamm* when you first came, so excited to have an older girl cousin living right here in the house. But she said no." Clara fidgeted with her prayer *kapp* strings. "Gets lonely sometimes."

Jane tapped her Bible. "I'm never alone. But sometimes it would be nice to go visit Emma all by myself."

"You're best friends, *jah*?"

"*Jah.* But I can only see her at *Gmay*, every other Sunday or at a work frolic when I go with your *mamm*." She didn't dare say more. Her aunt never let her leave her side. Aunt Miriam watched to 'make sure she didn't commit any of the sins passed on from her parents'. But Emma made up a secret signal to get away for short talks and her aunt never caught on.

"Emma lives one farm over. Why don't you just go over and visit?" Clara seemed hard pressed for an answer. "Aren't you allowed to have friends? Are you supposed to always pay for your parent's sins?"

Jane felt her cheeks grow warm. *Shame.* It was her enemy. It claimed her and she didn't know why.

"Jane, I have to confess that I heard a lot more in the barn today. I can't tell you, but I'm afraid for you. You need to make friends, who can help you."

"Help me? Help me what?"

"I can't say," Clara blurted, her chin quivering.

The room was warm, being unusually muggy for a September night, yet Clara was shivering. What on earth was she talking about? What couldn't Clara say?

"I'm taking you in the buggy over to Emma's tomorrow, understand? I'll tell *Daed* that I need you to go with me to town to carry bags. I really do need to go to town, so it's not a lie. *Mamm*'s list is a mile long. But we'll stop by Emma's on the way home to make a plan."

"A plan for what?"

Clara leapt forward and latched onto Jane. "I'll tell you tomorrow. Just promise me you'll go with me to town."

"I promise."

~*~

Jane couldn't sleep that night and did what she always did to calm herself. Write in her secret journal, hidden under a loose board on the floor, she wrote out all her feelings locked deep.

Slipping out of bed, she tip-toed over to the board, flipped it up, and retrieved the cheap essay tablet used in Amish schools. Nothing fancy, but it was a treasure. Jane took up her pen and sat under the window, the glow of a full moon having to be enough light. If she lit a candle, her aunt and uncle may see the glow under the door and barge in. They always just barged in, no privacy was given to this little room.

Dear Diary,

I can't sleep. Clara tells me that I resemble my mom and memories of her keep invading my mind, along with fear. Why is Uncle Malachi upset that I look like my mom? My mom was beautiful. She'd brush my hair one hundred times every night, tuck me in after prayers, and give me a telling. Such good stories she came up with.

I don't know why people won't talk about my parents. Had Uncle Malachi told a falsehood about his brother, tainting his name? My parents were good people and loved the Bible, but Malachi reads it at night during family so-called worship with harshness. A log has more love in it than Uncle Malachi. Aunt Mariah has shown some kindness over the years, but only when her husband is absent.

The pen slipped from Jane's fingers as sleep overtook her and she lay on the cool hardwood floor and dozed off.

~*~

The bang on her head woke Jane up. "Ouch."

Soon Uncle Malachi's face, with morning breath wafting out, was up against hers. She lay on the floor, feeling paralyzed. "What is this?"

He jutted the diary up against her face, so she only saw darkness.

"Answer me!"

She turned, trying to get up, but he pushed her down hard. "You write about me in here? How much you hate me?" He threw the diary up against the wall, making a dent in the plaster. "Rubbish is what you write, spiteful girl! You ingrate. Have you ever paid one red cent for your keep? N-O. Do I or your aunt get any thanks? N-O." He yanked at her arm, pulling her up.

Jane wailed at the pain in her arm but the slap on her face sent her flying up against the window. Her hand bashed through it, the glass stabbing her hand. *He hated her.*

"Look what you've done? Smashed the window!" He gripped her shoulders and pulled her face close. "You'll pay for it."

As blood dripped to the floor, Jane's knees buckled and Uncle Malachi let her fall. "Clean up this mess and get downstairs and help your aunt, you lazy thing."

Jane closed her eyes, as each step he made out of her room seemed forever. When the door slammed and his loud descent down the stairs was heard, she let the sobs out. "Lord, help me", she said over and over, a simple prayer from her heart mingled with hope that she would be rescued.

~*~

"Why does Jane have to go with you?" Aunt Mariam asked, hands on her amble hips.

"*Mamm*, your list is mighty long. I can't carry all the bags."

"Take one of your *bruder* with you, Clara. Jane fell and hurt her hand. She can't go."

Clara glanced over at Jane's bandaged up hand. "Can you still lift bags, Jane?"

"*Jah*, I can."

"I can do it," fourteen-year-old Jeremiah offered.

"I want to go to town," his twin, Jacob, said.

Clara glared at the twins and slightly shook her head.

"*Ach*, let Jane go," Uncle Malachi barked as he stabbed his pancake. "Nobody wants her here."

All eyes landed on Uncle Malachi, and then fearful looks to each other. His wife was busier than usual hovering

13

over her stove.

Jeremiah shifted. "Jane, I'm glad you're here."

"Me, too," Jacob said.

When Sarah started to speak, Uncle Malachi pounded the table with his fist, making the dishes clatter. "Hush now. I'm the head of this house and what I say goes."

"Jane, let's get going and quick," Clara said in a demanding tone. "Quit dawdling."

Jane pursed her lips. She was not a dog to be given such commands, but she followed Clara out the side door and to the horse stalls in the back.

Clara turned to her. "I didn't mean to be bossy, but I want to leave." When Jane got into the buggy and Clara led the horse to the driveway, she sighed. "Why's your window broken?"

Jane couldn't tell her the truth. "I'm clumsy."

Clara slid into the buggy, snapped the reigns and they were off. Jane looked at the farmhouse from the road. *A whitewashed tomb*, she thought. Lately, Jane really did think her uncle capable of seriously injuring her, his anger had no boundaries. And his anger said over and over, *I hate you.*

The rural country road was riddled with fallen acorns and pinecones. Jane couldn't appreciate the delights of autumn today as she tried to steady her throbbing hand as the buggy bumped along.

"Jane, I'll miss you. Truly I will."

This startled Jane. "I'm not leaving. What are you talking about?"

"You have to believe me. I've never lied to you and

neither has Emma."

"*Nee.*" Jane gulped, her throat hurting from her morning cry.

"I said I heard more than I told you last night. Now I'm free, but you have to promise you'll never tell my *daed* it was me who told you."

"I promise. Clara, what is it?" Jane asked, fear gripping her. "It can't be that bad. My *mamm* always told me this as a child."

Clara slowed the horse. "*Daed's* going nuts. I've never seen the twins talk back like they just did." She raised a hand. "I'm shaking. *Ach,* Jane, the older you get, the more you look like your *mamm.* I know what the quarrel was between our folks. *Daed* loved your *mamm* and she rejected him."

"What?"

"Everyone knows about it and still talks. Now that you've grown into a woman and look as beautiful as your *mamm,* they think my *daed* is going batty in the head."

Jane put her bandaged hand up. "Clara, this is really true? Uncle Malachi loved my *mamm*? And she rejected him because she loved my *daed?*"

"*Jah.* Both *bruder* loved her and *Mamm* knows it. She said in the barn, she can remember the fight they had."

"But Amish are pacifist."

"*Daed's* temper was hot back then, too. He held a hammer up to your *daed's* face and threatened to kill him. *Mamm* saw it all. She was the one who screamed and it made my *daed* stop." Clara's eyes misted. "My *daed's* a *gut* man when he's not mad. I think it's his nerves. Never had *gut* ones. But Jane, you have to leave."

Jane had wanted to leave, but not like this. Out of fear?

"My *daed's* been acting funny in the head. He's called *Mamm* 'Abigail', your *mamm's* name, *jah*?"

"She went by Abby, but *jah.*"

"*Mamm* said he could have a breakdown and be hospitalized. Talking foolishness."

"Like what?"

"Making you marry Luke Miller to get you out of the house."

Luke Miller...a rare friend. "He never asked."

"This is what I heard in the barn," Clara continued. "Luke's never courted a girl but wants a family. My *daed* said you'd marry Luke. Said he'd pressure you into it. If you resisted, he'd take out the belt."

Indignation ran through Jane like a train, whistle blowing and all. Make her? Never. "He can beat me to a pulp, but I won't marry someone who doesn't love me. I won't be like Leah in the Bible. No, I want someone like Boaz."

Clara's face grew red. "Me, too. A man like Boaz who's kind and protective of Ruth. I love that Bible story." She glanced over at Jane. "You'll need to leave like Ruth and go into a foreign country."

"Foreign?"

"I don't mean literally. Emma has friends in New York. I ran to her place after hearing *Mamm* and *Daed's* fight. She has a plan. That's why we're going to her place after shopping."

Excitement and fear ran through Jane's veins. Could she

get away? But was her uncle really losing control? Was she in real danger? She'd have to verify many things with Emma, especially if it was right to run away. Her aunt and uncle had given her a home. She should be thankful they took her in. Was she wicked to think of leaving and never even caring if she saw their faces again?

She took in a deep breath. Emma could help her.

Karen Anna Vogel

Chapter 2
Luke Miller

*J*ane tried to hide her bandaged hand under the sweater she carried. Yoder's Surplus Store sold everything from food to specialty pet food. Run by the Amish who used solar lighting, Jane always found it a treat to come with her aunt. But today she was walking the aisles alone and she felt grown up

She walked up the ramp that led to the antiques. Her eye was immediately drawn to the paintings that lined the walls. She sketched in her room, but threw what she'd made in the woodstove when finished. No one knew except Emma.

A picture of two Amish children running behind a dog made her gasp. The young boy was what she remembered her *bruder* looking like. Bowl cut, lanky and always running free in the fields with his dogs. Sammy, he was too good to die young. How her *mamm* wailed at the news of the farm accident, but Jane barely remembered the funeral, being in shock. Sammy was two years younger and they did everything together. The next year, the fire took her parents and she was sent away.

Jane had been a hollow tree since that day. The wind could blow her over and break her. Her aunt and uncle could boss her and she obeyed. She was like a dog. Go fetch this and that, Jane, was all she heard and quickly obeyed. And she was isolated. Being on a farm out of the sight of neighbors made it easy for no one to step in.

"Like the picture?"

Jane heard Luke Miller's voice. Luke had welcomed her to Punxsutawney, being the same age, and he reminded Jane of her deceased brother. She repeatedly ran off with him to skip rocks across a pond or go creek walking on a hot day. But the price she paid at home became more and more severe, until she decided to only see Luke in groups.

"Jane, what's the matter?"

Knowing the kind voice of Luke Miller, she couldn't turn to face him. She didn't want to leave a hint with anyone that she may be leaving and Luke had a way of pulling things out of people. She continued to pretend she was interested in the painting. "Nothing's wrong."

Luke stood beside her. "Jane, are you alright?"

Trying to discourage a conversation, she simply said, "The boy looks like my *bruder*."

"Still miss him?"

"My parents, too, even though it's been six years."

Luke softly touched her bandaged hand. "Are you hurt?"

Jane usually felt shame for the many 'accidents' but today, she was feeling bolder. It wasn't all in her imagination. She was tired of saying she was clumsy in the kitchen or make up some story to cover her uncle's violent behavior. But if she told him the truth, her uncle may find out and get worse. But she *was* leaving. "My uncle hit me and I fell into the window." She jutted her chin out. There, she'd said it. Maybe she did want the whole town to know.

Luke's brown eyes darkened and his face screwed up.

"So the Amish grapevine's right! He's abusive?"

What? Did the whole community know he was a wicked man?

"What do you think of my uncle?"

Luke placed a hand on her shoulder. "I pity you. Always have wanted to help. My *daed*, too. But we needed proof."

Jane mechanically walked to a nearby chair and sat. "Proof of abuse?"

Luke squatted on the floor, looking up at her. "My *daed* being an elder, I overhear things. The bishop talks to your uncle about his temper but he weasels his way out a kneeling confession. It's like they feel sorry for him, but they didn't know he's physically abusive." He took off his straw hat and fidgeted with the rim. "Jane, has he hit you before?"

"Jah. I've learned it's better to keep my mouth shut or he'll take it out on one of my cousins."

Luke's chin quivered as his eyes filled with tears. "No more," he murmured. "Can we talk more on a buggy ride?

Jane saw Clara nearing them, eyes wide. "*Jah.* I'd like that. *Danki* Luke. You've helped me."

"When?"

"When what?"

He leaned near her and mumbled. "Go riding."

"Tonight," Jane found herself saying, really needing more time to tell Luke more. Why she just opened up like a spring flower around him was a mystery, or maybe it was because she knew deep down she'd be leaving.

He winked and then his face flushed up to his ears. "Midnight?"

"*Jah.*"

Clara was tapping her foot, making her presence known.

"Hi Clara," Luke said. "Buying up the whole store?"

"*Mamm* needs lots of stuff. Hasn't been to Yoder's Mall in two weeks."

"Can I help carry bags out to your buggy?"

"Sure," Clara said, looking over at Jane with a glare.

~*~

Emma led Jane and Clara into her bedroom. "Charlie? Billy? Are you up here?" she yelled down the hall. When no one answered, she shut the door. "Okay, we can talk in private. *Ach,* Jane, I'm so worried about you. I'm afraid your uncle will kill you someday."

"My *daed* wouldn't do that," Clara sputtered.

Emma, a tall slender woman the same age as Jane, didn't beat around the bush. She pointed to Jane's hand. "I suppose that was an accident?"

"Jane tripped," Clara informed.

Emma towered over Jane, her features softened. Dark green eyes and black hair peeking through her prayer *kapp*. She was the image of kindness to Jane. "Clara, leave us alone for a minute. I want to talk private-like," Emma said.

Clara nodded and stepped out of the room and Jane whispered, "My uncle pushed me."

Emma embraced Jane, kissing the top of her head. "We're getting you out of here."

"I talked to Luke Miller. He said the whole community knows my uncle's a mean man? Is that true?"

Emma nodded. "Clara woke up to it all yesterday, poor

child." She stepped away and opened the door. "Come on in, Clara."

Clara looked pale and fear was etched in her eyes. "Did my *daed* do that? I want to know."

Jane slowly closed her eyes and nodded. "I had to break my fall after he hit me." Jane took off her prayer *kapp* to reveal the goose egg bump on her head. "These *kapps* come in handy," she said, forcing a faint smile.

"My friends tell me all kinds of stories about my *daed*," Clara blurted. "So they're true? My *daed*'s an abusive man?"

"*Jah*," Emma nodded.

Jane could barely take all this in. She felt alone in her opinion of her uncle, thinking he was considered the perfect man in the community. What Luke said was true.

Emma ran to Clara as tears fell from her cheeks. "Your *daed* needs help. What you told me yesterday, you had every right to reveal. It's not you who said it?"

"Said what?" Jane asked, her hands growing cold.

"Tell her, Clara."

Clara clammed up and started to shake, leaning into Emma for support.

Emma looked down pensively. "He wanted you as dead as your parents, but he doesn't really mean it."

Something akin to being punched in the stomach pounded into Jane. She'd seen it in his eyes and feared it. Rage like Cain and Abel in the garden. Rage that killed a brother. She was a niece. "He does. I see it. He wants me dead." Jane needed to sit down, fatigue washing over her in waves. "What do I do?"

"I have a plan, but it can't leave this room. I need you both to take an oath that you won't tell anyone about this."

"I promise," Clara said.

"*Jah*, I promise," Jane whispered.

"You can run away to New York. My pen pal lives there and I told her all about you. Rose wants you to come stay with her. Something about needing a new school teacher, or was it a shopkeeper... Can't remember, but she seems lonely and you'd be doing her a favor."

Jane put her head in her hands. "Run away? Live where I don't know a soul and not tell my aunt and uncle? They took me in when I could be homeless."

"That's rubbish," Emma spurted. "They took you in to do chores. Clara was ten when you got there, remember? You had to be a grown up at fourteen, Jane. Fourteen, the age Jeremiah and Jacob are." Emma glowered. "That's being like a slave. And they didn't let you go to school?"

"They taught me at home...kind of. Well, I read and write *gut*. And I can do all the math."

"Because you learned with Clara, right? Isn't that true, Clara? Your *mamm* tutored Jane along with you when doing homework."

Clara's eyes never looked so ashamed. "As far back as I can remember, you were always with me during homework time, but *Mamm* was never there. You must have taught yourself, *jah*?"

Jane wanted to run. This was too much to bear at once. Had they only taken her in to do chores? How could they?

Jane mindlessly picked up the book next to her. *Jane Eyre.* The woman on the front looked sad. Or was she an overcomer? Needing to escape, she blurted, "Can I borrow this?"

Emma gasped. "Jane, you don't believe a word we say?"

"*Jah,* I do. But it's like swallowing a mountain of sorrow. I can't."

"But you can't just stay here. Go to New York and take this job. We won't tell anyone where you are. You'll be safe, Jane. Please."

It was all too surreal. "I can't," Jane said nonchalantly. "I'm going on a buggy ride."

"What?" Clara blurted. "You found your Boaz and didn't say?"

"I didn't find a Boaz and it's only one buggy ride…tonight. I need fresh air and peace."

"With who?" Emma asked.

"Luke Miller."

Emma clenched her fist. "Your uncle is going to make you marry him. What do you think of that?"

"Clara told me. I say I won't marry anyone who doesn't love me. Luke offered to take me for a ride tonight and I'm going."

Clara ran to Jane and cupped her cheeks. "Jane, my *daed* will find out you're gone. He may hurt you again."

Jane knew what she was doing was risky, but telling Luke about her personal hell had helped so much, she felt like a little bird that escaped from a cage. She was flying high. Maybe a little too high to think right, but she knew the truth. Her uncle was known for his brutality. *The truth will set you free*, she thought. How true that Bible verse was.

~*~

Luke Miller stabbed the hay with a pitchfork and heaved it into the cow's manger. The image of Malachi abusing Jane had made him ill. Ill and filled with rage. The way he dealt with it all was how he'd learned to deal with all his emotions; have an honest talk with God like David did in Psalms. David was a man after God's own heart, so his honesty was appreciated by God.

To think that Jane had been locked away so much from the community that she didn't know of her uncle's reputation? Nor her aunt's? Jane deserved better. *Lead, her, Lord. Help her and protect her. And give me words to tell my daed once I've calmed down my mind. Lord, I've had my eye on Jane since I was old enough to like girls. I think it was fourteen. We played after church and got to talking under the old hickory nut tree in my backyard. When it got struck by lightning that night, Jane said it was a sign that she wasn't supposed to be talking with boys. And she's avoided any attempt at talking until I plumb gave up. But no girl in the area's caught my eye like Jane. I know how unloved she is, yet she possesses inner serenity. I have a large family, love and stability are constants, but I lack confidence. No, I'm not as strong as Jane.*

He thanked God for his parents. They never compared their *kinner*, but said "Bring up a child in the way he should go and when he's old, he won't depart." They'd said that meant their natural bend, their temperament and disposition. His was more sensitive, so they encouraged him to be an animal rescuer. He couldn't enlist and fight in the military to battle injustice in the world and be

Amish. He'd almost left because of it. But he could help God's creatures. Some of the People said he had a way with horses to calm them and they'd slip him a few bucks to come over and spend time with their horses.

It was common sense to Luke. Time and love tamed an animal. It healed wounds.

Was he attached to Jane, because he saw wounds? Well, something had made all girls not match-up. Jane was a ruby, the kind of girl that could make him happy. There was something about Jane so beautiful, how she cared for her cousins and walked with her head held high.

Well, he'd put off long enough telling his *daed* about Jane's cut up hand. Justice demanded that she be rescued, like critters dropped off at his place. She needed a safe place to mend. But where could it be?

~*~

Jane couldn't look anyone in the eye at the supper table. Her emotions were volatile right now and she knew if her uncle said anything unkind, she'd explode and spew out all she'd been told about him today. What a hypocrite he was to his family.

"Aunt Miriam, I don't feel too *gut*. Can I go lay down?" she asked without faltering.

"Dishes need washed," her uncle snapped and he poked his pot roast with his fork.

"But her hand's all bandaged up. She can't," Clara blurted. "I'll do the dishes for her."

Uncle Malachi glared at his *kinner* and then wife. "What's this about?"

"N-Nothing that I know of," Miriam stuttered.

"Clara, you got plenty to do besides helping a girl who shrugs her duties."

Jane and Clara shot up at the same time. "Jane and I are exchanging chores until her hand heals, *Daed*. It's all decided." Clara gave a defiant look at her *daed*.

"Clara, what's come over you?" Aunt Miriam chastened. "You don't use that tone with your *daed*."

"*Ach,* just leave. Both of you. I want peace at my table," Uncle Malachi growled.

Jane shot a thankful look at dear Clara.

Clara motioned for Jane to follow her up the stairs, and Jane took the cue. When upstairs, they went into Clara's room. Jane always fought envy here. This room had the best of everything. Furniture, a soft mattress, and a hope chest, something Jane didn't have. Clara's was filled with China plates, linens, flatware, crocheted doilies, pots and pans. Jane had nothing to bring to a marriage, and the familiar demon of shame taunted her.

"Jane, don't go out with Luke tonight. I'm afraid that *Daed* is on to something."

Jane wanted to talk to Luke again. She'd forgotten how they talked a bit when she was younger.

~*~

Jane lit the loan candle in her room that night, daring to open *Jane Eyre*. Was it wrong to disobey her aunt and uncle and read something besides the Bible? Memories of her *mamm* reading in her rocker near the woodstove bombarded her mind. She read the *Little House on the Prairie* series out to the family, her *daed* joking that he could never match up to Mr. Ingalls. Her *daed* was such a kind, mild-mannered man. How could her Uncle Malachi threaten his own *bruder* with a hammer?

She bowed her head in silent prayer, waiting for her nerves to be soothed. Opening the book, she read about a little girl in a window box, reading a book. Jane Eyre was a young girl and hiding from her older cousin who beat her regularly.

Jane couldn't believe this. How many times had she hid when first coming to this house, only to be found by Uncle Malachi, and a lashing always followed?

Jane read on to see that Jane Eyre's aunt, who she was living with, blamed Jane for everything, thinking her children innocent and above Jane Eyre.

Jane had known this all too well.

But then Jane Eyre loses control. She defends herself, telling her aunt she's a cruel woman, and wishes she could leave. She may be poor, but she'd be free.

This thought started to vibrate in Jane's heart ever since she turned eighteen. Why did she stay? But where could she go?

Jane gripped the book when she heard the bishop and elders downstairs, talking loudly to her uncle. The back door was slammed shut and soon the men where outside, right under Jane's window. Her name was mentioned, she thought, but the wind muffled sounds.

Jane went to her window and cracked it open. She heard Luke Miller. He was accusing her *daed* of abuse. "She'll come live with us," Luke demanded.

His father gave a hearty "Amen" and "I'll not have that lamb living under the same roof as a wolf."

Jane felt oddly calm. She could live with the Miller family? She and Luke could be like brother and sister?

The voice of her uncle violently accusing Luke of luring his niece away to take her from him.

Line after line of insult to Luke made him speak up. "*Jah*, I care about Jane. Who wouldn't? She's the best girl I know."

A growl and then the sound of scuffling made Jane rise to see what was going on. The bishop and elders were holding her uncle back from attacking Luke. Her uncle was acting like an animal. He shouted out, "You accuse me? I took in Abigail and she cost me a fortune to raise." He collapsed and pawed at the ground like a dog.

Abigail? Her mother's name. Her uncle was becoming delusional.

Soon her aunt was outside, shooing the men away from him. She wagged her finger to shame them.

"We're taking Jane to our house," Luke said firmly. "You've been as cruel to Jane as your husband. It stops tonight."

Aunt Miriam chided them all at the top of her lungs, saying Jane was staying.

Luke ran away from the group and Jane's heart sunk. How she wished Luke wasn't a pacifist, going the other direction in a heated argument. But the front door banged open and the pounding of footsteps was heard. What on earth? But soon Luke was yelling, "Jane!"

She ran to her door and opened it. Luke ran to her and Jane found herself clinging to him.

Chapter 3
Jane Eyre

The next morning Jane awoke in a beautiful room with an oil lamp on the nightstand. Oak furniture, a full-sized dresser, and a blue oval rag rug near covered the shiny oak floors. She curled in her toes. It was Luke's house.

But it was daylight. She'd never awoken to daylight. How odd. Not wanting this family to think she was a sluggard, she started to wash up in the provided basin and pitcher. Warm water. What a treat.

Jane let the water run off her fingers. *The Lord shall guide you continually, and satisfy your soul in drought, and strengthen your bones: and you shall be like a watered garden, and like a spring of water, whose waters fail not.*

This scripture she'd memorized long ago, but never thought it could happen. Her soul could be satisfied away from her uncle. She would be strengthened and be a well-watered garden.

As much as the scriptures gave her peace deep down in her soul, she was so naïve about other books and opinions. Well, God would lead her, she was certain. She may have been abused and neglected like Jane Eyre, but she'd read the back of the book and Jane Eyre marries a man who's not perfect, but one her equal, one who she could bring comfort. For the first time she longed for this, not snuffing out any romantic emotion.

Luke rescued me, she thought. How he'd tenderly let her

cry, and then helped her pack up her meager possessions, while the bishop and elders tried to calm her uncle down. And here she was, out of prison. She splashed her face with water and giggled. She tried to stop, having never shown such lack of self-control, but she couldn't. She was set free and what liberty.

~*~

Jane ran down the steps to see that no one was home. She ran to the Grandfather clock to see that it was eleven o'clock. She gasped. *You lazy girl, Jane,* she heard her aunt's voice clamor. She held her hands to her head. "I left you, Aunt Miriam. You can't talk to me like that anymore."

You stupid foolish girl!

Jane's short-lived happiness crumbled. The voices in her head played as if they were actually real. Would she ever escape her aunt and uncle's words?

Jane's eyes misted. Maybe kind words would take the place of cruel ones until they were erased. She must give herself time to adjust.

The back door opened and Ruth Miller came in. Upon seeing Jane, she ran to her and held her tight. "I'm so sorry. You're safe here."

Jane's heart rose to her throat. Her *mamm* embraced her like this. How long it had been since she'd been shown such tenderness. "*Danki,* Ruth."

"It'll take time to adjust being away from that awful uncle of yours." Ruth cupped her mouth. "I'm sorry to speak so unkind."

"*Nee,* it's true," Jane said freely. Jane Eyre had woken

up and said the truth about her aunt, and she would too. Her life had to improve.

Ruth went to the speckleware coffeepot and poured a mug of coffee. "Here. You sit down at my table and I'll get you some pie. I made blackberry for breakfast. Saved a piece for you. Luke can eat his weight in food every day and is still skinny."

When Ruth put her hands on her thin waist as she spoke, it was obvious to Jane where Luke got his tall, lanky frame. "*Danki* for saving me a piece." Jane had never been in the house of another Amish family. She'd snuck over to Emma's plenty of times, but paid for it later. Jane felt like she was in a foreign country.

Ruth placed a quarter piece of pie in front of Jane. "Eat up."

"*Danki*, Ruth."

Ruth sat across from her, tender light green eyes misted like a spring day. "What would you like to do today?"

Jane near dropped her fork. No one had asked her this in years. Blinking rapidly, she shook her head. "I'm sorry. You must think I'm daft, but I've never thought of it before"

"What?"

"What I'd like to do." Jane felt her cheeks burning in embarrassment.

Ruth shook her head and clucked her tongue. "Well, I'm asking. What would you like to do today for fun?"

Jane knew exactly what she'd like to do, but she had no money and that would be awkward.

"Out with it. What do you like to do?"

"I love to sew. I'm *gut* at it."

Ruth slouched. "You mean you had to sew? Sew clothes for your cousins?"

Jane lowered her head in shame. "*Jah*. But I made it into a hobby."

"I knit for charity. It sooths me to feel the yarn wrapped around my fingers and that my efforts will pay off. Plus, a child in a poor country will be warm and not fear frost bite."

"You send them to another country? How?" Jane felt the need to give rise up. By giving to others she would get her mind off her woes. And what better cause then to help children.

"We'll go to Punxsy-Mart and get some yarn and I'll tell you all about it. Maybe get some material for a few new dresses for you."

"I don't have any m-m..."

"Money? *Jah*, you will soon. Your uncle's being made to pay for some essentials he's denied you out of sheer neglect. Moses and the other church leaders are hammering out the details right now. Makes me sick with anger." She cupped her mouth again. "I can't say more. All I know is that we have fifty dollars to spend on yarn and material for new dresses and more is coming."

Jane shot up. "My uncle isn't rich. The kids will all suffer if money's given to me."

"*Ach*, Jane. Your uncle's a malicious man. When he so-called took you in out of love, there was a will. Your family had a thriving farm and it was all left to you, but your uncle's nearly spent it all. Like I said, the bishop and elders are pressing for answers and more money that is rightfully yours is on its way."

Jane dug her fork into the table. "He said the family was poor."

Ruth ran around the table and hugged Jane from behind. "It's alright to be angry. This was a great injustice."

Jane's body started to shake uncontrollably, like she had the chills. She heard Ruth say she was in shock, but she'd slipped into a dreamlike state, seemingly half awake. And then she saw all white. "My head,"

"Does it hurt?"

"I see white."

"A migraine. I used to get them. Let's get you into your room."

~*~

Jane woke with a start as someone pulled up the blind, and she held her head. When she groaned, the room became dark again. "Sorry. Just pulled it up an inch, so I could see."

Jane relaxed "It's alright, Luke."

"Still feeling lousy?"

He pulled a chair up to Jane close enough to see her in the dim room. Jane wished he'd take her hand to comfort her, but he didn't. "*Jah*, lousy. My uncle's wretched behavior makes me sick."

"*Mamm* told me after the doc left. You still have some money though."

She'd get up and shout if she had the strength. "Luke,

I'm so angry. He's as cruel as Aunt Reed."

"You have an Aunt Reed?"

"She's in a novel I'm reading. She was supposed to take care of Jane Eyre, but never loved her. Treated her like everything was her fault. I've lived like that since fourteen and I can never forgive."

"In time you will. It's our way."

Jane clenched her fist and hit a quilted pillow. Seething pain jabbed her head, but she let out, "Our way? I don't know what I believe anymore."

Luke took her hand, but Jane withdrew it, now raging, her emotions like a yoyo. "Look, this has been too much for you too fast. In time, your mind will settle and things will go back to normal."

"Normal? What's that?" Jane truly wanted to know. She'd been lied to for so long, held captive like a caged bird. "Why didn't anyone at *Gmay* save me? They had to know I wasn't treated right."

"Don't you remember?" Luke asked. "I was fourteen when you moved here. My buddies and I kept an eye out for you."

Jane vaguely remembered a time when she tried to make friends at school. Her uncle came and picked her up, demanded she get into the buggy and Luke and Emma asked if she could walk home like everyone else. It was a special bonding time she was denied, either her aunt or uncle picking her and their other *kinner* up. And then it was announced to her a week later that she'd be taught at home.

"I'm sorry, Luke. It wasn't your fault," Jane said in a

trembling tone.

"I tried after that, too, but every time anyone tried to talk, you walked away. We all thought you were shy or stuck-up. But I never thought so." He reached for her hand and she grabbed it. "I saw fear long ago, but the elders and bishop, your neighbors, too, have only had cause to pry into your family business lately when it…"

"What?"

"Lots of reasons. Odd behavior. Your bloodied hand made me real suspicious and I told my *daed*." He caressed the bandaged hand. "How is your hand by the way?"

"It wasn't a deep cut, mostly blood from shards of glass. The doc looked at it and your *mamm* re-patched it up."

"Jane, I'm glad you're here. You'll get to know my family and see how peaceful it is. What a real home is supposed to be."

"I like your *mamm*."

"She likes you, too." Luke cleared his throat. "She'll be your *mamm* if we get married."

"Married? You're joking."

He took off his straw hat. "I know Emma told you my *daed's* plan. But hear me out. My *daed* wanted to get you out of your house and I told him how I felt. My *daed* talked to your uncle and he agreed."

Jane lay her head on the pillow, trying to remember to breathe. "Luke, you don't love me. It's *furhoodled* to think we could get married."

He leaned towards her, touching her shoulder. "I do love you Jane. I always have."

He loved her? And then a most unwelcome thought ran like a train through her mind. She was being pitied by Luke, not loved. "I don't even have a hope chest," she challenged. "No quilts, China, crocheted doilies or other family heirlooms."

"I don't care about those things. I make a decent wage in the clock shop. Even have land out back picked out to build a house, to share with you."

Her eyes were now well adjusted to the room and she could see genuine love pouring from Luke's eyes. His voice echoed his sentiments. He was kinder right this moment than anyone had ever been. But soon fear gripped her by the throat. What if he's cruel to her when married? Forcing herself to calm down as her head throbbed, she said quietly, "*Nee*, I can't marry you."

"But why? I'd treat you like the Bible says a wife's to be treated, ready to lay down his own life for her." He forced a grin. "And if I ever get cross, since I'm not an angel, you could tell my *daed* and he'd put me in my place. We'd live right outback, not too far from this house."

Jane turned away and stared at the opposing wall. "I need to rest."

"You think about it, Jane." He got up and kissed the top of her head. "Hope you're feeling better soon."

After Jane knew Luke had left the room, hearing the door shut, she let out the sobs. Her *mamm* and *daed* used to kiss her on the head and no one had until right that moment. *God bless Luke*, she prayed. *Lead me to healing, Lord. I can't go on living without love and companionship.*

~*~

Over the next few days, Jane's headache prevented her from doing much except read and finish *Jane Eyre*. Ruth bought her a beginner's book for knitting along with brown yarn and two large wooden needles. Start with big needles and thick yarn, Ruth had advised. She managed to cast on some stitches, despite the pain in her bandaged right hand. But the wound was bandaged properly, much tighter with white tape, and she thought she'd try to knit today.

Ruth and Luke came in regularly with trays of food and tea, and she'd never felt so rested in her life. She was beginning to feel lazy, but the headache was still painful enough at times that nausea overpowered her.

Jane Eyre left Longborn, the shabby school she was sent to, being abandoned by her aunt, but she bore it and made the best of it. After a new master came to the school, things became better and Jane Eyre gobbled all the education she could handle, even becoming fluent in French.

Aunt Miriam had told Jane she was stupid, but she learned English as a second language quickly when only five. Memories of her *daed* praising her for being a quick learner cheered her on. *What else can I learn? And how can I find out?*

Well, she knew. She had to leave like Jane Eyre, and maybe she'd meet someone like Mr. Rochester. Someone who she could be one soul with. What did she know about life?

But she knew what she was risking. The ban. Being a baptized member of the Amish church, even if forced, was still a vow before God. She'd be breaking it unless she found a bishop who would approve of her joining his flock. She clenched her teeth. Maybe she wanted more. Maybe she didn't know her mind and would have to leave to find it.

The job Emma told her about in New York came to mind. She could write to Emma's pen pal, Rose, but she was Amish. What Jane needed was to stay with the *English* to see what they had to offer. Well, she'd have to start with Emma's pen pal at first, and then see what became of it.

One thing was for sure and certain. Jane Eyre had been like a companion through this whole ordeal. What other books had she missed out on, only allowed to read the Bible? But a soothing river ran through her soul. She loved the comfort the Bible gave; Jane could identify with it, especially Joseph, held prisoner for seventeen years. The story of Daniel being taken prisoner, treated like a slave, thrown into the lion pit, only to have the lions purr at his feet. Her life since fourteen had been wretched, but if it was a Bible story, how would it be written? Should she wait patiently here to find out or leave?

She asked God for a sign. If the job in New York came easily, she'd go, if she didn't get it, she'd stay, but would have to leave this house. She'd be forced to see her uncle and aunt unless she moved in with someone from a nearby church district. Maybe back to Plum Creek. Contact old friends from childhood? *Lord, lead me.*

~*~

Ruth had been to a work frolic most of the day, but

checked in on Jane at night. "I saw the light on. Light sensitivity gone? No more migraine?"

Jane lowered her Bible. "Feeling much better."

Ruth held a hand to Jane's cheek. "You're so pale."

Jane needed advice from an older woman in the church and felt instantly at ease with Ruth. "I feel like a naïve woman, being so sheltered. Is it wrong for me to want to go out and see the world?"

Ruth's kind eyes didn't flinch. "*Nee.* You've been too bound-up and now most likely you resent that. It's like being on a strict diet only to find yourself hungry and so you binge, eating due to starvation. Give it time, Jane. Your emotions will settle soon."

"But I can't be in the same church district as my uncle. How could there be unity? And I can't bear to look at him."

Ruth smoothed her apron. "Your uncle's been given his final warning. He's under the ban."

"He was given warnings? About what?"

Ruth took Jane's hand. "I'm not even told. If he repents, he's forgiven. The elders and bishop know. But this last one I do know was about repenting of abuse and stealing."

"He stole?" Jane put her hands over her ears like a child. "I can't stand to hear any more about his sinful ways."

Ruth slowly lowered Jane's hands. "Stealing your inheritance. Malachi reasoned that it took money to raise you."

A sob deep in Jane's heart wanted to come out, but

she stifled it, making her throat ache. "The farm must have sold for much more than the cost of keeping me."

"*Jah*, we all know that, but your uncle's an irrational man."

Jane knew this to be true, and he was getting increasingly worse. It made her shudder to think that as she matured and looked like a woman, her mother, he may have looked upon her with lust. Did he? Is this why Aunt Miriam looked on her with increasing contempt? "I need to get away from here," she blurted.

"You're safe here, Jane. And we care about you."

"My aunt will be at *Gmay, jah*? Only my uncle is under the ban, right?"

"*Jah*. But Miriam seems to have woken up, not defending her husband's behavior. You may find her kinder."

"That would be a miracle," Jane scoffed.

Ruth put a finger to Jane's lips. "You're a beautiful woman. Don't let bitterness ruin you."

Jane slowly pushed Ruth's hand down. "I *am* bitter. How can I not be?"

"You're not bitter yet. This has all been a very emotional experience for you. Bitterness grows over time due to a lack of forgiveness. Forgive your aunt. I believe she cares about you."

Jane trembled and then let the stifled sob escape. She sobbed and leaned with open arms to Ruth. She was held tenderly by this dear woman. At this moment, she felt as if her *mamm* was comforting her through Ruth.

Chapter 4
Rescued

*J*ane surveyed the breakfast spread she'd prepared to surprise Ruth. She'd serve this dear woman, not letting her do the dishes afterwards. After their long talk last night, she realized that Ruth was the woman she could confide in.

Loud pounding down the steps seemed to make the wooden house shake. Luke ran into the room and headed for Jane. "*Ach*, it's you Jane. Was going to give my *mamm* a kiss for making such a breakfast."

Jane laughed. "You like to eat, *jah*?"

He nodded and took his seat at the round oak table, but said nothing more.

"Can I get you some coffee?" Jane asked, picking up the coffee pot, heading his way. "When *mamm* and *daed* sit down and after morning prayer."

Jane fumbled for words, once again feeling so stupid. At her uncle's place it resembled pigs vying for the best slop. "When will they be down?"

Luke shrugged. "In a few minutes." He shot up and grabbed a newspaper from the basket on the wall. "Wanted to show you this. The Antique Mall is hiring. Thought you might be interested."

When he handed her the paper he took her hand. "I have lots of work today. A buggy ride tonight?"

Desire mixed with fear made her mute for an uncomfortable spell, but she nodded.

"Autumn smells *gut* and we can take a walk, then check what my birds ate up."

Jane let out nervous laughter. "What your birds eat?"

"*Jah*. Birds migrate in autumn and I have a feeding station for them to rest a while. Have to fill it most nights, because the cracked corn and suet are gone by the end of the day. I can show you my injured birds, too. I nurse them until they can be released."

"Really?" Jane admired this and couldn't help but gawk. What a caring man.

Luke reddened. "I can't stand to see an animal suffer. I don't see it as anything special."

Jane poured two mugs of coffee and sat across from Luke. "You're busy in the clock shop but take time to care for hurting birds."

"Not just birds. Folks drop off all kinds of critters. I'll show you some later today." He sipped his coffee. "Got sprayed by a skunk a few weeks back and *mamm* was fit to be tied. Soaked my dungarees in tomato juice for a week to get the stink out."

"Your *mamm* is so nice like my *mamm* was. Crabby old Aunt Miriam made me forget that there are plenty of loving people out there."

"Pray, Jane," Luke advised. "Pray for your aunt. She's going through a hard time."

Jane felt like she was being scolded like a child. Couldn't she vent to anyone? She shot up and headed towards the utility room. Getting her bonnet and light cape, she ran outside, feeling like she was being suffocated.

Luke followed her. "What are you doing?"

"Trying to breathe!"

"Do you have asthma?"

She spun around, hands clenched tight. "*Nee.*"

"Allergies?"

"*Nee.* I panic sometimes, like I'm trapped. I need space."

"Did I do anything wrong?"

Such sincerity made her melt. "*Ach,* Luke, I'm so furious. It'll take time to forgive my aunt."

"I know." His eyes widened. "I'm only telling you that your aunt's in a bad way."

"What do you mean?" Jane asked, surprised that she cared a smidgen.

"Miriam has to live with Malachi as a shunned man, but he won't sit at a different table. He won't abide by the ban and is pressuring Miriam to leave the Amish with him."

Tender, nurturing feelings surfaced in Jane. "What a terrible example they are to the *kinner.*"

He motioned for her to go inside. "My stomach's rumbling. Let's go eat."

She followed him in, but decided what she'd do today. Visit Emma.

~*~

Jane thanked Ruth for letting her use their buggy, but felt afraid, not driving a buggy since she was thirteen. Memories of her *daed* letting her hold the reins for the first time and taking it out for the first time gave her more determination to be independent; it was obviously what her parents wanted. But, here she was at twenty, afraid to drive.

"Do you want me to teach ya?" Ruth asked, shielding her eyes from the morning sun. "But it's like riding a bike."

"A bike? Amish don't ride bikes here," Jane blurted.

"I was raised in Lancaster and had a bike." She pat the seat of the black buggy. "Jane, it's only a mile away and you can take the dirt road, and come out onto the back of Emma's house."

"But what if my uncle sees me?"

Ruth lowered the rolled up shades on both sides of the buggy. "He'll never know it's you."

"*Nee*, I can't."

Ruth puckered her lips, staring at the ground. "Want to take one of Luke's dogs?"

Remembering the dozen or so dogs Luke was tending to, strays people dropped off along the road, her mind settled on the chunky Golden Labrador. "How about Peanut?"

Ruth laughed. "He's still bouncy like a puppy, even though he's two. Are you sure?"

Jane nodded and ran back to the barn and called for Peanut, who quickly came to her side. "You have a job to do today, boy. Calm me down."

Jane embraced Ruth as Peanut jumped into the buggy. "I'll be back in an hour."

"Why so soon?"

Jane scoffed. "Because I was always told to be home in less than an hour when going to Emma's."

"Really?"

"*Jah*. I ran over with eggs that Emma didn't need but paid me for them. It was our secret, although deceitful."

Ruth slipped a few strands of hair under her kapp. "Stay all day if you want, but be back by tonight."

"Tonight?"

"*Jah*. Luke told me you two are taking a buggy ride."

Jane felt pressure on her face and knew she was blushing. "See you in a bit."

As she gently snapped the horse's reins, she guided the horse towards the back pasture and onto the road behind the Miller farm. Red apples dripping from the dwarf trees took her back to when Sammy was alive. He'd hang on a branch, shaking it so the apples fell freely. Their *mamm* would make them each an apple pie and let them eat it over four days. "That was Happy Farm," she said to Peanut. Instinctively, the dog leaned closer to her, and she rubbed him behind his ears. As she made her way down the road, she realized she *did* know how to drive and confidence filled her.

She noticed a barn off to the right, and grasped that this was the land that Luke had told her about. The land her parents bought up, a gray barn still standing, where Luke would build his house and raise a family. She stopped the buggy and stared. Such beauty she could barely take in. A meadow dotted with golden rod and purple chicory, an old stone pathway from the barn that led to springhouse.

She let her mind ease for once, no time restraints on her. She envisioned Luke older and *kinner* running around a big house off to the right of the barn. A tire swing could be hung from the massive oak. But who was the wife? Jane had known Luke since fourteen and he seemed more like a *bruder* at times, but other times, she felt romance towards him.

She nudged the horse along the dirt road, but fear that her uncle or aunt would come in the opposite direction gripped her out of nowhere. She massaged Peanut's massive neck and the dog put his head on her lap. "You're a sweet dog," she exclaimed.

When times seemed bleak, she'd learned to memorize scripture that seemed to instantly anchor her trembling mind.

"Our Father which art in heaven, Hallowed be thy name.

Thy kingdom come, Thy will be done in earth, as it is in heaven.

Give us this day our daily bread.

And forgive us our debts, as we forgive our debtors.

And lead us not into temptation, but deliver us from evil: For thine is the kingdom, and the power, and the glory, forever. Amen."

The prayer that soothed her most soaked into her soul, and the rest of the buggy ride she pondered other scriptures. How odd it was that her aunt used the Bible to punish Jane. Did her aunt not know the comfort and peace it brought? Maybe not? Maybe her aunt never saw the love of God in the Bible, only the wrath and fear. Pity forced its way, very unwelcome, into Jane's heart. "*Ach,* God, don't soften my heart towards my aunt," she cried in exasperation. Peanut lifted his head and whimpered, his ears down. Was her tone that hateful? Dogs sensed things humans didn't, Luke told her. "I'm sorry if I scared you, boy."

Turning into the dirt lane that separated her uncle's house from Emma's, her stomach lurched and nausea along with dizziness assaulted her. She clung to Peanut and feeling his heartbeat, it soothed her and her symptoms lessened a little. "*Danki,*" was all she could mutter to the dog.

She heard children playing and Uncle Malachi yelling for them to stop making such noise. Jane refused to peek out from the black blind, and hastened to Emma's. Quickly tying the horse to a post, she led the dog by his collar, fear still shadowing her.

When she entered through the side door, she stopped short when she viewed Aunt Miriam.

Miriam didn't turn to face her, but Deborah, Emma's *mamm*, put a hand on her shoulder. "Miriam, it's alright."

"Is Emma home?" Jane asked, wanting to leave the room.

"She's outside hanging laundry," Deborah informed.

"*Danki.*" Jane gripped the dog's collar, not sure if she should do what half of her heart told her to do, so she just stared at her aunt. "Aunt Miriam, even though you won't speak to me, I want you to know, I care about you."

Her aunt said nothing, but Jane soon realized by her aunt shaking shoulders that she was crying, hiding her face in shame. Deborah smiled at Jane as if to say she appreciated what was just said, but motioned for her to leave.

Jane took the cue and met Emma on the other side of the house where the thirty-foot clothesline pulley reached to the heavens. Seeing laundry flap from the two tiered line, she knew Emma was near finished. "I came too late to help," she said, sneaking up on Emma.

Emma spun around and hugged Jane. "What a surprise."

The dog, now free to run, ran circles around them, his tail wagging. "Helping Luke with animal rescue?"

"*Jah*. For now." She reached down to pick a dandelion. "Have time to talk?"

"*Jah*, but *Mamm* told me to stay out of the kitchen. Miriam's in there and in a bad way."

"I know. I just saw her."

"What?"

"I always use the side door." Seeing Emma's face blanch, she frowned. "What's the matter?"

Emma hung up a tea towel and then led Jane to a cedar bench under a maple tree. "Your uncle slapped her. And she has a nasty bruise on her face."

Jane called for Peanut to come near and she hugged him around the neck. "Stay here."

"Did you hear what I just said?" Emma asked, perplexed.

"*Jah*, I did. He's getting worse, then, taking his rage out on his family."

"Miriam won't let Malachi eat at the same table, since he's under the ban, and she made up a real pretty table in the kitchen. Looks like an *eck* table at a wedding. But your uncle refuses to sit there, turned the table upside-down, food went flying everywhere, and when Miriam tried to reason, he hit her." Emma's shoulders slumped. "She has a black eye."

Digging her fingers into the dog's fur, Jane narrowed her eyes and glowered. "What are the bishop and elders going to do?"

"I don't know. *Mamm's* hoping she can smooth things over, help Miriam bear her load."

"Someone should call the police."

"It's not our way," Emma gasped.

"Well, maybe it should be. If someone had called the police, maybe I would have been rescued long ago."

Emma turned towards Jane, eyelids flapping. "Jane, in two short weeks, you've grown a backbone." She pat her back. "*Gut* for you. Of course, I don't agree with calling the police, but you've got gumption like I've never seen."

Jane grinned. "So much gumption, I'm ready to write to your friend in New York, enquiring about that job."

"Really? *Ach*, Jane, do you have to leave? You're safe now."

"Not really. I'm still in the same *Gmay* as my uncle..."

"But he's shunned."

"I know him. He'll do a fake confession. He'll never change, once cruel, always cruel."

Jane looked up at the maple leaves, but felt Emma boring a hole threw her head. "What's wrong?"

"Jane, why would you say something like that? A fake confession? You know he'd have to kneel before the

People and confess his faults, his abuse. And if he does, we give him the right hand of fellowship again. We've been forgiven and we must forgive." Emma gripped Jane's shoulder. "You suffered so much over there, but we have to forgive others just like we've been forgiven."

Emma's words stung. The Lord's Prayer she'd said coming over stung as well, for those words were in it. "I can't forgive my uncle. I already told Aunt Miriam I forgave her, but it was half-hearted."

"But it's a start," Emma encouraged.

"Emma, I'm reading books now besides the Bible. I need to return *Jane Eyre* to you actually, but I see my uncle like Jane's abusive cousin. He ended up always being bad and it shortened his life. I see my Uncle Malachi like that..."

Emma sighed and stared ahead. "I read a biography of the author, Charlotte Bronte. She wrote from her family experiences, her brother was the mean kid in the story and he died in real life from alcohol and drug abuse. He became an opium addict. But, Charlotte never gave up on her brother. She loved him."

"How?"

"Charlotte felt pity for him and being a strong Christian, she knew her duty. She had to forgive."

Jane had only been fed Amish doctrine, so to hear that an author from the eighteen-hundreds held to such strict views was a shock. "Was she Amish? Quaker?"

"*Nee.* Church of England. Lost his wife to cancer and he had to raise a bunch of kids. He educated them at home, sheltering them from other *kinner* in the neighborhood because of bad influences."

Jane felt like she had camaraderie with Charlotte Bronte. "Can I read her biography?"

"When you get a library card, you can check it out of the Punxsy Library," Emma quipped.

"I, ah, haven't been to the library since I was a kid. And I won't be living here much longer. I'm determined to go work in New York. Maybe my Mr. Rochester is there."

Emma burst out laughing. "Jane, Mr. Rochester was an immoral man. I know you're joking."

"Mr. Rochester came to an understanding of who God is through the goodness of Jane Eyre."

Emma thrust up a hand. "It's fiction, Jane."

"Can I have the address to your pen pal in New York? I've made up my mind. I want to be independent."

Emma groaned. "Just like Jane Eyre, *jah*?"

"*Jah*," Jane admitted, holding her head higher.

~*~

Jane hugged the dear Golden Labrador tight as she stopped the buggy alongside the dirt road. "How can I explain to Emma my fears? Uncle Malachi is taking his anger out on his wife, and my cousins will be next."

She closed her eyes, confessing her concern for the *kinner* as opposed to her concern for her aunt being a polar opposite. Yes, her aunt's sobbing tugged at her heart. How horrid to live with a man who had little respect for Amish ways.

Since moving in with the Miller's, memories of her parents bombarded her at times: birthday parties, nature walks, fishing, picnics, bird watching.

Jane, I don't like you, her dad would say with a twinkle in his eyes. *I love you.*

You're the prettiest girl in town, next to your mamm.

I pray that when you grow up, you'll find someone you love and respect as much as I love your mamm.

Her *daed's* voice rang in her mind with rapid force. Had she intentionally blocked these precious memories in order to cope? She wasn't to mention the death of her parents, while in her uncle's house. She was a dam, bursting now, overflowing at the most unexpected times.

She needed a place to heal. But how? Big problems don't get solved in a day, she remembered her *mamm* saying. Jane straightened and urged the horse forward.

Jane breathed in autumn in all its glory for the first time since fourteen. She'd been like a slave at her uncle's house and dreaded the harvest season. Her eyes misted. She'd never had time to soak up the beauty of autumn because of abusive overwork, and come to think of it, her cousins worked harder than most kids.

When she was half way back to the Miller's, she heard a buggy, horse hoofs pounding. Her heart started to bang against her ribcage. Only my uncle pushes a horse like a lunatic. She sped up the buggy but soon she saw her uncle, bareback on his horse. "Pull over!"

She met the hatred in his eyes and sped the buggy up. He sped further ahead and then cut her off. She pulled back on the reigns and her uncle grabbed the horse's bit.

"Get down, now!"

"*Nee,* uncle. Come to your senses."

"Abigail, you come to yours," he said as he flung one foot over the horse and dismounted. "We have *kinner* to raise."

"I'm Jane, not my *mamm*," she screamed, tears now running down her cheeks.

As he approached, grabbing her by the wrist, Peanut crouched down and growled viciously.

"Shut up you old mutt. Getting my woman."

"Stop it," she yelled, as he pulled at her bandaged hand.

Peanut barked and Malachi backed away, but the dog jumped from the buggy and darted after him. He ran into the ditch on the side of the road and took out a thick stick and started beating Peanut's head. Even though blood oozed from his head, Peanut kept snapping and finally bit Malachi on the leg.

"Peanut, come," Jane commanded and the dog twirled around and cocked an ear, as if not understanding. Malachi lifted a rock and pounded the dog's head and Peanut ran to Jane, yelping in pain.

Jane coaxed Peanut into the buggy and took off just as Malachi reached for the horse's reigns, but Jane jerked them away and he was soon out of sight.

Karen Anna Vogel

Chapter 5
Independence

Luke tried to comfort Jane later that night that it wasn't her fault that Peanut was badly bruised. She didn't have to pay the vet bills, either, like she insisted. Why did Jane think everything was her fault?

"How about we go out for some ice cream?"

Jane, still trembling, agreed. "I want to check on Peanut first."

"*Daed's* with him. *Mamm's* treating him like a *boppli*. He's in *gut* hands." He took her hand and led her to the buggy, glad that she didn't resist. Her long fingers clenched onto his, but was it her nerves, or was it a sign of affection?

As they made their way onto the main road, he noticed Jane was shaking. "Are you cold? Autumn nights can get nippy."

"*Nee*, I'm fine. Have my shawl if I need it."

Luke felt like one of his *mamm's* canning jars in a pressure cooker. He'd kept his feelings for Jane in too long. "Jane, what are you thinking about?" he probed.

She leaned towards him as if needing support. "I know who hit Peanut."

Blinking rapidly, Luke tightened his hands on the reins. "Who?"

Jane's head dropped. "My uncle."

"What?"

"*Jah*. It's true."

She started to weep, and Luke put an arm around her. "Tell me what happened. Did your uncle try to hurt you? Did Peanut try to protect you?"

"I can't say," she whimpered. "It's too horrible. My poor cousins."

Her cousins? It only being six-thirty and plenty of sunlight for a while, he turned onto a quiet, less traveled road. He brought the buggy to a halt and tried to lift her sagging shoulders. "Jane, what did your uncle do to your cousins?"

"I hate him," she yelled, and then let Luke cradle her in his arms as she wept.

Luke had always dreamt of this day when he could embrace dear Jane, but not under these circumstances. He wondered if he should take her back home to talk to his *mamm*, the two having a budding bond.

"Can you tell me what happened or do you want to tell my *mamm*?"

"You," she was able to get out.

Luke let her sob until she was wrung out and able to talk. Oddly, he felt like he was in a holy place. That this was his purpose in life; to marry Jane with all her scars, love her to wholeness. *Lord, You see this. You know me and my desires. I believe You put them in me. Guard and protect Jane's and my path which I believe will be intertwined someday.*

She remained still in his arms. "My Uncle chased after me on his horse," she said in monotone. "And my aunt has a black eye."

Luke's mind tried to take in both revelations, but he couldn't. Holding her tighter, he asked, "Did he try to hurt you?"

"He thought I was my *mamm*. He called me Abigail, and then wanted me to go with him and…"

"Peanut protected you. He has *gut* instincts."

"He bit my uncle, though."

"*Gut*. He provoked the dog." Luke wanted to say her uncle was meaner than any dog he'd ever seen, but kept this to himself.

"I went to see Emma. My aunt was there crying in the kitchen. *Ach*, Luke, I feel so bad about Peanut."

He slowly rubbed her back. "It's not your fault. A dog can sense fear in people and you have every right to want to run from such a madman."

She shook her head violently. "He's an immoral man. I saw lust in his eyes. He disgusts me and I'm not even sorry about it."

"Your uncle leaves a trail of destruction behind him."

Jane turned towards him, red swollen eyes wide. "*Jah*, he does. What can we do?"

Luke sighed. "We'll have to tell my *daed* and he'll take care of it."

"Really?" Jane asked, sarcastically, squirming out of his arms. "The Amish act like their blind when they see sin amongst themselves."

"How can you say that?"

"*Ach,* it's all brushed under the rug. And Luke, I'm so angry about not being rescued sooner, I don't think I believe in many Amish ways anymore. Why not call the police? I wish someone had when they saw bruises on me."

Luke hadn't seen Jane's face so contorted in anger before. It didn't even look like her, eyes too wide, mouth pursed. His *mamm* never yelled or spilled out bitterness like this. Could he handle being married to such a wounded woman? A minute before he imagined a life with her.

"You know that we tried. And my *daed* will do something about your uncle." Indignation arose in him and he turned the buggy to head back home. No one knew the sleepless nights his *daed* endured out ministering to the People, keeping peace, without ever getting one cent.

Jane was silent for a spell, and then asked, "Luke, was I wrong to tell you about my uncle? My aunt, too?"

Now he felt like as soft and pliable as dough. "Of course you should have told me."

"But it made you mad."

How could her emotions teeter from hatred and rage to humility? "I was mad that you accused the Amish of sweeping things under the rug. My *daed* works hard at being an elder."

"I'm sorry."

"We're going to talk to my parents. Maybe they can make heads or tails about everything."

"Everything? My uncle and aunt?"

"About lots of stuff."

~*~

Jane sat at the Miller's oak table next to Luke as they waited for his parents to enter. She'd cried on his shoulder and felt so protected, loved, but then it all abruptly changed. She would have said yes to a marriage proposal the way she felt in Luke's strong embrace; she never knew such a feeling. But he loved the Amish more than her apparently, because as soon as she criticized, he became angry...

Moses and Ruth entered the kitchen hand-in-hand. Jane could barely believe that marriage could be so beautiful and she wanted it more than ever.

Moses pulled at his long brown beard and took a seat across from them. Ruth put on the tea kettle. "Jane, Luke said you have something to disclose."

Disclose. It sounded so serious. Well, it was serious. No more closing the door on abuse and hypocrisy. "*Jah.* My uncle gave my aunt a black eye. I saw her when I visited Emma. And on the way home, my uncle came after me, thinking I was my *mamm*. Peanut protected me and that's how he got the bruised head."

Moses' eyes' bulged. "Are you sure?"

"*Jah*, I am. If my uncle denies anything, I'll accuse him to his face."

Moses cocked his head back. "You've become so brave."

"*Jah*, I have. I'm tired of hiding the truth."

Luke clucked his tongue. "She thinks justice won't be done, so I wanted to assure her that you took your duty as an elder seriously."

Ruth put two teacups in front of Luke and Jane. "Luke, I don't like your tone. What's wrong?"

Luke lowered his head and rubbed the back of his neck. "I know what you've sacrificed *mamm*, being an elder's wife."

"We look out for each other. It's our duty," Ruth said.

Rage roared in Jane and she shuddered and stammered for words. "No one looked out for me," she yelled, darting up.

Ruth ran around the table and pulled Jane to herself, even though Jane tried to push her away. "You're going through grief, Jane. Anger is part of it."

"*Jah*," Moses added. "Jane, you have every right to be angry, but don't sin. In your anger sin not."

"What does that mean?" Jane snapped.

"Don't water it like a plant, helping it grow. When you feel that righteous indignation coming up, pray to the Lord above and know that He sees. Justice will be served."

Jane tried to piece together what Moses just said. She had the right to be angry, but not nurse it. "So righteous indignation is okay?"

"*Jah*," Moses continued. "A bonfire is okay but don't go pouring kerosene on it. Understand?"

Ruth ushered Jane to her seat and poured hot water into her cup and placed a little basket of tea bags on the table. "Jane, I don't think you should go past your uncle's place anymore. It scares me to think what he could do to you."

"I agree," Moses said.

"But Emma's my best friend." Jane felt like she was a *kinner* again. How she longed to be independent, on her own. "I may as well tell you my plans. Emma has a friend up in New York, an elderly woman who's lonely. There's a couple of job openings and I'm going to apply."

"Where will you live?" Moses asked, face reddening.

"I don't have the details worked out."

"You'd live among the Amish, *jah*?" Ruth pressed.

"Well, it's an Amish woman I've written to once, just to get details. If I don't find lodgings with her, I'll pay my way."

"At a hotel? Live with the English?"

"I don't know."

The silence in the room was heavy, but soon Luke let out an 'ouch'. He looked at his *mamm* quizzically. "Why'd you kick me?"

She sighed loudly. "Go on, Luke. Say something."

He slowly got up and took his hat off the peg. "I need to check on Peanut."

Jane's heart plunged. Why was Luke so quiet and distant?

Moses followed Luke and Ruth teared up. "Jane, what I did was wrong."

"Kicking Luke under the table?"

"*Nee*," she said with a forced smile. "Urging him to tell you what's been on his mind."

"What wrong with him? He's so angry."

Ruth poured more hot water into her teacup and took a sip. "Luke's waters run deep. Maybe too deep."

"What do you mean?"

"His waters run deep. Very deep, but they're a constant river in him that you can depend on."

"Ruth, I don't understand you."

Ruth pursed her lips as if to keep from speaking, but

then looked Jane in the eyes. "He loves you. You talking about New York upset him." She fidgeted with her teacup. "Sure would love to have you for a daughter-in-law, but only if you love my son."

Jane did feel something when Luke held her. She imagined a life with him. Was this love? "I don't know much about love. I've been so sheltered, and it's why I need to leave. Need to mature and learn to have thoughts of my own."

Ruth's eyes brimmed with tears. "Just promise me one thing. You'll live among the Old Order Amish in New York. We have friends up there."

"Do they live near Cherry Creek?"

Ruth nodded. "Farther north, but the mail from New York to Punxsy is a busy route for the post office. It's only three hours by car."

"Really? That's a relief."

"Why?" Ruth probed.

"It's not too far from here."

~*~

Jane flipped the pancakes, while Ruth scrambled the eggs. They both gasped when the back door pounded, making the kitchen windows rattle.

Ruth ran to open the door and Marshall Springer stood erect. "Hello Ruth," he said. "I hear one of your dogs bit someone yesterday, nearly killing him."

Ruth stared back at Jane, eyes round.

Jane was as puzzled as Ruth looked. The Amish didn't call the police or get them involved with their troubles. Should she tell the police what happened?

"Excuse me, but I have work to do. Can either of you show me a yellow Lab?"

"Our dogs don't bite," Ruth said evenly.

"Well, like I said, one of your people came and filed a report. Malachi Schmucker. Nice man, when you get to understand his ways."

Fear surged through Jane. This man seemed to know her uncle like a friend. Now he was threatening them with a police report made up by her uncle?

Luke appeared in the doorway. "Mr. Springer, do you want something?"

"Yes. I need all the shot and medical records for your dogs or I'll shut you down."

Luke's eyes narrowed. "Your threats didn't work last time."

Ruth wrung her hands. "Just give him what he wants."

"Follow me," Luke scoffed. "*Mamm*, tell *Daed* he's here again." Luke's chiseled jaw was so fixed, Jane never realized how handsome he was when angry. How masculine.

When they left for the barn, Ruth cupped her cheeks. "That man scares me."

Jane went to Ruth and took her by the shoulders. "This isn't the first time he's intimidated you?"

"*Nee*, but I never knew his sources."

"Sources?"

"*Jah.* Your uncle's the one who tells the police our business. We've gotten threats."

Ruth was visibly shaking now and Jane couldn't help but take her like a child to the table. "Sit down. Want another cup of coffee?"

She shook her head. "Was Malachi responsible for the barn fires? Is that why my husband and the bishop fear the police more than usual? Fear Malachi?" Jane felt numbness move through her legs and she took a seat. "You're afraid of the police? You avoid them?"

"*Jah*. Most Amish don't, Jane. Most have a *gut* relationship and can call them without fear"

"But?" Jane prodded.

"They've gone door to door helping with elections and petitions, saying the Amish need to do their part. When we don't comply, we get our share of headaches." She closed her eyes and breathed in deeply. "Bishop Stoltzfus had the EPA come survey his land for toxins going into the streams…"

"EPA?"

"Environmental Protection Agency," she said slowly as if in a dream. "People trying to help keep God's green earth clean."

"What happened over at Bishop Stoltzfus'?"

"Nothing. It was a false report and the EPA told him it's usually the non-Amish that are upset with an Amish person to call them. Ninety percent of the time they can't find a thing. I just never thought Malachi would do such a thing."

Jane recognized this police officer. He came by and talked to her uncle real friendly and Jane thought maybe he came to get him to treat his family better. She imagined an *Englisher* heard him rant and called the police. "Ruth, are the *Gmay* leaders afraid to call the police to help me?"

She shrugged her shoulders quickly. "Maybe?"

The clip clop of horses hoofs were heard outside and Jane felt protected, since Moses was finally home. Ruth peaked out the window and stepped back. "Malachi's here. Headed out to Luke's kennel."

Jane felt like disappearing, but an unusual boldness arose in her. A need to defend Luke. She dashed out the door, hearing Ruth call for her to stay inside.

~*~

Luke jabbed at the ground with a stick, making the groove deeper and deeper as tension rose. "Officer, *nee*, I don't have a license to care for wounded animals."

"Well, the law says you need one."

"I take in critters at my own expense. If they need anything, we have a vet friend who volunteers his time." He shifted. "Was he doing something illegal, too? Helping a non-certified animal shelter?"

Malachi appeared around the corner, nostrils flaring. "Did you put the dog down?"

Luke stared at Malachi, trying not to show his utter contempt for this man. "He was protecting Jane from you!"

Malachi raised up a pant leg. "See this here bruise. Made by your dog."

"You deserved it!" Jane yelled from behind Malachi.

Luke's stomach lurched when Malachi turned a raised hand to strike Jane. Rushing to her side, he pushed Malachi away. "Leave her alone."

"She's a no *gut* woman, just like her *mamm*."

Jane dug her fingernails into Luke's arms. "My *mamm* was a loving woman. And she loved my *daed* with all her heart. More memories are coming back now that I don't live in constant fear." She turned to face the officer, Luke still hovering over her. "Officer, this man was abusive to me and I'd like to file a report."

The officer's brown eyes protruded, making him look unnatural. "You're Amish. Ah, don't you work things out?"

She pointed to her uncle and jutted out her chin. "Seems like some of the Amish make reports, right Officer?"

"Yes. I can take you down to the station if you'd like."

"I'm going with her," Luke insisted, putting an arm on Jane's shoulder. "This should have been done years ago."

Malachi spit some chewing tobacco near Luke's foot. "Like what?"

Luke ignored him. "Officer, are you done inspecting here?"

He meekly nodded, and then grimaced at Malachi. "Nothing's wrong here." Turning to Luke he asked, "Is it Dr. Fox who volunteers with your critters?"

"*Jah*. He's a *gut* vet."

"Well, if you can get paperwork done to be approved as an animal rescuer, it would be better."

Luke nodded. "I'll think on that."

~*~

A few days later, Jane reflected on how empowered she felt, telling the police all that she'd suffered at the hands of her uncle. Luke patiently waited while she spoke for over an hour and his reactions to the many cruelties showed her something; he loved her.

But her decision to go to Cherry Creek had materialized and another confrontation with her uncle at the corner store made her want to leave the area for good.

She'd miss Ruth, too. It'd been ages since she could talk to someone like a *mamm*. Such a wise woman with *gut* advice.

Her mind wandered to the land promised to Luke and she wanted to say yes and be his bride. Jane would have this wonderful family as her in-laws. Being in a loving family at last.

But, she told Luke no again after his many pleadings last night. She felt wretched, since she did care for him a great deal. But was it love?

When Luke said he'd visit her in New York, she wanted to jump into his arms and scream for joy, because she'd be lonely for him. Once again, she felt like Jane Eyre. She had nothing to bring to a marriage and she didn't really know herself. Jane learned by living in a place foreign to her. And she came back to Mr. Rochester. Was Luke her Mr. Rochester? Truth be told, she hoped so.

Karen Anna Vogel

Chapter 6
Cherry Creek, NY

That night, Jane lie in her comfy bed, the oil lamp's warm glow casting light onto her Bible. Battling anger towards her uncle, hatred if she was being truthful, she hugged the precious book to her heart. *Lord, I've never felt so at home anywhere in a long time. And now I have to go because of my wicked uncle. I know I'm to forgive and let You serve out justice, but right now, I don't even have words to say how lonesome I'll be in Cherry Creek. Luke thinks I'm trying too hard to make a point; he sees me as an intelligent, independent woman, but I don't. Is this pride or good sense? I have no dowry, just like Jane Eyre.*

Jane heard what sounded like hail hitting the window pane. She jumped out of bed and peered out and could make out two lights. Flashlights. She cringed. Had her uncle come to take her back home? Was he in allegiance with the police officer she'd poured her heart out to?

Her racing heart lunged until she could make out the figure. Two women. Or a woman and a young girl. Opening the window, she heard Clara and Sarah calling her. *Ach, my precious cousins!* "Come in through the back door," she yelled.

She tiptoed downstairs with her oil lamp and set it on the kitchen table. Jane looked up to see Clara and Sarah, with tear streaked faces. "*Ach*, what's wrong?"

Sarah tilted her head down and fumbled for words while Clara straightened. "We hear you're leaving. Is it true?"

Stunned, Jane sat at the table, motioning for them to take a seat. Did they really care if she left? "*Ach,* girls, I am. Up to Cherry Creek to work."

"It's because of *Daed, jah?* He's threatened you?" Clara asked, chin quivering.

Jane, angry enough to not hold back and cover for her uncle, nodded slowly.

"He's so mean now," Sarah blurted. "He's mean to all us *kinner* and *Mamm.*"

"Has he hurt yinz?" Jane gripped her hands together, trying to remain calm.

"He only hit *Mamm* a few times," Clara said, "but he's given us and our *bruder* so many chores, we can't keep up. I can't even see Benjamin." Clara reddened. "Benjamin Weaver and I have been courting for a few months and I'll lose him if I keep locked up like a caged animal."

Part of Jane wanted to yell, 'Now you understand what my life's been like,' and the other half, 'Tell the bishop and get help.' Trying to breathe evenly, she reached across the table and their hands all met. "I'll be praying for *yinz* and maybe you can come visit me."

"How?" Clara asked, tears trickling down her pretty face.

"Well, Luke's going to visit."

Sarah forced a grin. "Seems like he's helped you a lot."

"*Jah,* he's a *gut* man."

Sarah slipping her hand away, covering a smirk. "Is he your boyfriend?"

Jane's eyes misted unexpectedly. "He is a *wunderbar gut* man, but he's not my beau."

"The Amish grapevine says he wants to marry you," Clara said. "Well, Emma said," she added.

"Maybe someday we'll wed. I need to go away to make money."

"You're afraid of *Daed*," Clara protested. "Marry Luke and don't go. You'd have the whole Miller clan as kin. *Daed* can't stand up to the whole Miller clan."

Jane laughed. "*Nee*, I don't think so. But you know how you've been feeling like a caged bird lately?"

They nodded in unison.

"That's been my life for six years. I want to get away. Maybe I'm running away, but it feels right."

"Will you come back?" Sarah asked, eyes droopy.

"I'll come back soon. Can't imagine celebrating Thanksgiving with strangers."

Sarah clapped her hands.

"We can celebrate Sister Day," Clara said with feeling. "We're like sisters, *jah*?"

Jane darted her gaze from each girl back and forth, like a deer while crossing the road. How could she have missed this? Her dear cousins truly loved her. She'd been too tired and so knotted up inside to even recognize it. "Is it true?" she whispered.

"Is what true?" Clara asked.

"That you love me like real family."

"Of course we do," Sarah said. "You didn't know that?"

Sadly, Jane did not know that. How many missed opportunities to create happy memories and bond, but her uncle's cruel iron fist ruined it all? Bitterness grabbed her by the throat, but is was soon eased as Sarah and Clara came around the table and embraced her. *Ach, Lord, how can I leave now?*

~*~

"Are you sure?" Luke prodded.

"I'm sure," Jane said. "I was *furhoodled* after seeing my cousins and realizing they cared about me, I teetered, but I need to do this." She put a finger up with a smile though. "I'm coming back for Thanksgiving and Sister Day."

Luke's eyes twinkled. "Can you save a date for me?"

"Amish don't date."

"I mean a day," Luke said, twisting up his face into a grin. "If the pond freezes by then, we can skate."

Jane wanted to hug Luke. *No,* she wanted Luke to hold her. She felt so safe in his embrace and the fear of going to New York today was overwhelming. Their eyes locked and Luke's brown eyes seemed to enlarge. She stepped back, realizing he was trying to kiss her. She turned towards the farmhouse and saw Ruth looking out the window, and let out nervous laughter. "Your *mamm* will think I just turned you down again."

"What?"

Jane leaned into Luke. "Your *mamm's* watching us through the window."

Luke's brows shot up. "We can give the *Gmay* something to talk about." He pulled her to himself and kissed her on the cheek.

Jane hugged him around the middle. "*Ach,* Luke, you're a rascal." She leaned her head on his chest. "And

I'll miss you." She heard the thumping of his heart and didn't want to retreat. But a big yellow dog soon edged his nose in between them.

Luke chuckled. "I'm hugging her, Peanut, not hurting her."

The dog was a statue in front of Jane, warding off any intruders.

Luke's eyes narrowed. "Would you like to take Peanut with you? He's protective and it would make me…it would ease my mind."

Jane gulped and dug her fingers into the blonde fur. "I'd have to ask for permission, right?"

Luke scratched his chin and stared at the dog. "You ask and write me. I'll deliver him to you."

Jane bent down to hug the dog, but her arms yearned to hold Luke. "*Danki*, Luke. *Danki*."

~*~

Seeing the sign 'Welcome to New York' was so strange to Jane, she may as well have been on a trip to Africa. How sheltered she'd been, never crossing the state line. But as she stared at the massive moving water, it was further away from her cousins, who'd been on her mind constantly. Not allowed to come over to say goodbye, being held like prisoners in the home, made Jane wonder what she could do to help them.

Celebrate Sister Day with us, kept replaying in her mind and it slipped a smile from her heart to her face. Her *mamm's* maiden name being Raber, maybe Ruth was right in thinking she had cousins in New York. Her *daed* only had a *bruder*, Malachi, but her *mamm's* relations she could barely remember. Why none of them took her in was no longer a mystery. Malachi demanded he take her and the sale of the farm. It was what his *bruder* wanted, he'd always said. With no will written, the People believed it. They also believed he'd be good to her.

Her stomach ached as it twisted at the thought. Bitterness again seized her, but she'd talked to Luke and Ruth and they warned about the dangers of holding a grudge. It holds you to the one who wronged you, Luke had said. Ruth loved to talk in Amish proverbs, especially, '*It's better to forgive and forget than to resent and remember.*' They said the same thing in a way and the last thing she wanted was her mind to be constantly bombarded with images of her uncle.

As the van full of Amish visiting relatives in New York came to the first stop, Jane was surprised at how large the barns were and situated so close to the farmhouse. A woman from Smicksburg said that New York was so cold and snow so deep, they needed the barns nearby. The farms themselves were much farther apart and she soon learned that they were mostly massive dairy farms. Amish lived nearer to each other in Punxsutawney, having small hobby farms and home businesses, not full-fledged farms. The wide open flat spaces tall with wheat ready to harvest gave way to mountains, vibrant with autumn colors. They were in their peak, someone mentioned. The colder weather was two or three weeks ahead, because of the elevation. "Winter's six months long," a passenger quipped. "You need to be mighty hardy to live up here."

Mixed emotions filled Jane. Winter was a resting time

for the Amish as the fields rested, but she never had a *gut* constitution, given easily to colds and sore throats. Maybe the Amish family she was lodging with would actually let her stay in bed if running a fever.

She opened the letter from Rose, the woman she'd be staying with:

Jane,

I'm looking forward to your arrival. Like I said in my last letter, the job at the store got filled. But we need a more mature teacher, and since you have experience helping kids learn, like you said, I'm hoping you'll take the position.

You say your mamm was a Raber. Lots of Rabers here. Did she come from these parts? I asked some of the womenfolk and I'm sure they'll be asking about an Abigail Raber.

You have my address and I think you'll find my place cozy. Since Matthew died, I've lived alone, but don't like it. You'll be a comfort to me, I'm sure.

Rose Hershberger

"I hope so," Jane said.

A young man who had slept the entire trip, his black wool hat over his face, turned around. "You hope what?"

Startled, she looked away and folded her letter back up. "Just talking out loud."

"You headed to Cherry Creek or East Otto or another settlement?"

"Cherry Creek."

He readjusted his hat. "I live there. My name's Jonas Hershberger."

"Really? Do you know Rose Hershberger?"

He chuckled. "All seven of them."

Jane showed him the address on the envelope and he nodded. "She'd be my *grossmammi*. You must be Jane, the woman who'll be the new teacher?"

Jane gawked at the coincidence. "*Jah*, I'm Jane. But I haven't accepted the job position yet. I'd like to not teach in a way."

"Why's that?"

"Well, I love *kinner*, but I've tutored my cousins since I was fourteen and would like to try something else." She put a finger to her cheek to hide her blush line. "I'd love to work in a craft shop or with antiques, like Yoder's Antique Mall in Punxsy. Have you ever been there?"

He nodded. "Can get lost in the place. An Amish mall seems kind of funny, don't you think?"

Jane had never been to an *Englisher* mall and didn't quite understand his meaning.

"You know those fancy malls with escalators and whatnot. I work construction and mingle with the *English*. Getting back from a month long job." He smiled, accenting his dimples. "Puttin' up money while I'm single."

Jane didn't know why he was divulging so much information. feeling ever so awkward as he kept staring, his blue eyes fixed on her. "So you're getting married then? Planning on making money while you can?" As soon as she said this, she felt her face flush from the tip of her hairline down to her neck.

He gave a crooked grin. "Maybe someday. You

working while you can before your wedding?"

Should she say she was kind of courting Luke? She did hope in time that this restlessness would cease and she'd clearly see that Luke was the one for her. "I'll be writing to a *gut* friend who's a man. He'll be visiting soon to bring up my dog."

His lips made a thin line. "*Grossmammi* won't allow a dog in the house, if that's what you mean. She lives in a small *dawdyhaus.*"

Jane's heart sank. "But maybe she'll let me keep him in the barn?"

"Mighty cold in the barn. You're moving to what some folk call the 'Heart of the Snowbelt'. But maybe I can help…since I live in the main farmhouse."

"We'll be neighbors then?" Jane asked.

"*Jah*, and I can show you all around Chautauqua and Cattaraugus Counties. You seem like the adventuresome type. Ever meet a Native American?"

Once again, shame filled her. She was twenty, yet met only the people in her *Gmay.* Memories before fourteen were fuzzy. "*Nee*, I don't recall ever meeting one. I'd like that."

~*~

Jonas opened the door to the tiny house. "*Grossmammi*, don't want to scare you by walking in so late." He placed Jane's suitcase inside and entered, Jane following. The dim glow of an oil lamp illuminated Rose's sweet face. Jane was amazed at her angelic like appearance, dressed all in white, a cotton nightgown with white slippers. Jonas bent down to kiss her and she placed her hands on his clean shaven face. *"Ach,* Jonas, I've missed you."

"I've missed you, *Grossmammi."* He pulled her tight. "Miss your pies."

She chuckled into his blue overcoat. "I made cherry pie today."

Jonas smacked his lips. "My favorite." He turned her in the direction of Jane and the woman appeared startled. "How? When did you get here?"

"We were on the same van. She was *gut* company," he quipped.

Jane stepped forward and offered a hand and Rose took it. "Nice to meet you, dear. What do you think of the mountains?"

"They're majestic," Jane fumbled. "I've never seen any so high. The farms are much bigger, too. The houses in Punxsy are closer together. I can run over to my best friend's house in no time."

Rose shook her head in disbelief. "Can you believe I've never seen much in my seventy years? I'm like a tree, planted right here in Cherry Creek."

Jane found comfort in this. So, other Amish women had never traveled far from home.

"I'll take her suitcase to the spare room," Jonas said. "Need to say hello to my folks."

"They've missed you something fierce," Rose said.

Jonas lifted the suitcase, flexing his muscles. "They only miss me because I milk the cow when home."

"I can help," Jane offered. "Milked plenty of cows."

"You're my guest, and will have a job soon," Rose chirped. "Well, it's past my bedtime and I need to show

Jane her room." She went on tip toes to kiss and pat his cheek.

Peace enveloped Jane. By Rose's tone, she'd prepared a lovely room for her and was eager to show it. How odd that kind words could make a house seem like home in no time.

~*~

Jane could easily make her way around Rose's tiny kitchen and made scrambled eggs and bacon in no time. She peered into the icebox to find a loaf of store-bought bread. She'd make homemade a different day.

Rose appeared, her head up, sniffing the air. "I'm dreaming. I smell breakfast."

"Not a dream. I made breakfast most days for my aunt and her *kinner.*"

"Smells *gut.* And *danki*, Jane. You didn't have to cook your first day here."

Jane placed a plateful of food on the small round drop leaf table. A lacey runner came over the side and a vase full of wildflowers in a mason jar made the table so inviting. Jane took her plate over and sat across from Rose.

Rose bowed her head in silent prayer and Jane did as well. She thanked God for smoothing her path to Cherry Creek, enjoying not only the chatter with Jonas, but him escorting her to her destination. This *dawdyhaus* was so lovely, white walls with dark blue curtains pulled back to one side, large planked oak floors so shiny, she knew why this delicate, fancy-type of plain woman would never permit Peanut to invade her dollhouse.

Rose cleared her throat, the signal that prayer was over. "So, Jane, are you homesick at all or is that a silly question? You're a grown woman."

Jane dropped her fork, making a clatter. "Didn't Emma tell you my situation?"

"*Ach*, she mentioned you lived with your uncle and aunt along with four cousins."

"Anything else?" she prodded.

"Not really. Not that I recall, but a *gut* cup of coffee can jar my memory." She rose and headed towards her speckleware coffee pot. "*Danki* again for making the coffee."

"My aunt can't function without it," Jane said, surprised at how tenderly she let the words roll out of her mouth.

"You miss your aunt?"

"Rose, truth be told, the bishop removed me from her home. Her husband, my uncle, was abusive to me." Abusive. She said it with ease. Her shame was lifting.

Rose sipped her coffee as she crossed the kitchen to her seat. "Some men are idiots."

Jane just stared. This bright-eyed angel of a woman had spunk. "*Jah*, idiots. I'm glad you said it before I did."

"I don't mince words. Some men aren't worth spit." Her face contorted. "My first husband was *furhoodled* in the head."

"Your first husband. So you've had two?"

"*Jah*. Jonas is like his *grossdaddi*, my first husband. So is Johnny. Well, it's because they're his blood *kinner*."

"How did your first husband die?" Jane asked,

shocked that their first conversation wasn't small talk at all. Were folks from New York so blunt?

"He drowned when out fishing in Chautauqua Lake. His funeral was a celebration to me. I don't want anyone to burn in hell, but that man. Well, Lord forgive me. I hope he's not in hell."

Jane sprinkled salt on her eggs. "I've imagined my uncle getting hit by a car and going to…well, God knows where."

Rose chuckled. "So you don't have to hide the shame that comes with living a lie?"

"Live a lie?"

"*Jah*, you know, put on the happy face at *Gmay* only to fear the whole service he doesn't slap it within the week."

"Your husband slapped your face?"

"*Jah*, he did."

Rose said it so matter-of-factly, it puzzled Jane. "How did you get over such abuse?"

Her eyes misted. "Love. Love from a *gut* man. I remarried at thirty and had two more *kinner*. Michael lives in the farmhouse and you'll meet him today. My other son, Micah, has a farm ten miles away."

Jane leaned her elbow on the table. "Weren't you afraid to get married again?"

"Well, I was a bit more cautious and mature. I married my first husband, when only seventeen. He preyed on me like a hawk on a mouse. He was ten years older. At twenty-nine, when I was released from him, I started courting Matthew. Do you know Matthew means 'gift from God'? Well, that's what he was to me."

"When did you meet him?"

"I grew up with him. He liked me since grammar school. I never did experience such unconditional love in all my days. I'd do anything for that man. Anything. His love healed my heart." Tears pooled in her eyes. "He's in Glory for sure and certain. No doubt about that. And I'll be meeting him soon."

What a love story, Jane wanted to say, but didn't. "Rose, why do you say you'll be in Glory soon? Are you ill?"

"Fit as a fiddle," she quipped. "But I'm seventy and the Good Book only guarantees three score and ten years. So, I have an expiration date stamped on me and I'm more than willing to go."

Jane near choked on her eggs. "Rose, don't talk like that. You can see how your grandson loves you."

"Jonas was closer to Matthew. He's still grieving and mad. Ever since the funeral, he's had a strong leaning towards the English way of life."

"How? By working for them?"

"Nee, not those things. He's lacks *gelassenheit*. Too proud. It's those dimples he inherited from my Matthew. Knows he's handsome."

"Is he baptized? At his age, surely?"

Rose shook her head slowly, the ends of her prayer *kapp* swaying. "And that's why I say he has pride like the English."

Jane thought Jonas was a chatterbox, but didn't see any arrogance or unhealthy individualism in him. Well, she was here for work. "Rose, can I ask a favor? I see how dainty your house is. My friend wants to bring my dog up for me. Could he live in the barn? Jonas said he'd help tend to it."

Her eyes were aglow. "Jonas promised you that?"

"*Jah.*"

"Then I say it's fine with me."

"Also, can I go into town today to see if there's any work in a shop we passed by on the way here? It had a help wanted sign."

Rose grinned. "I'll have Jonas take you."

.

Chapter 7
Unexpected Temptations

Dear Luke,

First of all, I'm so excited. Rose, the elderly woman I'm be living with, has agreed that I can have Peanut here with me. Well, not exactly in her house, but in her son's barn. Do you think Peanut will be warm enough in a barn? I don't have all the details about heat and whatnot. It gets much colder up here, so maybe I can knit him a large wool blanket. Rose is a knitter, like me, and we plan to sit and knit and sip tea when the cold weather hits.

Luke, I was so afraid, when I passed over the Allegheny River. I wanted to have the driver stop right there and then and tell him to let me out at the nearest town. But I really believe I'm supposed to be here. Rose understands me. She's had great hardship in her life and can empathize. She's been checking though the Amish grapevine and found that I have an uncle. It's my mamm's brother. He's not Amish anymore and is shunned. Bishop Byler isn't too sure I should meet him.

I got a job in a variety store in town. I'm relieved. I didn't want to be a teacher. They need one, but I saw a sign in an English shop, but it sells lots of things to the Amish. The owner is Stella and seems right nice. I start in a few days.

Will you bring Peanut up like you offered? If it's not convenient for you, I understand. To be honest, Luke, I'd like for you to come with me to meet my uncle. I'm afraid again. I've read Jane Eyre five times now and she finds relatives she never met and it was all good for her. What if my cousins aren't good people? They left the Amish years ago.

Like I said, if you can't come, I understand. I'm making a few new friends here. Maybe I can ask one.

How is Aunt Miriam? Rose had a marriage like my aunt's, can you believe it? How are Jeremiah, Jacob, Sarah and Clara, all my cousins? I haven't had any letters yet.

Give your parents my love.

Your friend,

Jane

~*~

Luke read the letter again and then let out a '*whoopie*', throwing his black woolen hat in the air. He ran into the kitchen without taking his boots off and placed a kiss on his *mamm's* cheek. "Jane near begged me to go to Cherry Creek."

Ruth spun around. "She said yes? Jane's coming home?"

"*Nee, Mamm*. I'm taking Peanut up to her. She also wants me there to meet her uncle. Do you know anything about an Abigail Raber from New York?"

"That was Abigail's maiden name, I'm supposing." Ruth rubbed the back of her neck.

Luke led her to the table. "Let me massage that for you. All this canning with no help. Why couldn't anyone come to help you?"

"I just started, Luke. We women will have our frolics."

"Jane says she's canning pumpkins already. Seems like the weather up there is mighty different than here. A bad frost can come mid-September. She said the wind off the lakes have made most of the leaves fall off."

Ruth put her hand on her son's. "Luke, I'm concerned

for you. All you talk about is Jane. I do love her, but do you think you need to court other girls to know if she's the right one? You've never courted anyone."

Luke applied his nimble fingertips onto his *mamm's* shoulders. "You're so tense. Relax."

"I'm trying, but you've been sulking around here since she left. It could be God's will that she make a life in New York. Have you considered that?"

He made his way around the table and took a seat. "*Mamm*, Amish court in secret, *jah*?"

Ruth nodded, fiddling with the strings of her prayer *kapp*.

"How do you know I haven't courted anyone?"

She grinned. "Because you're my son and an open book. I'd know." She shifted. "Have you? I mean, is there someone else besides Jane?"

Luke took his *mamm's* hands. "It's a secret. But I can give you a hint."

"What?"

"She's a lot like you. *Mamm*, I don't say it much, but I think the way you reach out to others in need, take care of this old farmhouse after all us kids left, except me… well, you never make me feel like a burden."

"Because you're not."

"You and *Daed* could be in a *dawdyhaus* if it weren't for me."

Ruth's lips parted in disbelief. "I love this place. And you'll have your own house on the land out back." She eyed him. "Are you saying you'd like to live here, being the last to marry, and have a *dawdyhaus* built on the land intended for you?"

Luke knew his *mamm* was hopeful he was making plans. That maybe he was secretly courting someone. But he had an undisturbed peace, almost like a knowing, that Jane would be his wife someday. She just needed time to find out who she really was. Time to find out she isn't a character in a novel like *Jane Eyre*. "*Mamm*, you stay here in this house you love so much. Give each minute to God and the hours will take care of themselves."

Ruth grinned. "Luke, you mess that proverb up all the time. It's 'Live each short hour with God and the long years will take care of themselves.'"

Luke simply nodded in agreement, but knew he was right. He couldn't stand to think of 'long years' away from Jane, so he decided that when he fretted, or sulked as his *mamm* put it, he'd give each of his cares to God, even it was every minute.

Dear Emma,

I'm sorry I haven't written yet. I'm just so busy settling in. I live with Rose, right in her little dawdyhaus.

I met someone up here. His name is Jonas Hershberger. He's so attractive, but he's not baptized and he's twenty-three. His grossmammi is Rose. Somehow I think they believe I can straighten him out.

Emma, do you think he's like Mr. Rochester? He was a wild one and Jane tamed him, even making him a believer. I do find comfort in my Bible, dear Emma. Don't worry about me.

Have you seen Aunt Miriam? Let me know. I'm praying for her. How is Uncle Malachi handling his shunning? Has he been kinder

*to my cousins? Maybe you can pop in and check on them from time
to time.*

*I'm going to meet my mom's brother and his kids. Can you believe
it? I don't understand why he didn't come to her funeral. It's all so
odd. Maybe he's a bad man. Jane Eyre's cousins she finally met
were nice. Pray for me. I'm nervous about this meeting.*

*I just wrote to Luke to see if he can bring Peanut up. Maybe you
could come with him. I know it's puttin' up time, so most likely the
answer will be no. I'm helping Rose put up lots of pumpkin pie
filling. She makes all the pies for Thanksgiving for her extended
family, so we're canning a lot.*

Your friend,

Jane

~*~

Emma hitched up the horse and buggy and headed
straight over to the Miller's after reading Jane's letter. Jane
was becoming *furhoodled* in her head. For a smart woman,
she was taking the whole *Jane Eyre* novel too seriously.
This new handsome man was not for her!

Truth be told, she could read Jane like a book and
knew Jane loved Luke. Jane just hadn't figured it out yet.
Her complicated life with such hardship made her think
everything in life was a struggle or some kind of mystery.

As she passed Miriam's place, she noticed Sarah and
Clara in the garden picking beans and Jeremiah and Jacob
filling the corn crib. Since there was no sign of Malachi,
she decided to stop and visit a spell. Hitching the horse to
a post near the kitchen garden, Emma almost lost her
balance when Clara near toppled her over, hanging
around her neck for support. "Clara, what on earth is

wrong?"

"I'm so glad you're here. *Mamm's* acting mighty funny," she cried, swiping a tear from her cheek. "She's not making any sense."

"What do you mean?"

"Follow me and I'll show ya." Clara darted to the kitchen door, while Emma shot up a prayer. This family had more stress in it than some with fifteen *kinner*. When she entered, Emma was not prepared. Miriam clutched an Amish doll to her bosom and cried. She looked up at Emma and clutched the doll tighter. "Miriam, what are you doing?"

Miriam's body racked with sobs and Clara led her to a wooden chair. "*Mamm*, why are you crying?"

She cradled the doll in her arms. "*Yinz* were all wee ones once. And we were happy."

"*Jah, Mamm*," Clara said evenly. "I'm happy now."

"You'll all leave. I'll be alone."

Emma sat in the chair opposite Miriam. "You are never alone. You have the People and Lord above." Emma, pinched the backs of Miriam's hands. Just what she suspected. "When was the last time you drank anything?"

Miriam's tears only spilled out all the more. "Don't know."

"Well, you're dehydrated. Have you eaten today?" Emma prodded.

Clara spoke up. "She hasn't cooked in two days. We're eating stuff out of the pantry."

"And where is your *daed*?" Emma asked Clara.

Clara thrust her palms up. "Don't know. Suspect he's out scouting land for hunting." She poured lemonade from the icebox and handed it to her *mamm* who pushed it away.

"Miriam, you need to drink. Why are you doing this?" She held the doll close. "I have no desire. No will."

Emma had heard from her own *mamm* that Miriam was at her wit's ends living with a shunned man who wouldn't abide by the shunning. She turned to whisper in Clara's ear. "Any more bruises from your *daed*?"

Clara shook her head. "*Nee*," she said, leaning in to whisper into Emma's ear. "But he's been ornery. It's like he's driving her crazy over the whole shunning. *Mamm's* determined to carry it out in the home by him sitting at a separate table and they sleep in different bedrooms, and such, but *daed* makes it hard."

Emma had never seen an Amish man with so much rotten fruit. A tree is known by its fruit, the Bible said, and Malachi was one bad apple. Her *mamm* had said to try to have pity on him. Why? Was there something her *mamm* knew? Something that Miriam knew and was she so torn she was losing her mind?

"Clara, I'm headed over to see Luke. He's headed up to see Jane soon and we need to talk."

Clara pressed her hand on her heart. "I hope she marries him and we can live with them," she said softly.

Emma's eyes narrowed and she studied Clara. Sheer terror was etched into her face. She turned and hugged Miriam, telling her that her *mamm* would stop over and lead Clara outside by the elbow. "Are your *bruder* and sister afraid to live here? I can tell the bishop. Someone may have to come and live here, until things settle down."

Clara slowly closed her eyes. "Who?"

"I don't know, but I'll tell my *mamm* and we'll find *yinz* help. And Clara, run over to my house if you need anything."

Clara nodded in compliance, but Emma doubted she'd take her up on the offer. The entire farm seemed to be draped in a veil of fear. "What a mess," she said under her breath.

~*~

Jane pulled her black wool cape tighter as she stepped out of the variety shop, another *wunderbar* day, another *wunderbar* memory to put in her journal. October felt like winter here in New York. She inhaled deeply and let out air that made white wisps. Jane observed the little town she was so blessed to be planted in. She'd seen pictures like this at Yoder's Antique store. Wooden plank shops, many decked with gingerbread trimming lined both sides of the road and a sidewalk with huge maple trees with autumn foliage at its peak. She'd never seen such shades of reds, the colors in Pennsylvania being more subdued.

When Jonas pulled up to the curb, she grinned. She'd grown so fond of this fun-loving man. She almost forgot what a hard belly laugh felt like. "Hello, Jonas," she said as she stepped into the buggy. "*Danki* for picking me up."

He ogled at her large bag. "More yarn? My *grossmammi* making all her *grandkinner* blankets for Christmas?"

"I don't think so. We're knitting for charity. Making plenty of scarves."

Jonas leaned towards her as he urged the horse onto the street. "Will you make me one?"

"Are you poor, in need of charity?" she asked seriously.

He elbowed her. "Just kidding. Jane, I think it's my mission in life to cheer you up. Would you like to do something fun?"

"Go back to the library," she blurted. "I've never seen anything like that place in Jamestown."

He took her hand. "I was thinking about dinner at the Grainery."

Jane gulped. Weren't they supposed to get to know each other at Singings? "Are you going to the singing this Sunday?"

"*Nee.* I'm too old for that kind of thing. And, I said I want to cheer you up."

Jane slipped her hand free. "Singing's the best cure for a homesick heart."

He turned to her. "Homesick. For anyone special?"

"Well, I have friends. And my cousins who I'm mighty concerned for. My uncle's shunned and making life miserable for my cousins. I'll find out more because Luke's coming up anytime he can get a driver."

"Luke? *Ach, jah.* You mentioned he was bringing your dog."

She nodded as warmth filled her heart. "I can't wait to see ... Peanut, the dog."

As he turned the corner, the wheels slid and the horse clasped at the ground, gaining balance. Luke pulled Jane close. "Ice already."

"You were driving mighty fast before turning"

"*Nee*, it was an icy spot. We can get a foot of snow by the end of October." He slid closer. "You're shivering."

Jane wasn't shivering, she was shaking, trembling at how much she liked being near him. But how did a woman act around a man? She had no experience and felt once again anger arise towards her uncle. *He handicapped me.*

"What are you thinking Jane?"

The warmth of his breath made her cheeks burn. "Nothing."

"You look sad."

"I don't know. Sometimes I think of my uncle and get upset. I hear he's driving my aunt nuts."

"Well, being under the ban would be hard," he informed. "I've seen it and truth be told, it's why I'm not baptized yet."

"But it's for the *gut* of the People. What if everyone broke their vow to the church? We'd have no community to fall back on. It should be harsh."

"Harsh enough that you couldn't meet your uncle?"

The words hung like a spell in the air. "What?"

"Your uncle. He's shunned. Not welcome to your *mamm's* funeral all those years back. Now, I think that's cruel."

Jane gasped. "I'd rather he'd come for me than have to live with my Uncle Malachi."

Jonas slowed the horse to a slow walk. "He never had the opportunity. He left a decade ago."

Jane froze. "That's how your *grossmammi* knew about

him?"

"*Jah.* Had a job up in Buffalo once." He let out a forced laugh. "My *grossmammi* thought I had a girl there."

"An Amish girl, of course," Jane added.

"Maybe," Jonas said straightening, his head high. "I can do anything outside the *Ordnung,* until I get baptized," he quipped. "And until then, I plan to live. Jane, have you ever wondered what it's like to live? Live unrestrained?"

Something in Jane wanted to run wild. "Sometimes," she said softly.

"Come with me on a trip."

"What?" She pushed him back as he tried to steal a kiss. "I'm baptized. And I could never. *Ach,* we're not married."

"A day trip, not overnight," he said, his eyes looking overly rejected. "We could go bowling, have lunch out and take a sleigh ride. And then eat dinner."

The dancing of his blue eyes intoxicated her, as did his dimples when he smiled. "Let me think about it. It's not against the rules to have fun, *jah*?"

He pulled her close. "Jane, I thought girls like you were only in my dreams." He brushed her cheek with his finger. "I'm starting to really care for you."

The pounding of her heart against her ribcage didn't stop, but only hammered harder. Was this love? Was he the answer to her prayer?

Karen Anna Vogel

Chapter 8
A Canine Companion

Luke leaned against his driver's car. "Vinny, maybe we should just leave the dog and get going back to Punxsutawney. Rose said Jane's usually home by now, so something must have come up."

Vinny leaned against the car near Luke. "You have the hots for this chick, don't ya?"

Luke had been friends with Vinny since *kinners*, but his mind concerning women wasn't his. "The hots? Seriously, Vinny, you're not fifteen anymore."

He nudged Luke. "Hey, Buddy, Jane is hot. If she wasn't Amish, I'd take a try."

Luke rolled his eyes. "All you see is the fur or feathers."

"Come again? Man, Luke, sometimes you're weird."

"Okay, bad comparison. Take a turtle. A nice painted turtle's colorful, but they can bite."

"*Oooouch,*" Vinny howled. "I see what you mean. But Jane seems, well, nice on the inside, too. She's the total package, if you know what I mean."

He did know what Vinny meant. If only Jane could see what a treasure she was. He heard horse hoofs, laughter, and saw the flickering of lantern lights. Soon a buggy pulled into the Hershberger's driveway and Luke could see through the dusk that it was Jane with a man. *Lord, help me.*

A loud squeal and then Jane jumping out of the buggy,

running towards him disarmed him. He opened his arms and she flew into them. "Luke, you're here. I didn't know you were coming."

He held her tight and then stepped back to take in the sight of her. Jane seemed younger and more carefree. It was like the girl he'd met when he was fourteen and she'd come to Punxsutawney. "I've missed you."

"That's an understatement," Vinny blurted. "You're all he talks about. Jane this and Jane that." He pushed them together. "Get married already."

Luke wanted to punch his friend at his crass remarks. Jane's eyes fell and she fiddled with the end of her cape. Vinny slapped her on the back. "I'm only kidding. It's me. Vinny, remember. The kid with the big mouth?"

Jonas approached and slid a protective arm around Jane. "Is everything alright?"

Jane stepped towards Luke and slid an arm through his. "This is Luke, my friend I've been telling you about. And Luke, this is Jonas Hershberger. His parents live in the big farmhouse."

"And this is Vinney, my driver," Luke informed.

Jonas tipped his black wool hat. "Have you brought the dog? I'll be taking care of her."

"It's a him," Luke corrected. "And I've already talked to your folks and have him bedded down in the barn. It's mighty cold up here, though."

"If it's a real cold night, I'll let him inside," Jonas said, his eyes not wandering from Jane's.

Now Luke knew he needed to repent because within five minutes, he wanted to punch two people. This guy was an unabashed flirt. "Jane, can we take a walk before I leave?"

"Leave? *Ach*, Luke, you can't leave."

"Hey Sunshine," Vinny crooned. "We waited a few hours for you. Had supper with the grandma. Real doll of a woman and man, can she cook. But I need to work in the morning."

"A quick walk," Luke pleaded.

Jane's eyes misted. "But I didn't know you were coming. Why didn't you write, Luke?"

"I did. Didn't you get my letter?"

"*Nee* or I'd have come home right quick from work." She turned to Jonas. "Was there a letter for me? I know you check all the mailboxes before anyone else."

Jonas fumbled for words and then said, "*Ach*, maybe. The writing wasn't too legible. I suppose I thought it was for my *daed*."

Luke wiped beads of perspiration off his upper lip. This guy had made Jane late on purpose. He took Jane's hand. "I'll stay overnight if you want me to. We can spend the day together tomorrow."

Vinny flicked him on the side of his head. "How about me, Bozo? I'm not driving through those mountains by my lonesome. There's a highway marked 666. That's the devil's number."

Jonas laughed. "I've heard that one before. Afraid someone will come out with a pitchfork?"

Vinny kicked a stone, trying to look brave. "No, just afraid of falling asleep at the wheel."

"Stay here and get up early," Jane suggested. "You

have to try Rose's cooking." She glanced over at Luke. "I'm collecting recipes."

Luke's heart melted. Was she implying she was thinking about meals she'd prepare for the two of them when they wed? As much as this Jonas irritated him, he knew Jane could be trusted to not fall for a charmer. *She'll see right through this guy.*

~*~

Luke threw down his napkin, showing he liked Rose's stew.

"Do you want more?" Rose asked.

Jane leaned to meet Luke's gaze. She shook her head slightly, hoping he'd catch her meaning. Rose wanted company but Jane needed to talk to him before he went back home.

"Danki, Rose, but we need to get on the road. I need to talk to Jane about her aunt."

Vinny raised one hand like he was in school. "I'll take more of that stew. Man, do the Amish know how to cook or what? You should start a restaurant."

Rose's face glowed. *"Ach, danki,* Vinny. You can have a big breakfast if you stay overnight. Plenty of room over at the big farm."

Vinny hit his chest with a fist. "You're killing me. I'd love to stay, but I have work in the morning. Six o'clock sharp."

"That's late," Rose chuckled. "We get up at four. Why not leave in the morning? Ham and eggs, fresh from the farm."

Vinny shot a look over to Luke. "You could have a

longer walk with your girlfriend, if we had breakfast here."

Rose's mouth gaped. "You two are courting?"

Deep down, for some reason, Jane hoped Luke would say yes. But he only shook his head, saying they were good friends. Well, it was the truth, but why did it sting?

"I think we need to leave tonight," Luke said. "Jane and I can talk quick-like."

Now Jane's heart was in her toes. Didn't he miss her? She took his lead as he rose to get his jacket off the peg board near the door.

Frigid air hit her face as she stepped out onto the little porch. Luke took her hand, leading her down the steps. "Is there a nice place to take a walk?"

"Why can't you stay?" she blurted, and then covered her mouth. Her tone was more like a yell than a question.

Luke's mellow brown eyes could be seen by the light of a full moon. "Jane, does it mean that much to you?"

"*Ach, nee,*" she lied. "You have work to do with all your animals. I understand."

He looked unconvinced, a brow raised.

"I'm a little homesick, but I don't know why. Rose treats me like a real *grossmammi*. The whole Hershberger clan does."

He let go of her hand and they ambled out onto the driveway. "Let's take the road to the back of the farm. Busy road out front." He cleared his voice. "Jane, your aunt's been hospitalized for stress."

"Are my cousins alright? Who's watching them?"

"Well, Malachi's gone missing. No one knows where

he is. No news through the Amish grapevine." Luke sighed. "*Daed* was wondering if you'd keep your stay here short and come home to help her out. With Malachi gone and all."

"What?" Jane asked indignantly. "My uncle could show up at any time if I was there, and I wouldn't feel safe. Why ask me?"

Luke put both hands up. "Like Vinny says, 'I'm the messenger, not the message'." He put an arm around her. "Your cousins have been asking for you. Sarah's been crying, missing you. The boys say they miss your cooking and Clara's at her wit's end, trying to tend to everyone."

The faces of her cousins flashed before her. Poor kids should have had a stable home. More memories of her own childhood had come back and Jane knew the blessing of parents who loved each other and the Lord. "Luke, I can't come home right now. I hope to meet my uncle and cousins. My other ones." Shyness overcame her but she forced herself to speak. "I'm mighty nervous and was hoping you could come with me."

He stopped and studied her. "Jane, I'd do anything for you. Is the meeting tomorrow? Is that why Rose is asking us to stay?"

She shook her head. "The meeting isn't even set up yet. My uncle and cousins left the Amish and are shunned. I have a meeting with the bishop tomorrow. I need permission to go."

He jutted his jaw, showing his chiseled features which Jane found so appealing. Having not seen him in a few weeks was harder than she imagined. "You let me know when the meeting with your uncle is and I'll do my best to be up here."

Rejection crept into Jane. Why couldn't Luke stay overnight? He could get a bus back home tomorrow. He was being inflexible. Or was she being unreasonable? But still the same, she felt distanced from him. "Luke, is there something wrong?"

His countenance fell. "I was hoping you'd come home and help your aunt."

She gawked. "Luke, my uncle could show up anytime at his farm. I left out of fear. He's not near New York. Or is he? You don't think he's looking?" She wrung her hands, just the thought made her squirm.

"I'm sure you're safe," he reassured. "And you have Peanut here now to protect you."

"And new friends," she said evenly. "The Hershbergers are the kindest Amish folk I've met outside of Punxsy. I thought other Amish would be like my uncle, but now I see he's a rare bird."

He gripped her shoulders. "Come back, Jane. We all need you."

She pushed him away. "Everyone needs me to do something. I know this sounds selfish, but what about me? I have the chance to meet long lost cousins, just like Jane Eyre.

Luke rolled his eyes. "*Ach,* Jane, you and that novel. It's fiction, you know."

"So are parables in the Bible. But they teach us lessons and make us think about our lives. And for the first time since my parent's death, I'm thinking about me. I don't care if it's right or wrong."

Stepping back, Luke appeared dazed. "I think Rose is rubbing off on you."

Rose? What did he mean? "She's had a hard life and is helping me."

"She's so outspoken is what I'm saying. Are all Amish folks like that around here?"

Indignation filled her. She was starved for a listening ear and Rose took more than ample time, taking in every word, every hurt. "Rose is a gift from above. She listens and gives *gut* advice."

"And she wants you to marry her nephew," Luke exclaimed. "Ever notice how many times she praised him to the hilt during dinner? She looked shocked at the thought of us courting. Didn't you ever mention me to her?"

Jane felt too choked up to speak. Jutting out her jaw to stop any tears from forming, like she'd always done, she bit her lower lip and just stared at Luke.

"I take it that she has no idea who I am. That I hope to marry you someday, when you've found your footing." Luke clamped a hand over her now quivering chin and lifted it gently. "Jane, what's going on? Have we drifted in such a short time?"

She didn't know, so she remained silent. This new Jane she was becoming was foreign to her, so how could she explain it to Luke? "Luke, there's so much emotion in me, it may take years to sift through it all."

He drew her to himself and rubbed her back. "I'm here for you. Don't ever forget that." He kissed the top of her prayer *kapp*. "We'll catch up during Thanksgiving, when you come home."

"If I do."

Luke stiffened. "Why say that? Your cousins are expecting you, along with my *mamm*. Big dinner at our house with you and your cousins."

"Rose asked me to stay here."

"Why?" Luke asked, holding her by the shoulders, his gaze demanding an answer. "She has *kinner* all around her."

Jane saw pain in Luke's eyes and it stabbed her. "I'll try. It's true she's gotten real attached to me, but I need that right now. As for Jonas, I'm not fooled by his flirting. I don't trust him."

A smile swiftly slid across Luke's face. "*Ach*, Jane, I was worried. He's a charmer."

"I know, but I'm strong. I won't fall for his."

"His what?"

"*Ach*, he tries to steal kisses as a joke."

"As a joke? How odd. But you don't."

"*Nee*. I always turn my head. Believe me, the more he does it, the less appealing he seems."

Luke cupped her cheeks and leaned into a kiss that lingered. "I love you, Jane. Don't you forget our plans."

Her first kiss from Luke was so tender, so loving, tears welled up to near overflowing. *He loves me even though I'm scarred.* "Luke, I hope I find my way soon. I miss being with you." She went on tiptoes and puckered her lips for another kiss.

~*~

Jonas put a hand on Jane's shoulder as Luke and Vinny drove away. Rose pat her hand. "Don't cry, Jane. New York's your home for now.

"I'm so homesick. Never expected to fill this way," she said, blinking back tears.

Rose opened the door to her humble abode. "Let's have some hot chocolate with whipped cream."

"Sounds *gut* to me," Jonas quipped, taking Jane's hand. She withdrew it. "Jonas, I'd like to talk to Rose alone."

"Well, after some hot chocolate," he said with a wink.

Rose rolled her eyes. "Jonas, your *mamm* has a pot of hot chocolate at all times on her stove, *jah*?"

He made a phony pout. "Please, *Grossmammi*? You make the best."

Rose turned to Jane. "Do you mind if he joins us?"

She did mind. He was chasing her like a coon dog does a raccoon. But this was Rose's house, so she nodded an okay.

They circled around her table as Rose poured milk into a pan and fed her stove another log. Jane thought this hard work for an elderly woman. "Rose, don't they allow natural gas stoves?"

"We don't have the luxury up here," Jonas said. "You all live on the Marcellus Shale and can drill for gas, *jah*?"

"*Jah*. We even make a bit of profit off the wells drilled. Many in Punxsutawney have natural gas for free now and aren't beholden to the government, still being off the grid."

"So do you think it primitive up here?" Jonas prodded.

Jane hadn't mentioned how much she missed more

modern conditions. "I think the glow of oil lamps are pretty. I used to only have a candle."

Rose spun around. "So your uncle didn't have natural gas?"

"He did, but he said he didn't trust it. We used oil lamps in the house, just like here, but my *mamm* had a natural gas stove."

"But you said you had a candle," Rose said. "Not a lamp?"

A dark shroud covered her. "*Nee*, not me, only my cousins."

Jonas reached for her hand across the tiny table. "They were horrible to you."

She nodded. "My aunt's ill because of all the stress. My uncle left and Luke asked if I could come back home and help my cousins."

Jonas and Rose stared hard at her.

"My cousins need me, but I said I want to stay a while to meet my uncle."

"Luke doesn't give a hoot about your safety," Jonas snapped. "How could he ask you to be in the same house where you were abused? Your uncle could show up."

Why had Luke asked such a dangerous thing? she wondered. "I'm sure the elders and bishop have a plan for my safety now that the cat's out of the bag about how abusive my uncle is. My best friend lives next door and could check in on us all regularly."

Jonas cracked his knuckles, the popping echoing around the walls. "Did you say best 'friend'? And she lived next door?"

Jane nodded, not understanding where this conversation was heading.

"Jane, she had to have known about you being abused. She didn't care."

Jane felt that old feeling of being short of breath, being taken by surprise. "I didn't tell Emma. I was brainwashed, thinking my uncle's abuse was normal."

He leaned forward. "And why would you think that? It's never right to strike a woman and keep her locked up, treating her like a servant girl."

"I hid it all from Emma."

"*Nee*, Jane," Jonas yelled. "She didn't care. Your cousins didn't care or they'd have found you some help."

Rose set two mugs on the table. "Seems to me many were paralyzed by fear." She slid into a wooden chair and folded her hands. "I know what that's like. Jonas, you're being too outspoken about things you don't know about."

"I don't want her going back there," Jonas said in surrender. "Jane, don't go back. You deserve better and can get a new start up here."

Jane noticed Rose smile warmly. Rose loved her and did want her to be a part of the big Hershberger clan. "I need to read my Bible," Jane said, surprising herself.

"Sounds like a *gut* thing to do," Rose said. "Once you're done enjoying your hot chocolate. You have a meeting with the bishop tomorrow and need to seek God."

Jane's eyes misted as she met Rose's. This woman's love was a balm to her soul.

Chapter 9
A Season of Rest

"Our Father which art in heaven, Hallowed be thy name.
Thy kingdom come, Thy will be done in earth, as it is in
heaven.
Give us this day our daily bread.
And forgive us our debts, as we forgive our debtors.
And lead us not into temptation, but deliver us from evil:
For thine is the kingdom, and the power, and the glory, forever.
Amen."

Jane prayed on her knees, her hands folded, leaning against her bed. *Lord, I'm confused. Is it true? Am I so naïve to think Emma didn't see anything? Were the Amish in Punxsutawney so concerned with keeping the peace that no one dared to confront my uncle? But then Rose said she understood being silent, having had a hard first marriage.* But Luke suspected things weren't right. His kiss tonight told her much. It was gentle and caring, like him. Maybe he thought his *daed* and the Bishop knew and Luke didn't want to speak up over his elders.

She licked her lips, still feeling Luke's kiss. No, she would not believe what Jonas was trying to imply. He was driving a wedge between her and folks in Punxsutawney.

Lead me not into temptation, Lord. Deliver me from evil.

As much as Luke's embrace meant and his declaration of love, he felt so far away. Too far away. But she needed time here in New York to meet her relatives. How odd that Jane Eyre's story was so similar to hers. The only thing she was pretty sure of, Jonas was not her Mr. Rochester. She felt at home with Luke. Safe and at peace.

Lord, give me strength to be around such a handsome man as Jonas and not fall for his charms. Charm is deceitful, like the Bible says.

A light flashed in the window. What on earth? The light steadied on her window. Uncle Malachi? Had he come to New York?

She snuck over to the window and peaked behind the dark blue curtain. The flashlight was now on someone's face: Jonas's. She let out a sigh of relief. What did he want?

Jane lifted the little window. "Jonas, you scared me. Is this a New York prank?"

"*Nee*, a sign that we want to talk," he said in a raspy whisper.

How odd. No one in Punxsy did this. "What do you want?"

"What do you think?"

"I don't know. Is something wrong?"

"Come on down and I'll tell you."

She clenched her jaw. "I need to go to sleep."

"It'll only take a minute."

Jane's brows furrowed. "Alright."

Glad that she hadn't unpinned her hair and still in her Amish dress, she slipped on her prayer *kapp* and tip toed down the few steps to the landing. Getting her warm cape off the peg, she stepped outside. Before she knew it, Jonas enveloped her and kissed her.

"Stop," she was able to get out, but he only devoured

her more. She felt a strange desire course through her veins and found herself wanting to give in to his affection, and did for a little too long.

"Luke never kissed you like that, *jah?*" he breathed on her ear.

She met his eyes. "*Nee*. He has manners. Don't try kissing me again, understand?"

"Are you sure that's what you want?" he asked, leaning towards her.

"*Jah*, very sure," she said, pushing him away, but he didn't slacken his grasp but tightened it. Fear gripped her. "Jonas, let me go."

"I think I love you. I wanted to tell you. To show you. When that Luke guy came I thought you'd leave."

Jane had learned to live with ill treatment, not so much attention, and her mind whirled as if in a tornado and she needed something to hold on to. But it wouldn't be Jonas. No, she needed God's direction more than ever.

~*~

The next morning, Jane got on her knees once she slid out of bed. *Lord Jesus Christ, Son of God, have mercy on me, a sinner.* The Jesus Prayer book she'd bought in town was one she could say when her thoughts were jumbled. Her dreams last night, of her and Jonas, made her feel dirty. His kisses last night had prompted it, for sure, but something in her she'd never recognized, *lust*, was a sin and she felt humbled. Being so cooped up most of her life, she thought she'd learned about herself, but not sin. *Lord Jesus Christ, Son of God, have mercy on me, a sinner. Give me strength to be around Jonas and not fall into temptation. And give me strength this morning to talk to the bishop, alone. Ach, how I wish Luke could be here to verify and fill in if I lose my train of thought.* But he did need to get back to Punxsutawney. Rose was going to a quilting frolic and almost canceled, but Jane wouldn't have her do this. Her heart warmed. Rose would do anything for her and love was healing her brokenness.

She quickly washed in the basin and dressed and pinned her hair back. As she secured the last clasp, she wondered who would see her long blonde hair for the first time. Her husband, of course, but would it be Luke? Deep down she prayed so. He was the kindest man, even though his kiss didn't shoot sparks down to her toes, like Jonas's.

She padded down the steps, smelling bacon and eggs, her favorite. Rose knew this day would be hard and wanted to encourage her with little niceties. But when she turned to the right, entering the kitchen, she didn't see Rose at all. "Jonas, what are you doing here?"

He winked. "I'm taking *grossmammi's* place, going with you to the bishop."

Jane clenched her fists. "Don't bother. I'd like a woman with me."

"You asked Luke, but he was too busy. Well, I take time for weighty matters."

Weighty matters? Such fine talk. "It's only to ask permission to see my uncle."

"And if he says no, what will you do? And how will you feel?" He put a plate on the table. "I want to be there for you if you fall, Jane."

Jane felt like running out the door. *Running back to Punxsy.* He didn't want to catch her when she fell, he wanted her to fall, right into his arms. And he looked so handsome this morning, wearing his good clothes: black trousers and vest with a white shirt. She obeyed and sat as he spooned scrambled eggs onto her plate. "What do you mean if I fall?"

"Get upset." He put a hand on her shoulder. "I want to help you, Jane. This day will be hard, but I have a treat."

Jane didn't want to ask what this treat was. *A stolen kiss?*

"I hired a driver to take us to Salamanca to visit the museum this afternoon. You wouldn't' believe the stuff in there. Real Native American relics."

"Really?" Jane's heart leapt.

"I promised I'd take you to see the Native Americans and I keep my promises."

"I don't recall you promising?"

"In the van coming up, when we first met. My word's as good as a promise."

Jane couldn't help but smile with delight. Her world was opening up to meet people of all different kinds of backgrounds, something that appealed to her. Emma had a hobby of reading about Ancient Egypt and she'd always envied her that freedom. "Do they sale books at the museum?"

"*Jah*, plenty. There's one about longhouses. Do you know several families would live in one long house made of logs? The Amish don't have the corner on community, *jah?*"

"Have the corner? What do you mean?" Jane puzzled.

Placing bacon on the table, he sat in the seat across from her and dug into his eggs. "I work with the English and pick up lots of their sayings. What I mean is that lots of people have community, not just the Amish."

Jane frowned. "They don't live in those long houses now, do they?"

"*Nee*, in the past, but they have their own culture and stick by each other. When the government came in to try to take their land away, they set tires on fire on the highway. The highway went through their land and they blocked it. I like their bravery."

Jane jabbed at the bacon. "Maybe we can discuss this at the museum. I need coffee."

Jonas smacked the side of his head. "I forgot to make it." His dimples deepened as he grinned. "Not sure how *Grossmammi's* coffee pot works. *Mamm* always makes mine."

His whimsical look made Jane laugh. "I'll teach you."

~*~

Bishop Byler wiped moisture from his eyes after Jane answered question after question concerning life with her Uncle Malachi. "I just hope you won't jump from the frying pan into the fire. What if you're hurt by your fancy uncle and cousins? Worse yet, be pulled away from your faith at such a vulnerable time?"

Jane smashed her lips together, bracing herself for the blow.

"Dear one, don't you think you need a season of rest?

Enjoy your life in Cherry Creek. Rose is a *wunderbar gut* woman who will show you what a real *mamm* is like."

Jane rubbed her sweaty palms together. "I had a *mamm* once and now's the chance to meet her *bruder*."

"Will it be helpful?" Bishop Byler asked. "We Amish move forward."

"I'd like to know why he didn't go to my *mamm's* funeral and take me with him," she blurted, heat rising in her face. "He could have helped me. Saved me from years of misery."

"Or it could have been worse with him. He rejected the Amish faith."

Jane lowered her head, trying to gain control. "My so-called Amish uncle was abusive."

The bishop pulled out his pipe and striking a match lit it. After a few puffs, he crossed his arms as if in deep contemplation. "Jane, you can't undo the past, only forgive."

"Forgive?" Jane shot up.

Jonas took her hand, gently pulling her down. "I can go with her if it helps, Bishop. It could be a quick visit, just so Jane can meet kin."

The Bishop's eyes were round orbs. "Are you two courting?"

"*Nee*, we are not," Jane interjected before Jonas had a chance to speak. "But can I go if someone goes with me?"

The Bishop blew a smoke ring into the air. "Let me pray about it and consult the elders. You're far from home and like I said, vulnerable. I'll let you know in a few weeks. Don't want to rush the matter."

Irritation sizzled up and down Jane's spine. Somehow, this made the Amish seem so cruel. "I can't meet my *mamm's bruder?*" she whispered aloud.

Jonas took her hand. "He didn't say that. Bishop just wants to not be hasty. Your uncle is fancy and under the ban, just like your uncle in Punxsutawney."

Somehow this revelation helped this blow to Jane. What's good for the goose was good for the gander, as the saying went. Visiting banned Amish was forbidden. "I guess I'll wait then."

"I'll write your bishop back home in Punxsutawney. And maybe you can talk to him, when you visit for Thanksgiving."

"*Ach,* Rose wants me to stay for Thanksgiving."

"I'm sure she'll understand," Bishop Byler said. "She gets lonely, but not for long with the big Hershberger clan all around her."

Luke's suggestion that she stay in her uncle's house made her cringe. "I'm not sure I have a place to stay."

"Now why's that?" Bishop Byler asked.

"She'd have to live in danger," Jonas blurted. "Her uncle might come around."

The bishop pulled at his long gray beard. "Forget what I said about Thanksgiving if it causes confusion or grief. Jane, that's the last thing you need is to worry. I keep thinking you need to rest and stay put. So, enjoy your job the Lord provided at the craft store and do something *gut* for the nerves."

"*Grossmammi* says crocheting stops her from fretting,"

Jonas said. "She'll teach you. She also knows how to make those lacey looking round things."

Jane grinned. "Doilies. I've always wanted to learn to crochet, and working in the store, it would be helpful if I could make them to display."

Bishop Byler flipped through his black leather Bible and then leaned over to read:

To everything there is a season, and a time to every purpose under the heaven:

A time to be born, and a time to die; a time to plant, and a time to pluck up that which is planted;

A time to kill, and a time to heal; a time to break down, and a time to build up;

A time to weep, and a time to laugh; a time to mourn, and a time to dance;

A time to cast away stones, and a time to gather stones together; a time to embrace, and a time to refrain from embracing;

A time to get, and a time to lose; a time to keep, and a time to cast away;

A time to rend, and a time to sew; a time to keep silence, and a time to speak;

A time to love, and a time to hate; a time of war, and a time of peace.

He hath made everything beautiful in his time

His tender light blue eyes met Jane's. "Can we trust the Lord to make your life beautiful in His time, even if it takes longer than you thought? Even if it's not how you planned it?"

Jane's brother's funeral flashed before her. "That was read at my *bruder's* funeral."

"Your *bruder* passed away in the house fire, too?" Bishop Byler asked.

"My *bruder* died the year before," Jane said in a trembling voice.

The bishop's brow creased and he made another smoke ring. "Did you meet your uncle from these parts at the funeral?"

"*Nee*," Jane sighed. "That's odd."

"*Jah*," Jonas interjected. "Folks travel far for funerals, sometimes clear across the country."

Jane pondered this and her desire to meet her uncle waned. The bishop was wise. Take time to rest and not figure everything out. He makes all things beautiful in his time, had been one of her favorite verses, but she didn't realize it came after all that the bishop read, the seasons of life's ups and downs, the time to embrace and the time to refrain.

Bishop Byler was the image of what she thought a godly man to be. He was asking her to be cautious and rest. Rest, something she hadn't done in a long time.

Chapter 10
Lukewarm

*J*onas planned for the two of them to eat sandwiches he'd packed as they sat in the back seat of the man hired to take them to Salamanca. "I love salami and Italian bread, how about you?" he asked.

"*Jah*. It's *gut*. Never had it until I came up here."

"I wanted to stop to have a picnic, but then with all this drizzle..."

"It's fine," Jane assured him. "*Danki* again for taking me to meet the Seneca's." She glanced up at the towering mountains. "You say all this land belongs to the Seneca?"

The driver, Billy, yelled back a hardy, "Ya, and the white folk still don't like it."

Jane stared at Jonas for an explanation, but he gave none. "What do you mean?"

"Well, I personally like the Natives. Really awesome people, but hey, the city of Salamanca is on Indian Territory and the whites don't like paying a measly couple hundred bucks a year for rent. I say if you build a house where you know you won't own the land under you, that's your problem. George Washington gave it to them eons ago."

"I agree with ya, Billy," Jonas said, slapping his shoulder. "You always speak your mind, *jah*?"

"Well, I'm a quarter Iroquois. Maybe it's in the blood," he said wryly. "We were the most aggressive of the Six Nations."

Jonas leaned back and sat close to Jane. "We're almost there. Excited?"

A shimmering building that appeared to tower into the low clouds came into view. "What is that?"

"That's the casino. You taking your girl there?" Billy asked Jonas.

Jonas shifted. "*Nee.* We're going to the museum."

"Maybe next time then. How much?"

"Keep your eye on the road. You'll flatten a tire with all these potholes," Jonas said evenly, arching to clamp Billy on the shoulder. "And stop the talk about gambling. You know the Amish don't gamble."

Billy snickered and irritation ran down Jane's spine. Or was it suspicion? "Have you ever been to the casino, Jonas? During *rumspringa?*"

"Well, *jah,* and I don't like to talk about it. Lost some money, but you learn from your mistakes, *jah?*"

Jane nodded, but didn't understand because she never experienced *rumspringa.* This was her *rumspringa,* a running around time to know herself better, but she was baptized. Her life was so backwards.

"Here it is. Now you kids have fun. And don't believe anything Lenny tells you about the Iroquois. We were mean, but not cannibals. Well, at least my ancestors weren't."

Jane laughed at what she thought was a joke and went around the front of Billy's blue sedan, waiting on the sidewalk while Jonas spoke to Billy. Jonas seemed agitated and she wondered if bringing up his past bothered him.

When a few minutes went by, the drizzle became a

downpour and Jane entered the museum. She jumped back when she saw a black bear staring her down. A hardy laugh bellowed and a tall sinewy man with long black hair braided down his back came from around the counter. "He won't bite." He pat the bear's head. "Good for us that he's stuffed, right?"

Jane blushed, feeling so foolish.

"Lots of people have your reaction. I'm sure when you see the deer and foxes, you'll coo over them."

Coo. What did that mean? "I'm sure I will."

He offered his hand. "My name's George Washington Kettle."

When Jane shook his hand, she met his eyes and grinned. "That's not your real name?"

His brows shot up. "Just call me George for short. But my middle name is Washington. It's part of my presentation. I'm your guide through this place and I start with the fact that George Washington gave the Six Nations land in 1796. We're one of the few Natives that still own our land." He scrunched up his face. "Did you come alone or is there an Amish tour?"

"I'm waiting for a friend who's out paying our driver." Jane knew how it felt to be gawked at in her Amish attire, but she stared at this young man's features that she found so appealing. High cheekbones, kind dark eyes, muscular, and very tall. His leather shirt and pants had fringe and he wore earrings and necklaces with little beads.

He lifted up a necklace. "We sell them here, along with other Native clothes. Unlike you, I don't dress like this all the time, only when I work."

Jane knew she was blushing and that old feeling of anger arose in her. She'd been so sheltered; she didn't even know how to converse with this man.

Jonas appeared by her and offered a hand to their guide. "Hi, George. Lenny off today?"

He stared hard at Jonas and then snapped his fingers. "Jonas? You're wearing Amish clothes. Why?"

Jonas forced a laugh. "I wear fancy clothes sometimes, because I'm not baptized, but plan on it this spring."

George crossed his arms. "Is this a joke? Halloween is over, man. I never heard you talk about being Amish."

"It never came up."

"Don't be ashamed of your heritage," George chided him. "I see some Amish come by and they hide their faces. Stand tall and be proud of who you are."

Jane put a hand up. "They hide their faces so people don't take pictures of them. We don't believe in getting our photographs."

George nodded. "I know that. They still need to walk tall and be proud."

Jonas leaned towards George as the room filled with visitors. "We're pacifists and some take advantage of it, if you know what I mean."

"Got it," George said. "So you're a target to get hassled, since you can't fight back?"

Jane heard sarcasm in George's tone. "So you don't think we'd get picked on?"

His eyes fixed on Jonas, he answered, "No. Well, there's trouble everywhere, if you hang around the wrong people. Never heard of anyone picking a fight with an

Amish man."

Jonas shifted and Jane didn't know what to feel, sympathy or suspicion.

~*~

Dear Luke,

I had my meeting with the bishop today and he wants me to wait for a spell before I meet my uncle, if I ever do. There's a season for everything and for now, he believes I need to rest and stay put here in Cherry Creek. So I won't be coming home for Thanksgiving. I hope you and my cousins understand that I need this time to heal. The bishop is very kind, not bossy and I believe he's looking out for me.

I went to a Native American museum today and met someone who can trace his heritage back to the early settlers in these parts. I met an old man who lived on land given to them by George Washington but in the 1960's the government flooded the whole town to make Kinzua Dam. Hundreds of people lost their land and their stories help me in a way. I see more and more that life just isn't fair, but George Kettle, the tour guide who's pure Native American, is a Christian and shared with me scriptures from his pocket Bible. Life isn't fair, but God is good, George said. I hope to go back and learn more about these amazing people I didn't even know owned land and live close to each other, similar to the Amish.

How is your mamm? I haven't received a letter from her. Can you ask her to write?

Your friend,

Jane

"What does it say?" Ruth asked, holding out a warm

bottle as she sat on a bale of hay.

The baby raccoon, still trembling in his lap, tried to wiggle free, but Luke took the bottle and shook a few drops of milk onto his finger. A little pink tongue licked it and took the bottle with a vengeance. "Little girl's hungry."

"Luke, you look ill. So pale. Is Jane okay?"

"She's fine. She wants you to write. Not coming home for Thanksgiving. The bishop up there thinks she needs time away to rest and heal."

Ruth crossed her legs and hunched over. "I was planning on having her cousins over. They're the ones who need a rest. Clara's nearly raising the *kinner*."

"Emma goes over to help quite a bit."

"Luke, you know this can't go on forever. Miriam's nervous condition and Malachi missing, if outsiders find out, they'll call social services. Clara's considered a minor, not old enough to be running a house."

"But Miriam's upstairs in bed. There's a parent at home. *Mamm*, you're fretting."

Ruth gingerly rose, flicking pieces of hay from her wool sweater. "I am fretting. I don't like seeing my son down in the mouth frowning. Maybe you need to consider other girls if Jane's staying up there."

An odd emotion surfaced in Luke. Something akin to rage, but not towards his *mamm*, but the man he believed was trying to lead Jane down the wrong path: *Jonas*.

Ruth sat down again, readjusting the black scarf that was tied behind her pinned up hair. "I'm sorry, Luke. Maybe I'm upset with Jane. Something in that letter has taken the wind out of your sails and I fear she met someone else? You wouldn't be so upset about her not coming home for Thanksgiving..."

"She's changing, *Mamm*. Her cousins were planning a Sister Day, when she came home. She's not keeping her word."

"Maybe she's afraid of Malachi still, have you thought of that? I never did think it a *gut* idea for her to come home and stay with the *kinner*, even though the bishop suggested it."

The little raccoon leaned into Luke and sucked in nourishment. "*Gut* girl." He pet her slowly down the back. "I feel like I need to talk face to face to Jane again. She misunderstood why I asked her to come home and help with her cousins."

Ruth raised a brow. "What's stopping you?"

"My critters and work." A barn swallow swooped from a barn rafter. "October's bird migration count is almost over. After that, I'll write."

Wagging a finger, Ruth said, "Forget about birds for once and think about your future. You love Jane, so why not visit her? You're courting, *jah*?"

"Kind of courting..."

"For Pete's sake, Luke, you're lukewarm! Be hot or cold about this relationship, but not double-minded and lukewarm." The gray tabby cat that came near Ruth soon scampered away. "You need to make her see how much you love her. If she's met someone else, go up and break things off or set a wedding date." Ruth cupped her mouth and then let out a long whistle. "I drank three cups of coffee this morning. Can you tell?"

Luke couldn't help but laugh. "But your words are wise nonetheless. I'll write Jane and see if it's okay for me to visit soon and find out where I stand."

"*Gut*. And now I'm headed back in to make a pot full of hot chocolate. When the weather cools, I can't fill myself with coffee to warm up." She snickered and ruffled Luke's hair.

He caught her hand. "*Danki* for being an example of what a Godly woman should be. I could be married by now if I lowered my standards."

She put a hand over a cheek. "You'll make me blush. I hope Jane realizes what she'll have in you if she accepts your proposal."

If. The two letter word that made his life like a teeter totter.

~*~

Jane decided to take a long walk with Peanut. After sitting all day sewing things for displays, her legs ached to walk. Rose was at a quilting bee and being in the little house made her afraid. Afraid of Jonas visiting before he left for a week to work construction and try to kiss her again. Why she felt like he was forbidden fruit, she didn't know, but something deep within told her to hold back from Jonas Hershberger, despite the desires that flowed through her.

Stepping onto the porch, bundled up with a heavier cape she'd purchased recently, the snow flew horizontally as the polar winds whipped across Lake Erie and dumped snow on the "Heart of the Snowbelt." Stories Rose told her of having to tie a rope to the main house to find their way back from the barn seemed thrilling to Jane for some odd reason. She was more adventurous than she thought.

Trudging over to the barn to visit Peanut, Jane decided to hold the dog close for a spell, intentionally relaxing, like Bishop Byler suggested. It made Luke seem nearer, and Emma's letter had quite disturbed her. Was she trying to make her jealous? Surely not Emma, but she did seem to spend a lot of time with Luke after breaking things off with her beau. Always meeting over at her old house to help with her cousins, Jane wondered if they were fulfilling the roles of parents and... maybe? Jane shook her head. Would feelings of unworthiness plague her forever? Feelings of being abandoned and discarded, easily forgotten.

As she neared the barn she couldn't believe how loud the wind was howling. Or was it the wind? *Nee*, it was Peanut, she was sure of it. She kicked up her speed and ran into the massive red barn, only to find Jonas taunting her dog. "What are you doing?"

Jonas flashed a smile. "Teaching him a trick. Doesn't he know how to fetch a stick?"

She ran to Peanut and felt his heart beating and a low growl rumbling his body. "He was a rescue dog. His old owner must have hit him with sticks, because he's really afraid of them. He can't play fetch." Jane hugged Peanut around his massive neck. "It's okay, Peanut. He won't hurt you."

Jonas came nearer and Peanut's body became rigid and that deep groan resumed. "Jonas, stay away. He's protective of me."

"He's a *boppli* dog is all and doesn't do much but eat and sleep. Can't go out and herd in cattle like a *gut* shepherd."

Jane tried to ignore him.

"Have you ever wondered if Luke hit the dog and that's why he's afraid of sticks? How long has he had this dog?"

"A few years, but Luke would never abuse animals. He nurses them back to health."

Jonas squatted down, the stick still in his hand. "After a few years, he shouldn't have this reaction. You see that Luke guy through rose colored glasses."

Rose colored glasses? Jane had never heard of this before, but she caught the meaning. "I've known Luke since I was a young teen!"

"Living with an abusive uncle and he was too sissified to speak up for you."

Peanut stared at the stick in Jonas' hand. "He'll bite and I can't hold him back if he tries."

Jonas smirked and tossed the stick aside. "Okay, you win. Now, I'm headed out to work soon. Like I said, I'll be gone for a week and I'll miss you. Can I write?" He moved near her, but Peanut stood as if a guard between them.

"See, he's protective of me. Doesn't like strangers getting too close." Jane could see Jonas wanted to kiss her good-bye and deep down, she wished he would. *Lust.* She'd memorized 1 John 2:16, "*For all that is in the world, the lust of the flesh, and the lust of the eyes, and the pride of life, is not of the Father, but is of the world."* Jane had been sheltered from men, but was catching on to what lust was. Physical attraction that doesn't last. And self-control was one of the fruits of the Holy Spirit and she needed it now.

Jonas stepped towards her, ignoring Peanut, and the dog tore into his pant leg, ripping it.

"Back away!" Jane yelled.

Jonas did out of fear. "He can't stay here. He's dangerous."

"*Nee*, he's not. You provoked him."

Jonas stomped out of the barn, muttering something under his breath. Jane noticed that when he was out of sight, Peanut's body relaxed. She scratched him behind the ears and his tale wagged. "*Ach*, Peanut, I hope Jonas is just blowing off steam. I need you here with me."

~*~

That night Jane tossed in bed as sleep evaded her. Something was oddly appealing and repellent about Jonas Hershberger. How could he be so mean to Peanut? His moods shifted, like Mr. Rochester's in *Jane Eyre*. Was she supposed to help him, as Rose suggested? Did she come here to meet him and help him "Look to God" as Jane Eyre repeatedly said to Mr. Rochester?

Jane lit the oil lamp and grabbed *Jane Eyre*, flipping to the passage that had become a prayer of sorts to her:

When you are near me, as now: it is as if I had a string somewhere under my left ribs, tightly and inextricably knotted to a similar string situated in the corresponding quarter of your little frame. And if that boisterous channel, and two hundred miles or so of land some broad between us, I am afraid that cord of communion

*will be snapped; and then I've a nervous notion I should take to
bleeding inwardly.*

Holding the book to her heart, she forced back tears.
Why did she yearn for Luke when reading this? She felt a
cord connecting them, although strained at times. But so
many Hershbergers thought she could make Jonas
straighten out, and she was attracted to him, but Jane
knew physical attraction wouldn't last or was something
to base a marriage on.

She recalled the talk she'd had with Rose. Her first
marriage was a disaster because she felt like an ugly
duckling and was proud that such a handsome man would
court her. Her second husband made her see what a
beauty Rose was and they enjoyed a lasting, steady love.
This is what Jane hoped for. *Could Jonas be steady at all?*

A flicker of light flashed in the window and she
cringed. Was it Jonas again? Out in the whipping wind?
Jane crossed the room and opened the window. "Jonas,
what do you want?"

"I want to apologize. I'm leaving tomorrow for a week
and couldn't bear to know you're upset with me."

The sincerity in his voice touched her. Was this the
real Jonas? He sounded like Mr. Rochester when he
spoke of being away from Jane Eyre. The cord between
them if pulled would make him bleed. "I forgive you,"
she found herself saying. "Be nicer to my dog, okay?"

"I'll buy him one of those coats the English put on
their dogs," he quipped.

She laughed. "No need."

"Can I get you something, Jane?"

"I have all I need."

He stared up at her without saying a word. The crisp cold air and the full moon cast a romantic spell on Jane. "Do you want me to come down and talk further? I can't sleep."

"*Jah*, Jane. I'd like that."

Jane felt a prick of her conscience. She should not be going out in the middle of the night with someone she found so appealing. But she ignored it, hoping she was seeing the real Jonas. The man Rose loved so deeply, and prayed for without ceasing.

She scampered down the steps, all the while slipping on her heavy robe and moccasin slippers. "Do you want to come in?" she asked, cracking the door open.

He took her hand and led her out onto the porch. "Do you like stars? It's a clear night and so many constellations out here."

"I've never watched stars. Always early to bed." She was so overworked, she'd fall asleep when Uncle Malachi read the Bible to the family at night, another reason to be chastened.

He took her hand and pulled her towards the porch steps but she slipped, falling into his arms. "I was hoping that would happen. Jane, you in my arms forever would make me a happy man. I love you."

Being in his arms made her heart race, her ears throb.

Jonas lifted her, cradling her in his arms. "You're so beautiful. How could you ever think you're plain?"

"Well, ah, my uncle called me Plain Jane."

"Marry me. I know you could make me be the man

you deserve." Jonas kissed her gently. "Please. I believe you've been sent here as a gift from God."

Jane weakened under such tenderness. This was the real Jonas, but he was like an unbroken horse at times that needed a lot of love and patience to train. Was that her job? Looking into his perfectly etched face, she believed she'd never tire of looking at him.

"Can you give me an answer?"

Rest, Jane, she remembered the Bishop advising. "I need to rest," she said, feeling her need to kiss him become stronger.

"I know. Who proposes at one o'clock in the morning?" He drew her closer and kissed her with a passion she'd never experienced or imagined existed. Wrapping her arms around him, she returned his affection until she heard a dog howling and getting closer.

Jonas near dropped her as he put her down and ran for the house. Peanut stood next to Jane, a stone statue not to be moved. Jane laughed. "He's jealous, *jah?*" Petting him, she took him by the collar. "You make a run towards your house and I'll take him over to the barn."

"*Jah,* okay," Jonas snapped. "That dog can't stay here if he's going to maul me." He took one step down the stairs and Peanut growled in a long even tone. Jonas ran back onto the porch. "I guess we have to talk from here. Will you marry me, Jane?"

"When I said I needed to rest, I didn't mean sleep. I need time. One month of resting and working through my emotions, which sometimes are mighty ugly. But, I can give an answer by next year."

Jonas's mouth gaped.

"In seven weeks or less," Jane teased. "Until then, I take to heart what the bishop said." Jane felt somehow so beautiful. She wasn't plain, but beautiful, Jonas had said. And he was so handsome, he could get any girl in both Cattaraugus and Chautauqua County. How many other lies did she believe about herself? Over the next month she'd find out. She gave a quick wave to Jonas as she led Peanut towards the barn.

Karen Anna Vogel

Chapter 11
Charlotte Bronte

Jane practiced crocheting with Rose as her instructor. She held up a finished doily. "What do you think?"

"*Wunderbar*," Rose exclaimed. "You're so *gut* with your hands."

The constant taunts of being clumsy by her aunt pricked her. Here was Rose saying she was well coordinated.

"What are you thinking, Jane?" Rose probed, her wire-rimmed glasses teetering on the edge of her petite nose.

Jane took yarn from her basket and began casting on stitches to her knitting needle. "I don't know. I'm not used to compliments, I suppose."

"I said I like your doily, that's not too much praise."

"*Nee*, but my aunt always said I was clumsy and not *gut* with my hands." She sighed loud enough to match the howling wind outside. "So glad I'm not seeing her anytime soon."

Rose set down her yellow yarn. "Bad nerves can make you clumsy. I was all thumbs during my first marriage but Matthew appreciated all I made to make a nice home and I realized that knitting and crocheting were relaxing and I was *gut* at both."

Jane desperately wanted to ask Rose for advice concerning Jonas, but knew she'd be biased. Rose thought Jane could straighten him out, but Jonas's free spirit was something that she found appealing. Jonas thinking she could keep him on the straight and narrow was also a mystery. He talked about taking baptismal classes so he must have the issues settled in his heart, being able to make the vow to be Amish.

"Jane, you're so quiet tonight. Are you tired?"

She smiled at this dear woman before her. "I feel hesitant to bring something up, but you've been married twice."

"Unfortunately, *jah*, I have. What're you hankering to know?"

Ever since Luke wrote, she realized she cared for him *and* Jonas. "How do you know if … well, how do you know if you should marry someone?"

Her eyes danced. "So Jonas asked for your hand?"

"*Jah*, he has."

Rose clasped her hands, her yarn lacing through her fingers. "I prayed for this. *Ach,* Jonas needs someone to ground him."

Jane couldn't help grinning. "So now you know why I'm hesitant to bring him up."

Rose reached for her tiny tea cup and sipped. "I suppose I'm biased when it comes to Jonas. He has the potential to be a Matthew, like his *grossdaddi*, but his *mamm*, well, she spoils him."

"I've noticed he can do no wrong over at the farmhouse, but didn't want to mention it."

"Well, he's still in *rumspringa* like a *boppli* and Mary Anna just coddles him, telling him he needs to make sure of his decision.'

"He told me he's going to be baptized," Jane said, as

she continued to cast yarn on her needles.

Rose began coughing yet with a smile. She punched her chest. "Almost choked. Are you serious?"

"*Jah*, he told me before he left for work."

A smile split Rose's face. "An answer to prayers for sure and certain. Jane, I tell you my grandson would be so blessed to have you for a wife."

Jane had been happy, almost ecstatic at the prospect, until her letter from Luke arrived and homesickness sunk her low. "Did you hear that my friend, Luke, the one who gave me Peanut, is trying to arrange a Thanksgiving visit? Once he gets someone to take his place at my uncle's house, he'll be free to come.

Rose sighed with a humph.

"Mary Anna has a spare room. Do you think she could house him?"

Rose clucked her tongue and rolled her eyes. "That woman is a jellyfish."

Jane only knew Mary Anna to be a kind woman, given to hospitality, reveling in it. "She enjoys taking in strangers, like the Bible says to do."

"*Jah*, because they might be angels." Rose put her head back on her rocker. "This fellow won't be an angel if he steals you away from Jonas."

Jane tried to stifle a laugh at Rose's quick wit. The Bible said to entertain strangers, because they might be angels. "Rose, I'm following what the bishop said about taking up a hobby and rest. I won't be making any major decisions for a month or so."

"I know. I'm anxious about Jonas. I've never seen

him so steady and it's you that changed him."

Jane thought she'd attempt a joke someone said at work to lighten the atmosphere. "Rose, if you took all the verses of the Bible, do you know what the one right in the middle would be?"

"What?"

"Trust no man," Jane quipped. Rose forced a smile. "It's true, I suppose. We can only trust God, *jah?*"

Their eyes met, the sudden warmth between them making the room much more snug.

~*~

Noticing the package on her desk, Jane ripped it open and saw the book, *The Life of Charlotte Bronte* with a letter enclosed. She opened the flowery stationery to read:

Jane,

I'm praying for you mighty hard. Read the biography of the woman who wrote Jane Eyre. You'll see you probably have more in common with her. I was so shocked when I heard you weren't coming home to help out, I just know this book will help you see clearly.

Levi and I were on the mend, but my workload has ruined my relationship with him. My mamm wanted me to live at your place. Levi's reaction to it all showed me he's selfish so that it all worked out for the best in the end, but Jane, you're needed here. Your aunt's in bad shape. You uncle hasn't been seen in weeks and the Amish grapevine says he got a fancy job driving trucks cross country. How he learned to drive a truck is a mystery to me.

Jane, I love you like a sister. Am I upset with you? I am. Do I forgive you? Yes. Do I understand your need to be away? Yes. I agree with your bishop up there, but my life is so hard right now. Won't you come home for a visit, even if it's for a weekend to see your cousins?

Your friend,
Emma

Jane bit her lip as she reread parts of the letter. *Emma's emotions are teeter tottering for the first time I've known her.* Was she upset about her beau, Levi? Jane decided she'd write a lengthy letter this week while Jonas was away, not that she arranged her schedule around him.

Digging into the book right away, she read until the sound of the Nightingale that started it's singing at two in the morning rang in the cold air.

Sitting up in bed, Jane was stunned at all she'd read. Needing to record all she'd learned in her journal, she wrote:

Charlotte lost her mother from cancer when she was only five and was raised by a cross aunt who didn't care for them but made them into servants, just like me, only Charlotte was so young to lose her mother. Her father was a preacher and busy, so when chores were over the aunt shooed them outside to play, but they weren't allowed to talk to other children in town, only run on the moors, the landscape that is throughout Jane Eyre. Three years later when a school for poor clergy opened, Mr. Bronte sent his four daughters and two died. This school is believed to be the school that inspired Charlotte to write about the awful school she wrote that Jane Eyre went to but it was much worse. So many children died of diseases, they had to close the school.

One thing about Charlotte I'm surprised over is how shy and nervous she was. Did she make Jane Eyre so independent and confident because she wasn't?

She sat the journal down as the pen slipped out of her hand and sleep overtook her.

~*~

A few days later, when Jane had a day off, she decided to hire a driver to visit the Seneca Museum again. Crocheting and knitting had calmed her, as did her new interest in Native Americans. Her reading a biography of the author of *Jane Eyre*, a story that inspired her to leave and be independent, she kept to herself. No one knew how well she could identify with this fictional character.

This was the only thing she didn't tell her dear bishop. Over the past weeks he'd checked on her to see her progress and said she looked years younger. Rose also said her rosy cheeks made her look like a fancy doll with make-up.

The ride to Salamanca made her heart leap at times. Snow blown onto the road was hazardous, even in the daytime, but at night it was much worse, the snow heaps taking motorists by surprise. When the car pulled into the museum, Jane thanked her female driver, Susan, who was visiting relatives in the area. With ominous clouds building up over the mountains, they decided to shorten their trip to a short two-hour visit.

The door to the museum opened before Jane could pull it. "Welcome back, Jane," George said, his face lifting into a smile, revealing gleaming white teeth.

Jane walked in, visitors stared and a little girl ran up to her. "Are you a Pilgrim? The Indians helped you so you had corn, right?"

George bellowed out a laugh and couldn't explain since her mother pulled her away, giving an apology to Jane. She met George's gaze and snickered. "Corn?"

"Out of the mouth of babes God's truth comes. Yes, we helped start America by helping the pilgrims. Do you know Quakers, who dress plain, helped us get this land off of George Washington?"

Jane slipped her cape off and hung it on the nearby coat rack. "There's a lot I don't know about Native Americans, but I came to learn and pick up a book."

"Follow me." George walked through the visitor's center and into a room with local history. "I don't think you saw this. Jonas talked a lot and my presentation got mixed up."

Jane gazed at the room, all the walls covered with painting. "Who are these people? Some look Native but the others Amish."

"It's the Quakers who came to live here and educate our kids. They were good people. When we wanted to keep our traditions, they respected that and didn't force us to dress like the white man." He shifted his weight and crossed his arms. "Others didn't agree with them and made trouble. Lots of booze was brought in to make us drunk and addicted."

"That's terrible. How long ago was this?" Jane asked, stunned.

"Colonial American Period. There's a book I recommend you read, after you spend some time in here asking me questions."

The two of them alone made Jane uncomfortable. Was George flirting with her? He appeared very serious.

"Jane, something troubling you? Is there something my people can do to help? I don't mean to be nosey, but sometimes we have more in common. People have asked me if I carried a bow and arrow. I tell them yes, during cross-bow season." He chuckled. "Or I tell a tall tale, and say something bizarre like, 'I like red scalps best. Have a collection of them'."

Laughter welled up in Jane and she let it out along with the stress George saw she was carrying. What a kind man. She took a seat and George sat in front of her, turning with intent eyes.

"When I was here last and found out about the land lost over at Kin…"

"Kinzua. Go on."

"I can see it still pains you all but you're building more on this land. How do you…"

"Forgive? Move on?" George prodded.

"*Jah*," Jane sighed in exasperation. "My bishop says I need to forgive my uncle, who raised me since I was fourteen, but I can't. And now my cousins and friends in Punxsy seem mad at me. Well, at least Emma does. She feels I'm not doing my duty."

"What duty? You're old enough to move away, right?"

Jane hesitated to say more, but George was so at ease, and he'd never meet her family. She needed a confidant. "My uncle was abusive and I left. Now he's taking his anger out on my aunt and cousins. My aunt has some kind of nervous condition and doesn't do much, so Clara has to do a lot, being the oldest. My friend, Emma, is the next door neighbor and helps."

"Where's your uncle?"

"*Ach*, who knows and who cares," Jane blurted and then set her jaw up in defiance. She really didn't care at all about her uncle. Not one drop of sympathy could she muster.

George walked to a nearby portrait. "This is Cornplanter." He grinned. "Remember, we helped build this nation with corn." He leaned to read the quote written on the bottom. "*We cannot waste one drop of our energy. We must live and change with the world around us. If we do not, we will never be able to stand against the weight of the white man.*"

Jane covered her mouth in awe. "Did he live on the flooded village? Had to forgive the white man?"

"The flood was long after he died. He lived in the 1700's and tried his whole life to seek peace and forgiveness. We Seneca stayed neutral during local wars with the white man, and George Washington appreciated that and gave him land. He lived to a ripe old age, nearly up into the 1800's in the ways his ancestors did."

"So why does he say he couldn't stand up to the white man?"

"You know, Jane, that's a curious thing. Cornplanter's father was a white settler, his mom was Seneca. He understood the white man better and was the one who invited the Quakers up to teach English and other useful skills." He paused, rubbing his chin. "Maybe he saw things the white man did. His brother became an alcoholic and nearly died. Cornplanter took care of him for a while."

"Were they close as brothers?"

"They were very different. His brother was a man of war between tribes and fought for the British against George Washington."

Jane's mind couldn't take all this in. So, a brother who was violent, was cared for by his brother? "Should I be taking care of my aunt?" she mumbled.

"Maybe?"

"*Ach,* George, everywhere I turn it seems like I'm supposed to go back home and help my aunt even though my uncle was violent."

George cocked his head and then slid into his seat. "Now how did you get that from my story?"

"Cornplanter forgave and took care of a violent brother."

"Wait a minute. I didn't say that you should do the same. Cornplanter had lots of help and protection if his brother became hostile when drunk. But his brother changed, but that's another long story. I am not saying you can change your uncle, but God can."

Jane shook her head slowly. "Sometimes I don't believe even God can change Uncle Malachi."

George took her hand. "Let's pray. *Lord, you see Jane's heart and care about her. She's torn between her family in Pennsylvania and her new life here in New York. Guide her path, making it clear as the noonday sun. Give her wings of strength, like an eagle. Reveal yourself to her uncle and change him. Have him throw off his old robe of wickedness and put on the robe of*

righteousness. I ask all this in Jesus' name. Amen."
Jane opened her eyes, seeing George's brawny hand
on hers. "Was that a Native American prayer?"
"Nope, Bible passages." He tapped her hand. "We
Natives do have some good sayings though. *Do not pray
when it is raining if you do not pray when the sun is shining.*
Jane snickered. "That's an Amish saying."
"No, you adopted it from us," George quipped. "Now
let's go around the museum again and then the bookstore.
I think you should read about the Quakers, since you're
both plain."
Plain Jane, she heard her Uncle's voice vibrate in her
head. A pain in her temples throbbed and she feared a
migraine was coming on, her first one in New York.
"Jane, what's wrong?" He led her to a chair. "Have I
upset you?"
"*Ach*, plain. My uncle calls me Plain Jane."
"Oh, sweetheart, you're anything but plain. You're a
very beautiful woman."
She looked into his clear, unfaltering eyes. He was
serious. "*Danki*, George. I need to lay down before my
ride comes."
"I'll tell you what. You can sit and watch a movie
about Kinzua in our little theater. We have soft chairs
there."
Jane nodded her head in agreement. She didn't care if
it was in a theater or not, any comfortable chair where she
could rest her head would do.

Chapter 12
Rumspringa

Dear Emma,

I miss you. Thank you for the book. It's an eye opener. Charlotte's life was hard yet she was a servant to her family, finding it an honor to serve. Humbled me heaps.

Emma, I need advice. I made a Seneca friend oddly named George Washington, but that's a long story in itself. I got a sudden migraine at the museum and even after a few hours opening my eyes was too painful. What happened was my driver knew the roads were getting bad and said she needed to leave to miss the storm. They come and go here suddenly so you need to drive when roads are clear. It's called a snow squall off the lakes. Anyhow, George ended up bringing me back late at night, around nine. Rose was worried, but I had no way to contact her. And I'm being looked at suspiciously about George. Though a very handsome man, I'm Amish and he's not.

So, there's a little wall up between me and the Hershbergers, even though they say it's not there. I talked to my bishop and he believes me, the dear man he is. Any suggestions on mending a relationship that's gotten a tear in it when the others deny it exists?

Miss you. Give my cousins a hug for me.

Jane.

Jane reread the letter, licked the envelope and headed towards the mailbox. After Jonas saying he couldn't tell if some letters were addressed to her, she decided to take out her mail and get it when she knew the mailman would drive by.

Peanut ran out of the barn and met her with his tail wagging. "Come on, boy. We'll get the mail and then I'll take you for a nice walk back in the woods."

When she stuck her letter in, she'd just missed the mailman, seeing letters that had just arrived. Maybe the storm warnings made him deliver early. But her heart jumped with delight when she saw a letter with a return address from Punxsutawney. "A letter from Luke," she informed Peanut.

Heading over to the barn, she ripped open the letter and read:

Dear Jane,

I wrote you last week twice, so this is my third attempt to contact you. Are you alright?

Like I said in my other letters, Clara's not doing too good. She's getting rundown and furhoodled at times, forgetting something's cooking. Burnt offerings is what Jeremiah and Jacob call them. Those boys are talking more with your daed gone. Opening up about lots. It's private man talk, so I can't tell you.

Emma asked Old Levi Yoder to fill the woodpile and go over often to encourage the boys. So everything's lined up for a visit.

I can't wait to see you on Thanksgiving. Can you find a place for me to stay?

Mamm sends her love. Me, too.

Luke

Jane pressed the letter to her heart as homesickness

enveloped her. A visit from Luke could be the balm she needed right now, but there were no hotels in town, only a Bed and Breakfast. The Hershbergers were prickly, but maybe it was her imagination. She'd ask Mary Anna, who seemed to thrive off of hospitality and was perpetually sweet. She did have two empty rooms.

But she told Rose she'd *redd* up the house this afternoon and so after a good rubdown to Peanut, she headed towards the little *dawdyhaus*. She found that Rose had just picked up her knitting and after hanging her wraps up, she took the seat near her. "Do you think Mary Anna would house Luke when he visits for Thanksgiving?"

Rose put her head back on her rocker. "Not if this fellow is coming to steal you away from Jonas and me."

Jane felt her cheeks rising with heat. "Rose, remember, I'm still resting and won't be making any big changes.

Rose slowly closed her eyes. "I'm sorry. I'm anxious about Jonas. He'll be back tomorrow and he won't like your friend being around"

Jane picked up her crocheting. Rose was being a bit too pushy about Jonas. No one could change Jonas. She could not keep him on the straight and narrow. It wasn't her place and in time, she wondered if it would wear her out, trying to do the impossible. She closed her eyes. *Lord Jesus Christ, Son of God, have mercy on me, a sinner.*

~*~

Dear Emma,

I'm upset. Luke is visiting over the Thanksgiving weekend, but the Hershbergers refuse to house him. Well, Mary Anna, who I just love, said it was fine and then Jonas came back from work and he got upset. Mary Anna said she understood, since Luke was competition. You'd think I was a quilt at an auction to be had by the highest bidder. My dear bishop said Luke can stay with him. He's a mile down the road and will even share his buggy. He's the kindest man alive.

I'm watching character now more than ever. My prayer is to have a husband like Charlotte Bronte had. Cannot believe her fictional Mr. Rochester was based on a man she fell in love with who was a married man! She got this man out of her system by writing Jane Eyre (and to make money, being so poor) and it worked. She settled down, grew up and married later in life. Maybe that's what I should do. Sometimes I think twenty is young. Well, I'll be twenty-one in January, so getting old, I suppose.

Charlotte's husband was described as a consistent Christian and a kind gentleman. Charlotte said, "These words touched me deeply, and I thought to merit and win such a character was better than to earn either wealth, or fame, or power."

I find that pretty shocking. She was famous by then and could have lived away from her childhood home, but decided to care for her old father. I think she was a content woman. She had more hardship in her life than I've heard anyone go through, losing her mom and siblings by the time she was in her late thirties. She nursed them all, too, exposing herself to contagious sicknesses.

My Seneca friend told me a Native American proverb. 'Certain things catch your eye, but pursue only those that capture your heart.'

I plan to do that. God put His spirit in us to guide and direct us. Bishop says it's ever so slowly, though, that still small voice of God, so he advised no hasty decisions.

Like I said, maybe I'm to marry in my thirties like Charlotte. Can characters in a book become too real? Am I getting furhoodled?

Write soon. I miss you and my cousins and even my aunt a tiny bit. I pray for her and my heart isn't as hard as stone anymore, to my surprise.

Jane

~*~

Jonas threw a package at Jane's feet. "Your Indian sent you a present."

"What?"

"Just got the mail and it's from George. Jane, what's going on with you? People will think you're a flirt. I'm starting to wonder."

Jane lowered her head, that old bad feeling of shame overcoming her. Rose was standing right there and Jonas was shaming her. *Was she a flirt?*

Rose put her tiny hand on Jane's shoulder. "No need for unkind words, Jonas."

"Unkind? *Grossmammi*, she knows I want to marry her and this Luke fellow's coming up and now a present from George? What would you make of it?" Jonas growled.

Rose ran for her broom and shooed Jonas out of her house. "You're making a fool out of yourself. Don't come back until you can act Amish."

Jane was too numb to get out a thank you to Rose. She picked up the package, her hands shaking.

"*Ach*, that Jonas is so spoiled. I'm sorry for his behavior, honey."

Honey? What tender words. "You don't agree with him?"

"*Nee*, not at all. You're a pretty woman who some men have their eye on. You can't help that. I've never seen you fish for a compliment or try to attract attention. You're not a flirt, for sure and certain."

Jane found tears welling up in her eyes. "I love being here with you."

"I love having you." Rose neared Jane and embraced her. "Things will work out. God makes all things beautiful in his time."

Jane was depending on it.

"Why not open your present? This George fellow is only a friend, so it won't be romantic."

Jane agreed and opened the little package. "My corn doll and book." She read the enclosed short note: "Hope your headaches get better and don't return. You left the corn doll you bought and the book about Cornplanter. Your friend, George." Jane held up the doll. "Isn't it cute? No face, just like Amish dolls."

Rose reached for it, flipping it over. "We could make these. So simple, just made of husks. I wonder if they have books on how to make them."

"I can get another one and you could take it apart to get a pattern."

Rose smiled at the doll. "*Gut* idea. I've never been to the museum. Jonas seems to go out to Salamanca often, but don't know why. Maybe his work's out there." She slid her arm through Jane's. "Let's have some tea and anise cookies."

Jane wished Jonas could be more like his *grossmammi*. Why was he so hasty in his speech? Amish learned from being wee ones to measure their words. Jonas was a mystery.

~*~

Luke read Jane's letter at the kitchen table, a steaming cup of coffee in hand.

"Well, what does she say?"

"I'll be staying with the bishop a mile down the road. I'm glad about that. Want to steer clear of Jonas."

Ruth pressed her rolling pin to her pie dough. "God's will be done. If she says no to your proposal, maybe God brought my old friends, the Kings, out from Lancaster for a reason." She twisted a grin at Luke. "What do you think of Lauren?"

"Just met her a few weeks back."

"Luke Miller, you're not binding yourself to her if you say she's pretty and very sweet. And single."

The lilt in his *mamm's* voice made him laugh. "You always have a Plan B."

"I want to see you happy. Now, make sure the sidewalk's cleared. Lauren and her *mamm* are coming over any minute."

"What for? A frolic?"

Popping a pie into the oven, Ruth turned, looking pleased with herself. "To welcome them to Punxsutawney and get to know my family."

"But *daed's* over at the hardware store."

"I know. I'll chat with Tabitha and you can chat with Lauren."

Luke was too stunned to talk. His *mamm* was encouraging him to speak his mind and not shy away from Jane, so why throw another girl at him? And then it dawned on him. "You think Jane will say no?"

Ruth replenished Luke's coffee and then sat on the bench near him. "I just have a feeling Jane's changed. She hasn't even returned my letters, and I sent three. Do you have the right address?"

Luke let his head fall into his hands. "Jane gets her own mail now. Seems like Jonas hijacks it."

"For Pete's sake, is he that jealous?"

"Suppose so. He's a real, I can't say."

"Wolf in sheep's clothing?" Ruth suggested.

Luke put up a hand. "We're not to judge. God will show Jane. I trust her."

Ruth groaned. "You think Jane's not flesh and blood. She's tempted and deceived like any of us. And being so cooped up over at her uncle's, her senses haven't been sharpened to determine *gut* from evil."

Fear gripped Luke. Experience helped a Christian gain discernment, and Jane had little if any with men. A knock at the door broke his train of thought. Amish didn't knock.

Ruth scampered to the door and was soon greeting

Tabitha and Lauren, telling them there was no need to knock. Amish just walked right in the back door. She took their capes and bonnets and when Lauren slid her outer black bonnet off, her white prayer *kapp* slid down, exposing her pinned up auburn hair. Luke tried to force his eyes away, but they remained on the beauty before him. Lauren timidly turned to him as she lifted up her *kapp* and their eyes met. Luke swiftly held up the letter from Jane, trying to hide his shame. *Lord, I'm sorry. Like the forbidden fruit in the garden, I looked at her hair that's intended for her husband.*

Lauren came his way and laughed. "Luke, you're blushing."

"Am I?"

"It's okay. My *kapp* slides down, because I don't tie the strings. No harm done."

She was so unpretentious and care-free, Luke found his lips lifting into a smile. "I'm sorry for staring. It was wrong."

Her shiny green eyes glistened. "If more men had a tender conscience like you, the Amish would be more respected."

"What do you mean?" Luke asked, motioning for her to take a seat as he grabbed a mug and the coffee pot.

"Well, there's more Amish in Lancaster County, so more trouble I suppose. Some of the young men there are real charmers. Folks here are more serious about being Amish."

Placing a mug before her, Luke took his seat. "We have some not so *gut* Amish here. There's a bad apple in every bushel, *jah?*"

"*Jah*," she said, smiling. "So, your *mamm* said you were supposed to show me the wounded animals you help, while she talked private-like in the living room. Do you know what it's about?"

Luke snickered at his *mamm's* spunk. "I have no idea."

~*~

Jane rolled over, her sore throat lingering all day, keeping her up this freezing cold night. Her knitting and tea time with Rose, tea with lots of lemon and honey, had eased it a bit earlier. *Honey.* Rose called her this now and Jane reveled in the love that poured from this woman. Truth be told, it was the one thing that made her want to stay in Cherry Creek. How disappointed that Ruth hadn't written. Had Ruth forgotten her?

A light flickered in the window and Jane cringed. Still upset with Jonas's remarks a few days ago and no attempt at an apology, only ignoring her, would make it easy to refuse his marriage proposal. Who could live with such a moody man?

But the light stayed on the window, Puzzled, Jane went to tell Jonas to let her sleep. Peering out the window, however, she saw a car pull away and a girl was standing with a suitcase. What on earth? The girl just stood there, looking around as if confused.

Jane slipped on her knitted socks and grabbed the shawl she'd just crocheted and tip toed down the steps, not wanting to disturb Rose. Stepping out onto the porch, the girl ran to her, sobbing. As her features came into focus Jane gasped. "Clara?"

"Jane!" Throwing herself into her cousin's arms, she clung to her tight. "I'm so glad the driver took me to the right place."

Reeling from the fact that Clara had on fancy clothes, she asked "What's wrong? Why are you here?" Jane took Clara's gloved hand and led her into the house. "We have to whisper or Rose will wake up."

Clara unzipped her purple puffy jacket to reveal a sweater and blue jeans. "I'm on *rumspringa* and I did just what you did. Run away from the crazy house."

Jane swallowed, pain shooting down her throat. "I didn't run away; I was forced to leave." Jane lit an oil lamp to get a better look at her cousin. "*Ach,* you don't look right in pants."

"They're blue jeans. So much more comfortable, and the sweater is wool and alpaca, really warm." She stared at Jane. "You look better than ever. Younger and ... I don't know. Happy. Jane, I've never seen you look happy."

Jane wasn't happy right now, so why Clara would say this was a wonder. "Where are you staying?"

"With you, of course. Jane, I had to leave. Well, at least for a weeklong break. There's new family in town. The King family. Lauren's your age and volunteered to help for a week. She has such a servant's heart."

"So it's just a week? Why pay for clothes you'll only wear for a week?"

"*Ach,* Jane, as frugal as ever. I borrowed them from my *Englisher* friend, Robin Edwardson."

Jane recalled with relief that Robin wasn't a wild one but a good steady girl. And what could a one week visit hurt? "Why didn't you write and tell me you were coming?"

"I wanted to surprise you."

Jane's heart filled and then sank. "I have to work. If I'd known, I'd have taken some time off. With Christmas sales, we're awfully busy." The 'Help Wanted' sign flashed into Jane's mind. "You can stay for only a week?"

Clara tilted her head. "Why do you ask?"

"Well, Luke's coming up soon and if you can stay a little extra, I could ask my boss to hire you for holiday sales." Jane snapped her fingers. "And you could stay while Luke is here and take my place. You know about Black Friday sales?"

"*Jah.* I could use the money and time away. So relieved to get some help and by someone who doesn't judge *Mamm.* I know the gossip going around that she's as crazy as my *daed,* but she's just beat down and worn out. Made the noon meal yesterday and we had the whole King clan over. Their family isn't huge, so we only had five extra mouths to feed. And Luke came because he helped, too."

"How does he look?" Jane asked meekly.

"Don't know. His *mamm's* right close to the King's and seems to be pushing Lauren and Luke together."

"What do you mean?" Jane asked, her mouth growing dry.

"You know how parents arrange for their *kinner* to be in the same place as the one they secretly hope they'll fall for."

Had Ruth forgotten her completely? Did she think this King girl better for Luke? Jane jiggled her jaw to stop it from trembling.

Clara covered her mouth. "Jane, did I upset you?"

Jane knew all too well how to hide her emotions and forced a smile. "Ruth hasn't returned my letters is all. She's a busy woman I suppose."

Clara slouched in the rocker. "So tired all of a sudden."

Jane arose and pulled Clara up. "Let's get you some pajamas and get to sleep. I have a full sized bed, plenty of room for both of us."

Clara smiled and hugged Jane. "Never thought I'd miss you this much. Can we have a Sister Day this week?"

Jane nodded. "Of course."

Karen Anna Vogel

Chapter 13
An Honest Prayer

*J*ane awoke early the next morning wondering if she'd dreamed Clara had come, but when she rolled over, there was Clara. She'd never imagined Clara ever wearing English clothes and traveling so far from home. Was she a bad example to her? *Rumspringa* was a freer time, but to not be within the eyes of the *Gmay* for boundaries was a bit odd. Too independent. Jane had a suspicion that their bishop in Punxsutawney hadn't agreed to this plan.

Jane crept downstairs, inhaling the aroma of eggs and bacon. Had Rose gotten up early? For an elderly woman, she sure was spry in the morning. But when she turned to enter the kitchen, there was Jonas, pulling out a chair for her. "I came by to apologize, Jane. I've been acting like an idiot."

Jane didn't disagree completely. "Childish, *jah*?"

He rushed at her and planted a kiss on her lips. "I want you to marry me, Jane. Anyone who gets in the way makes me nervous."

Her eyes couldn't look away.

"Say you'll marry me. Don't wait until next year. I'm dying. My nerves can't take it."

Jane remembered a line from *Jane Eyre* and said, "Look to God."

He sighed. "It's hard with that Luke guy coming up."

Jane wiggled out of his arms, desire for another kiss too strong.

A clomping sound down the steps, and soon Clara appeared in blue jeans and a red sweater. Jonas gawked. "Who are you?"

"Jane's cousin. I came in last night to surprise her. Who are you?"

"Jonas Hershberger. I live in the big farmhouse out front." He eyed her. "So you're not Amish? Gone fancy?"

"She's only sixteen," Jane informed, stabbing bacon with a fork. "She's on *rumspringa*. Clara, hurry up and eat so you can go to work with me and we'll see about that job."

Clara slumped in a chair. "I'm so tired..."

"The craft store is fun and nothing like back home. You'll like it."

"Jane, if she just got here last night, can't she just have a free day to have fun?"

Jane shot Jonas a glance of confusion. "She'd be all alone. What would she do here?"

He grinned at Clara. "I don't have plans after chores are over. I can show you around town. Jane, don't you think she'd like the maple sugar farm?"

Once again, Jonas was full of surprises. Here she was in a pickle, not really wanting to spring on her boss a new employee, and Jonas came to her rescue by entertaining her cousin. "I think you'll have fun. It's so cold out, Clara. You'll need to really wrap yourself up."

"My *mamm* has a really warm cape," Jonas offered.

Clara laughed. "An Amish cape with English clothes. Don't think so. I have a jacket in my luggage. It's a down feather coat that you can scrunch up in a ball."

"Jonas, take care of her," Jane cautioned.

"*Ach,* I will, for sure and certain."

~*~

All day at work, Jane had an odd feeling that things were just not right with Clara. She was being so impulsive, but Clara had been cooped up under the heavy thumb of her *daed* too long. She prayed that her cousin wouldn't stray from her faith. The Amish in Cherry Creek were very consistent and God-fearing people and maybe Clara needed to see such faithful people. The church service would be at the Hershberger's this Sunday and she'd see family and friends pull together, not like it was when they had to house the service twice a year back home. Uncle Malachi complained, didn't help unload the bench wagon but was somehow…missing. Just like he was now. Did he always run away from work or when things needed working out? What made him such a hard man?

A woman with three children entered the store and Jane greeted them. When she saw how they followed their mother around the store like little ducklings, a yearning to have children of her own and a home overwhelmed her. She would be twenty-one in January.

Rose had taught her to let God know how she was feeling, not be afraid to talk straight to him. So, Jane prayed an honest prayer: *Lord, I want what that woman has, but I want a Godly man like Charlotte Bronte's husband, a man of character and kindness. Jonas is a mystery to me and we'd have to court much longer than January for me to give him an answer. He's so fickle, but Rose thinks he's restless and I could settle him. But what if his mood swings continued into marriage?* She shook her head. No, she wouldn't marry him until she knew his character and she'd be watching like a hawk over the next months, asking God to reveal to her who the real Jonas was.

Her boss, Stella, a pleasant woman with cherry cheeks, entered the store. "Jane, what would I do without you? What would I do? You're never late." She stomped her feet, snow flying onto the entry runner. "That snow's coming down hard, I slid off the road. Thank God someone I knew, a man strong enough to push my car while I accelerated, came by, but it took a while. Do Amish buggies slide?"

"*Nee.* It can injure the horse."

"Well, I hope no one's out there in this. Freezing rain under all that snow."

Jane frowned. "You drive in from Sinclairville, over by the lake, so there's more snow, *jah?*"

"It's coming this way. Didn't you hear the blizzard warning?" Stella hung her coat, fur hat and gloves in the closet and then spun around. "You Amish don't have television. So you don't know."

"Know what?"

"That a blizzard's coming. Snow squalls could be three feet high."

Jane took up scissors and began cutting up strings of ribbon to make bows, a store courtesy to gift wrap purchases.

"I bet we'll be dead today. So few on the roads."

"Well, I can work on some knitting displays, some

long loopy scarves."

"Infinity scarves, Jane. You must learn the item's name. If anyone wants to buy a pattern, you'll know where it's filed."

Stella was apparently nervous. Should she even ask about Clara helping? "Are you still looking for extra holiday help?"

Stella pursed her lips as if in deep thought. "The day after Thanksgiving for sure. Why?"

"My cousin showed up last night for a surprise. She could work this week up until the Thanksgiving weekend."

"She can't stay until Christmas?"

Jane slumped. "Probably not. Her *mamm's* sick and Clara's here on a break."

Stella seemed to be more relaxed. "Aw, the poor girl. Is that your aunt she's caring for? The one with the nervous condition?"

Jane nodded, not wanting Stella to give Clara a job out of pity.

"Is she working to get a nice present for her mom? I do hope the log cabin quilt sells and especially to someone who spends lots of time in bed. So much color to cheer a soul."

Jane peered over at the queen sized quilt hung in the display window. She'd help make it and the idea of buying it for her aunt popped into her mind, but she dismissed it completely. Why would she do something like that? She was obviously sleep deprived with Clara tossing and turning in bed last night.

~*~

Luke sensed the aroma of lavender as he neared Lauren. "You smell like summer."

She grinned. "I make my own soap out of lilacs."

"Smells like lavender," Luke said, smiling at this sweet girl who came over regularly to help Jane's Aunt Miriam. "Well, I best get back outside and chop wood. Cold snap coming in."

"I can put on some hot chocolate for you when you come back in," Lauren said, taking out the flour canister. "Making pies. Miriam loves peach pies and there're lots of canned peaches in the pantry."

Luke tipped his black wool hat. "You sure do make the best pies." As soon as he blurted this out, he spun around and headed outside. Why on earth did he say such a thing? She'd think he cared. The best way to man's heart is food and he'd gobbled down all she'd cooked over the past week. *Did the Amish in Lancaster have different recipes?*

He balanced a log on a tree stump that was made smooth to be a good chopping block. Luke loved to split wood even as a *kinner*. Getting outside to exercise invigorated him. He chopped and then gathered up wood to stack on the back porch. When he unloaded a stack, he thought of Malachi. The Amish grapevine, which his dear *mamm* was a part of, said Malachi was spotted out in Ohio. What would he be doing out there? Word also had it that he was dressed like an *Englisher*, and he wondered if this news got to Clara before she left for New York. Malachi was being an awfully bad example to his *kinner*.

His thoughts went back to Lauren. Did God bring her out here for a reason? She was sweet and respected him by asking all kinds of questions and taking his opinions to heart. She even knew he loved peach pies.

He put the ax to a log and split it, releasing pent up energy. If Jane rejected him, he knew his *mamm* and *daed* were right. He needed to move on, looking forward, as hard as it would be.

Oddly, the phone in the barn rang. He ran to it and heard Clara's voice. "Glad you made it there nice and safe."

He listened as Clara told him she'd be staying until he went up and his heart sank. "I thought you'd be here with your *mamm* for Thanksgiving. It means so much to my *mamm* to have *yinz* over along with the Kings."

Clara just kept blurting on about how much fun she'd had on a sleigh ride and actually ice skated. "Does Jane know how to ice skate?"

She told him Jonas did and then went on and on about how wonderful Jonas was and Luke wanted to just puke. "You watch yourself around that guy. I don't trust him."

When she accused him of being jealous, Jane taking a shining to Jonas, his heart leapt into his throat.

"He's a flirt, that's why. Clara, I need to go. I'm chopping wood and it's freezing. Take care and come home in a week. That's what we agreed to."

Clara pouted about being overworked and feeling free for the first time in her life. Luke understood, but he was tired of taking on the responsibility of being a good example to Malachi's *kinner*. "You gave your word, Clara, and being Amish, I expect you to keep it. Be home in a week," he said and hung up the phone.

He took off his hat, though cold, perspiration forming on his forehead. Jonas Hershberger was a weasel and he didn't even like the idea of him being around Clara.

Grabbing another log, Luke split it, slipped and felt pain in his hand. His fingers.

~*~

Ruth paced the hospital floor in one direction, while Moses paced in the opposite. The entire King family had shown up, even Miriam. Ruth praised God for Miriam caring enough to come and sit and wait.

"Luke's chopped wood since a *kinner*. How'd he get so careless? Did he slip?"

"He was talking to someone before it happened," Miriam moaned. "He's upset that Clara went fancy, like Jane."

"Jane's not fancy," said Ruth defensively. "She's still plain, just living away for a spell."

"But she put notions in Clara's head. Why else would she go up to New York?"

Moses wagged a finger at Miriam. "You're too hard on that girl. All she's ever done is be kind to you. If Clara leaves, it's because of Malachi leaving, not Jane."

Oddly, Miriam's eyes pooled with tears. "You're right, Moses. I'm a bitter woman, God help me."

Lauren ran to sit next to her. "But you've forgiven Jane, *jah*?"

"I'm the one who needs forgiveness. I'm so used to blaming Jane for all my woes, it still spills out at the most unusual times." She pulled a hanky from her pocket and dabbed her eyes.

"Well, at least you see the error of your ways," Moses said in a softer tone. "Will you write and tell Jane? Ask for forgiveness?"

Miriam straightened. "I'll think about it."

Ruth groaned. "Don't put off until tomorrow what you should do today."

Miriam leaned into Lauren, clasping her hand. "I know. Give me time." She pat Lauren's hand. "This angel came to me and her sweetness is rubbing off."

Ruth grinned at Lauren. She'd noticed a skip in Luke's step lately and she knew why. As soon as he went up to New York and Jane rejected him, he'd come home and find Lauren, a woman who she could clearly see adored her son.

~*~

Dear Jane,

I'm writing with my left hand, so this is probably hard to read. I got clumsy while splitting wood and got a gash on my hand. Got a few stitches. My doc says I'll need to have someone remove the stitches up there, since I'm determined to not have this stop my visit. Can you check to make sure I won't get charged an arm and a leg, no pun intended, if I go to the ER up in Jamestown? Also, Clara needs to be here for Thanksgiving. I talked to her on the phone and she knows why.

See you in a week,
Luke

"Phew. Sure glad Luke's alright," Jane said to Clara and Rose as they sipped tea around the little kitchen table. "He was chopping wood and had an accident. Got stitches." She looked up at Rose, who was knitting so quickly, Jane could barely see her hands. "Is there a doctor up here who can take out stitches?"

"*Jah*. Not a problem. A doc comes here who's Mennonite and doesn't charge much."

Clara held her yarn to her heart. "It's my fault. I made Luke mad. He hung up on me."

Jane and Rose's eyes landed on her.

"I said I'd call and leave a message on the barn phone, but he was outside and picked up. We had a little quarrel."

"About what?" Jane probed. "Luke's so easy going."

"He wants me to go home for Thanksgiving. Said I need to be there for my *mamm*. I'm sick of it all. Why couldn't I have been born into a normal family?" She pushed back from the table and ran up the stairs. Jane sprinted after her and the two cousins were soon in each other's arms. "I didn't want to cry in front of Rose. She doesn't know me."

Jane rubbed Clara's back. "She has *gut* advice. Rose has seen my tears."

Clara's body stiffened. "I'm not going back, maybe never."

Jane stared out the window at the falling snow. *What had she done?* What kind of example had she been to Clara and other girls in her *Gmay* back home? *Jane Eyre* inspired her to be independent, but she didn't think this rippling effect would happen.

Her bishop's kind face came to mind. "Clara, come back downstairs and talk to Rose. Tomorrow, you can meet the bishop I've come to love like a *daed.*"

"Don't you work tomorrow?"

Jane sighed. "With all this storm dumping so much snow, Stella said she'd get word to me if she needs me, but most likely she won't."

"Can we have a Sister Day?" Clara asked.

"*Jah,* I'd like that," Jane said, holding Clara tight.

Karen Anna Vogel

Chapter 14
Rumspringa Run Amuck

The next morning, Jane knocked on Bishop Byler's back door and wind cut through her. She pulled Clara to her. "Sure do wish you'd brought some Amish clothes."

Clara stopped her shivering chin from quivering to get out, "*Rumspringa.*"

The bishop opened the door and hurried them inside. "No need to knock, especially on a day like today. Come on into the kitchen. Hot chocolate will warm you up."

Jane's toes were numb so she wiggled them inside her new black boots Rose had told her to purchase "before the snow flies". Clara kept her purple down jacket on, blowing heat into her hands.

As the bishop ladled the hot liquid into two mugs, he asked, "Jane, is this the girl from work you talked about?" After placing the hot chocolate on the table he offered a hand to Clara. "I'm Bishop Byler and you are?"

"I'm Jane's cousin from Punxsutawney. Came up to surprise her. I'm on *rumspringa.*"

Jane's numbness now ran up to her mouth. How could Clara act so blunt and unfeeling? It was as if she was challenging Old Order ways to her dear bishop.

Bishop Byler cleared his throat and took a seat. "What's the occasion?"

Jane, still feeling stiff, said, "Well, it's been near a month and I've been mulling over what you said, to rest and take up crocheting. Can't count how many doilies

I've made."

"*Wunderbar*. Can put them in a hope chest," he said, his eyes as attentive as usual. "Any other news? About Jonas?"

"Jonas?" Clara blurted. "Jane, you didn't say anything about him and you?"

Baffled, Jane's brow furrowed. "What do you mean, Bishop?"

He groaned. "He told me about his plans. His hopes."

"*Ach*, it's a secret," Jane said dismissively.

"Not to me. So, he wants to marry you? Did you tell him to get baptized and you needed to take a space of time to digest all you've been through? So much abuse?"

Jane pursed her lips, wishing this was a private conversation. "My Uncle Malachi is Clara's *daed*."

"*Jah*, he is," Clara confirmed, "but he up and left us. I needed to get away and came here like Jane did."

The bishop bowed his head and started to twiddle his thumbs. "So, Jane, you came by to introduce your cousin?"

"*Nee*. I was wondering if you thought about me meeting my uncle."

"You have an uncle here?" Clara quipped. "How nice."

The bishop raised a hand slowly. "Jane, I've made more inquiries and truth be told, talked to your uncle. I don't think it would be *gut* for you to visit. He's been in jail for fraud and only sorry he was caught. Served two years and then built up his wealth as soon as he could. The love of money is the root of all evil, like the Bible says. And he has the same opinion of the Amish as he did long ago."

"Which is?" Jane asked, her heart lurching. "Was he in jail when the funerals took place? That would explain it."

"Jane, I need to speak the truth to you, but it may be painful. I told him about you and he said he didn't want to have anything to do with his 'backwards' sister's family. He despises the Amish, believing lots of lies being told about us on television."

"Maybe we can tell him the truth," Clara said. "If he has lots of money, he may want to help Jane."

"Clara!" Jane cried. "What's gotten into you?"

"Maybe some common sense. Since *daed's* left, we're pinching pennies too hard. Relatives help each other."

"Will you be staying here long?" Bishop Byler asked Clara.

"I don't want to go back home. It's depressing. So depressing... my beau." Clara crossed her arms and jutted her jaw as a tear slid onto her cheek, followed by another. She swiped at them fast like swatting a fly. "I got upset about *mamm,* and he said I sounded like a crazy person and maybe it's hereditary."

Jane realized Clara was stuffing her emotions down like she did. *Clara's in deep pain.* "Clara, we'll talk about this later. I really care and want to hear all your woes." Facing the bishop, she asked if he forbid her to see her uncle.

"There's safety in a multitude of counsels and I've had to ask around quite a bit before asking you not to see him."

"I don't want his money, but he's the only link I have

to my *mamm.*"

"Jane, you need to honor the fact that he doesn't want to see you."

"Can you at least give him a message for me?" Jane dared to push the issue further.

"I have his address and can write. But Jane, I fear I'd be wasting my time."

Clara bolted up and asked if she could see the house. "I know Jane has private things to talk about."

"Go right ahead and take a tour," Bishop Byler offered.

"We have white curtains in our windows and you have navy blue," she said, pushing in her chair. "Will be right back."

Confusion over her cousin's behavior was baffling, but she did need some time alone with the bishop. When Clara was out of earshot, Jane asked him what he thought of Jonas' character.

"He needs to grow up and show more humility. At twenty-three, he's not baptized and he had no business asking an Amish girl to wed."

"He said he'll make the vow to the People before we wed. I thought he was seeing you about baptismal classes."

"He did come by to talk, but he has a few hurdles to jump." Bishop Byler pat her hands. "Jane, can I ask you to take another month and do what the psalmist David said to do? 'Be still and know that I am God.' Remember, God makes all things beautiful in his time, like we talked about. And there're seasons we need to go through, a time to embrace, a time to refrain from embracing."

"So, no decisions for a month? You know Luke's coming up next week and he may propose."

The bishop leaned forward. "Do you want to marry him?"

"George said, 'Certain things catch your eye, but pursue only those that capture your heart.' I find that wise."

"Who's George?"

Jane couldn't help but smile. "A man who works at the Seneca museum in Salamanca. He tells me all kinds of Native American proverbs."

"Nice people over there, but the casino is a temptation to the Amish."

"Amish go to the casino? Gamble?" Jane asked.

He shook his head. "You'd be surprised, Jane. It's hard to stay on the straight and narrow, when we're always on a slippery slope."

Jane sighed. "I slid a few times coming over. I'm learning to walk slower on snow." She searched the bishop's eyes and saw that same loving face of her *daed*. She wanted to run and hug him, but only said, "I see. Slow down so I don't fall."

"*Gut* comparison. But back to my question. Do you want to marry this Luke who'll be staying here with Martha and me?"

Jane felt heat rise into her face. "Sometimes I miss him so much, I think I do, but then I've known so little about other men."

The Bishop pulled at his beard. "Think about this.

Maybe you met the right fellow first. And could you imagine a life without him? Could you stand to see him wed another?"

Jane held her middle. An ache seemed to run through her entire body. "Luke married to someone else?"

"Well, *jah*. He won't stay a bachelor forever."

"But you said no big decisions for a month."

"If he loves you, he'll understand. Love is patient and kind, *jah*?"

"*Jah*," Jane whispered.

~*~

After what seemed like an eternity, Jane and Clara walked back to Rose's.

"I've never b-been this c-cold," Clara managed to say.

"I'm going to check on Peanut. He should be inside," Jane said and made her way over to the barn. Peanut met her, as usual, with his wagging tale and circling around with joy. She hugged him and pretended it was Luke. For some odd reason, Jane missed him more than ever. Polar winds shook the barn and Jane thought she heard someone calling out to her. "I'm in here," she yelled. But after a few minutes, no one showed up. Jane took Peanut by the collar and led him outside. "I said I'm right here."

No one was in sight. She thought of Mr. Rochester yelling to Jane and she heard him miles away. Was Luke calling out to her? Or was she becoming too *furhoodled* over the book? She shrugged and headed towards Rose's house. "She won't like it, Peanut, but it's too cold for you."

They ran to the little house and when they entered, Rose immediately planted two fists on her petite hips. "Not in my house."

"I'll keep him in my bedroom. Please? He'll freeze."

"*Nee,* he won't. Lots of animals in the barn and plenty of hay, blankets and whatnot. If it drops below zero, there's a woodstove to be fired up."

Jane stroked Peanut's cold fur. "I'm new here, I suppose, and have never felt such freezing weather, and it's only November."

Rose glanced up the steps. "Jane, I do care for you, you know that, *jah?*"

"*Jah?*"

"Too tight in here. Your cousin and now your dog?"

"I didn't ask Clara to come up. I'm surprised and, well, embarrassed. It's bad manners to just show up and expect to be housed."

"*Jah,* indeed. But it's only a short time, *jah?*"

The door blew open and Jonas appeared. "I saw you out in the barn, Jane. Everything okay?"

"I heard you call to me."

"I was upstairs and saw you from the window. Didn't call you. What do you mean?"

Jane pulled Peanut closer, as he started a deep low growl. "The wind must be playing with my mind."

Jonas stared at Peanut. "Wind can sound like someone's crying. Want me to watch him over at our house? Plenty of room."

Rose backed away. "*Nee,* he'll bite you. We can keep him here until you start a fire. Barn needs heated up.

Jonas glared at Peanut. "Such a pest."

Indignation ran through Jane and she led Peanut away from Jonas and went upstairs to talk to Clara.

~*~

Luke tried to tell Lauren he didn't need another pie. He wasn't recovering from open heart surgery, just stitches. But it was touching how much she cared for ailing people. The desire to marry kept increasing and this trip up to New York in a few days made him uneasy. This Jonas guy was pulling Jane away. He had no proof, but she seemed different in her letters. She was holding back, not telling him everything. And then she went on and on about George, her Seneca friend. Love was not jealous, so why was he fuming at times, sometimes feeling indignant.

Was it Lauren's sweetness? Was he comparing the two?

Lord,

Lead both Jane and me. If we're not to be together, then let us know. I can't talk to Jane and this letter writing makes her feel so far away. Give her a sign or turn her heart towards me if she's to be my wife. Help me be around such a pretty girl like Lauren and have only brotherly feelings towards her. It's getting mighty hard.

His *mamm* peeked in the kitchen. "Lauren gone already?"

"She's helping Miriam today."

Ruth crossed the room and poured herself a mug of coffee. "I have to say, Luke, I'm pretty surprised at how much I like Lauren. I used to think I only wanted Jane for you, but since Lauren's come..."

Luke slid his jaw around. "*Mamm*, how did you know you were to marry *Daed*?"

She sipped her coffee. "Well, you won't believe this, but I courted others. It's *gut* experience and why I push you so hard to do the same. How do you know what you have in your wife if there's no one to compare her to?"

"*Mamm*," Luke asked, his face scrunched up. "That doesn't make sense."

"Let me give you an example. You're *daed* isn't moody. I thank God for it and appreciate it since I courted a very moody man. Made me a bundle of nerves. I wouldn't even recognize your *daed*'s easy temper and consistent behavior if I hadn't courted Harry."

Luke understood, but didn't want to court lots of girls. He wanted to court the girl he'd marry, so he held back. Held back for Jane, until she was old enough to be out on her own.

"Lots of fish in the sea," Ruth chimed.

"*Mamm,* don't you like Jane anymore? You're discouraging this trip because of my stitches and now making me notice Lauren."

Ruth rolled her eyes. "I can't make you notice anyone. Lauren's just a nice girl, you just admitted you've notice, *jah*?"

"I didn't say that."

"Son, why do you feel guilty for noticing Lauren? You're not married to Jane."

She had him about that. Why did he feel guilty for enjoying another woman's company?

~*~

"Clara! You stole that from the bishop!"

Clara crumpled up the paper and threw it up in the air. "Jane, I only got the address of your uncle. He's rich and you need money. We'll write him and ask if he cares about your *mamm* and her poor daughter."

Jane paced across the massive braided rug and then plopped onto her bed. "Clara, your runspringa's run amuck! What's happened to you? The bishop said not to contact him. He could be trouble."

Clara threw up her arms. "My *daed's* trouble. Left us penniless and there's only so many ways you can cook hamburger. Jeremiah and Jacob say their starving all the time and sometimes, I think they are."

Jane gave Clara a coy look. "From what Emma says, lots of meals and financial help's been given to the family. Now, tell me what's really going on. *Rumspringa* doesn't mean you're to disrespect Amish ways, but form lasting friendships and have fun running around."

Clara's lips became a thin line and then her eyes followed suit.

"Clara, open up. Don't bury things deep down like I did all those years. I should have spoken up, but I was afraid."

Clara clenched onto Jane. "I hate my family. My *daed* and *mamm*. They're so weird and I feel like people are laughing at us. It's so embarrassing."

"Laughing at you?" Jane asked. "Why would you think that?"

"Jane, *Mamm* stays in bed and cries. No Amish woman stays in bed and cries. And then she has to see the psychiatrist for her medicine, which everybody knows about since the *Gmay* pays for her treatment."

"*Ach,* I didn't even know that."

"And *Daed's* been spotted out in Ohio with an English woman. How could he? I'm afraid for Jeremiah and Jacob because it's a bad example. Sarah's just off in her own little world, praying that *Daed* will come home. I feel like I'm the parents at home and I'm only sixteen. Makes me want to run away for *gut,* just like *Daed.*"

Sorrow filled Jane's heart. Did she cause this? Opening her mouth had started it all, when she told Luke about her hand being cut. "I'm sorry."

"What?"

"I'm sorry I caused all this trouble."

Clara took Jane by the shoulders. "Jane, you didn't start this. It's not your fault. You've kept us all sane over the years. *Daed* had an ax to grind about your *daed* long ago."

"Was he kind before I came?" Jane had to ask.

Clara stared at the floor. "He was mad a lot. Praised his own *mamm* and said no one matched up to her. Critical of *Mamm,* comparing her to our *grossmammi,* who we've never met."

"Wish I knew her. Clara, I never wondered if our *grossmammi* had a sister or brother. Who could tell us about her? Do we have great-aunts?"

"I think we would have met them by now. Even if we did, I still live in a nut house and want to live up here.

185

Jane, I can't live in that house without you." She clung to Jane again and sobbed.

Jane pat her back and said soothing words, but knew she herself couldn't go back anytime soon. This was her time to heal and learn independence. How could she get married, offer herself to someone when she was half-whole? The bishop was right and wise. No big decisions. Right now, if Clara begged hard enough, Jane would pack her bags and head right back to Punxsutawney, out of sheer pity, being moved by her fickle emotions. Having her time of independence came with more choices. Acting like an obedient puppet to her aunt and uncle gave little room for decision making. *Lord Jesus Christ, Son of God, have mercy on me, a sinner.* This simple prayer she lifted up to God when distressed, and found comfort.

Chapter 15
Heart of the Snowbelt

Dear Emma,

I'm mighty concerned for Clara. Is it that bad at home? She said Aunt Miriam appears to be better, but then sinks down into a depression again. She's running away like her daed.

Emma, I need you to pray for me. Luke's coming up soon and I think he's going to propose marriage, but my bishop said no major decisions for another month. He says I need time to heal. But it's really odd. I know you'll think I'm really nuts, but I feel like he's calling to me, like Mr. Rochester did to Jane Eyre. The wind howls and can sound like someone crying at times, but my heart is getting ever so tender towards Luke.

Jonas, as you know, proposed. I'm going to tell him after Thanksgiving no. He's a yoyo and his devotion to our People is questionable. He thinks I can keep him on the straight and narrow, as does Rose and the whole Hershberger clan, but I don't want a husband who is weak. I see how strong Luke is now.

I miss you.

Tell everyone over at my place hello, even Aunt Miriam, and that I'm praying for them.

Jane

A scream and a thud and Jane nearly crumbled her letter up. "What happened?" she cried out, running to the top of the stairs waiting for a reply.

Laughter? What on earth? She raced down the steps.

187

Rose was knitting in her rocker. "Did you hear that?"

Rose smiled. "Takes me back to my childhood. This is an old-fashioned hard winter. Jonas and Clara sledded off the roof."

Jane walked slowly to Rose. "I don't think I heard you right. They sled off the what?"

"The roof. You pack up snow along the house to make a hill, if there isn't a snow drift already there that's high enough. *Ach*, I had so much fun when winters were harder back in the day."

Jane pulled back the navy blue curtain to see Jonas and Clara throwing snowballs at each other. A toboggan was leaning up against a snowman. "Seems like their having fun, but I'm afraid Clara will break a bone. It's not safe."

Rose shooed at the air. "Never got hurt and I went down plenty of roofs, some much higher than this little house." She placed her knitting down, nostalgia written on her face. "Didn't Jonas take Clara to the maple syrup farm the other day?"

"*Jah*. Clara bought some candy."

"We can make maple taffy!" Rose rubbed her hands together. "I'm like a *kinner* again, when I play in the snow. You pour hot maple syrup onto the snow and it hardens into taffy." She scurried towards her kitchen. "I have the recipe all written down. You young folks can warm up the syrup. Takes about an hour to get it to 250 degrees." She scratched her head. "I think my candy thermometer's over at the big farmhouse. Tell Jonas to get it for me."

Jane laughed. "I've never seen you so excited."

"Like I said, it takes me back to my childhood, the

happiest time in life."

Jane nodded. "It's a real gift to have those memories. Everything's so simple and carefree."

"*Ach,* Jane, you look sad. Miss your parents?"

Do I miss my parents? She'd never really thought about them until she left her uncle's house. Fear had choked her of thinking beyond the next chore. "I *do* miss my parents," Jane found herself saying without thinking. "Memories are coming back and they make me feel safe and loved."

"Then you had a *gut* foundation. How many years did you have such a childhood?"

"My parents died when I was fourteen. So, come to think of it, I was pretty old. Passed the eighth grade. I did have a childhood. I always envied my cousins for having their parents alive, despite how horrible they were, and I had loving parents at their ages."

"Jane, be careful. Calling them 'horrible' is judging, and it's for God who knows the heart." She lifted her lips into a smile. "But I understand and I'm glad you're sifting through all your emotions here. Takes time to unearth them."

Jane and Rose fell into a mutual embrace. Rose had to unearth bitter feelings towards her first husband and now Jane had to dig up more childhood memories. She'd write them all in her journal, something she'd neglected.

~*~

Clara poured the hot maple syrup onto the white snow as Jane, Rose, Jonas and Mary Anna looked on. Jane saw the wonder in Clara's eyes, she was the ten-year-old cousin she first moved in with.

"Help her so she doesn't spill it," Mary Anna advised Jonas.

Jonas cupped his hands over Clara's and she tried to hide a smile.

"That's better, *jah?*" Mary Anna said.

Rose let out a sigh, ice crystals wafting up into the air. "Clara's young and strong, Mary Anna, and was doing fine. I can still hold that pot steady."

"I'm keeping her hands warm, *jah?*" Jonas asked.

Jane had one of her odd and unexplainable intuitions. *Jonas is flirting with Clara?*

Mary Anna slid an arm through Jane's. "Can we take a quick walk to talk?"

Jane wanted to try a piece of candy when it came right out of the snow. "In a minute? Never had this snow taffy."

Clara lifted a piece up. "Jane, look, it's like hard candy." She squealed with delight.

Mary Anna nudged Jane. "Go on and take a piece."

Jane obeyed and then she and Mary Anna took a walk towards the barn.

"Will you be having Thanksgiving dinner with us?" Mary Anna wanted to know.

"Well, Luke will be coming up, as you know. Bishop Byler's asked us if we want to have dinner with him."

Silence and Mary Anna stopped in her tracks. "Jane, we all believe you've been sent by God to help our Jonas. Don't you care about his feelings?"

Rose murmuring about Mary Anna treating Jonas like

a *boppli* was ever so true. *How unbelievable.* But then again, Ruth had said something similar about Luke. "Mary Anna, I'm here to work and get away from a very unhappy situation back in Punxsutawney. I'm sorry if what I say offends you, but I don't think I'm ready to marry anyone anytime soon."

"But Jonas says you'll be twenty-one in January.

"And Charlotte Bronte got married in her thirties," Jane said, feeling a tad bit defensive and needing her friend from the 1800's to come to her defense.

"Who's Charlotte?"

"*Ach,* someone I admire. She did lots of things before marriage. She taught school and wrote books."

"Was she Amish?"

"*Nee,* but she was a devout Christian who believed in waiting for a man who held his faith as dear as she did."

"And you think Jonas isn't as strong a Christian as you? Is that it?"

Jane had never seen this side of Mary Anna and stepped back out of shock. "I think this is between Jonas and me."

Mary Anna screwed up her face. "Well, it affects our entire family. He loves you and is afraid of this Luke fellow coming up."

Jane wanted to ask if she'd hold Jonas' hand to fall asleep if he was afraid of the dark! What foolishness. "Mary Anna, Jonas is twenty-three, a grown man. Why do you fret about him so?"

She crossed her arms. "I love him, plain and simple."

"Look to God." Jane was so unnerved that she blurted

this line from *Jane Eyre*.

"I do look to God, Jane. I'm Amish."

Jane felt beads of perspiration forming on her forehead despite the frigid air. "I don't mean to offend you. I really like your whole family, but Luke's been my friend since I was fourteen. And we'll be having Thanksgiving with Bishop Byler. But we can stop by for dessert. I'll bring pumpkin whoopie pies."

A slight lift of Mary Anna's thin lips and a nod gave Jane hope that she wasn't being too blunt or rude.

Clara ran up to Jane. "You'll never guess what else they make out of snow!"

Jane chuckled at Clara's overly huge eyes. "What?"

"Ice cream. Rose is getting things ready." She went up on her tip toes and clapped her hands. "I want to live here, it's so much fun."

"Do you now?" Mary Anna asked. "Lots of young fellows here that would scoop you right up like ice cream."

Jane stared at Mary Anna. Fear that she was insinuating Clara be a match for Jonas sent a shiver down her spine, and it wasn't from the cold.

~*~

The next day, Jane was called into work, but Stella had said she decided against hiring Christmas help. Her sister volunteered to help out, holding some quilting classes to draw in a crowd. Jane would be sewing Amish dolls for displays, which she was happy to do. But all day at work, she feared Clara would get herself in trouble by another adventure with Jonas. Was she going crazy with fear for her dear cousin? Seeing Clara in fancy clothes was still a shock, so maybe she was overreacting.

The day flew by and she was soon back home, taking with her material and doll patterns to cut. Jane found the feel of cloth, the simple act of cutting, to be a soothing thing. Her *mamm* had taught her to sew and more fond memories had come to her all day. She could almost picture her *mamm's* face. How she wished she'd had a picture of her.

Clara barged into the bedroom. "Jonas is too much fun. We went to that museum you told me about. The one with the Seneca Indians. It was interesting, Jane. I met George. He's so handsome!"

Jane offered a wry look. "What's on the inside counts more, *jah*?"

"You don't think George is handsome inside?"

"I never said that. Clara, you're putting words in my mouth. George is a *wunderbar* man."

Clara fell onto the bed. "But not Amish. Is that what you were going to say?"

"*Nee*. Clara what's gotten into you? I'm Amish and will only marry an Amish man."

Clara rolled her eyes. "My *daed's* Amish, remember."

Jane put a hand up and then continued to cut material on the fold up table Rose suggested she use.

"What were you thinking when I came in?" Clara asked. "Looked like you were going to cry."

Jane took a deep breath. "My *mamm*. I can almost see her face now. Just wishing I had a picture of her, but it's forbidden, so there is none."

"How do you know?"

"Because she was Amish, like I just said."

Clara lit another oil lamp to illuminate the room. "Maybe her brother took a picture."

Jane's heart leapt into her throat. "Do you think so?"

"You know how the English take pictures when they think we're not looking. They're far off, but the new phones can zoom in."

Jane gawked. "How do you know?"

Clara put up both hands in surrender. "Robin has a phone. I don't yet. So many interesting things on the internet."

Jane could see Clara was too fascinated with the English, but she needed this running around time to know her mind, just like Jane needed this stay in Cherry Creek to know her own. Who was she to judge? "So, Clara, when are you packing to go back home? You know Luke expects you to be home. Will you leave Wednesday?"

"In two days? Jane, I don't want to. It's so dismal at home."

Jane walked around the table and sat on the bed. "I agree. But you can come back when things get better."

Clara guffawed. "Get better? How?"

"Well, they can't get worse. We lived so isolated from the People and our dirty laundry wasn't aired out. Now it is and I expect some *gut* will come out of it."

Clara let her face fall into her hands. "Laundry. I hate laundry. I do it all."

Jane laughed at her play on words. "I'll miss you."

"Jane, I haven't agreed to go home. Actually, Mary Anna offered for me to stay with her. It was odd, but it upset Rose. Do you think she wants me to stay here?"

Jane fell down on the bed, feeling limp, drained of energy. "Rose thinks Mary Anna pampers Jonas too much."

"What's Jonas have to do with anything?" Clara asked.

"I don't know." Jane slowly closed her eyes. "I'll have to tell Luke not to come."

"Why?" Clara laid next to her cousin. "Don't you care about him?"

Jane clenched her fists in frustration. "He helps over at the house with Jeremiah and Jacob. But Luke always puts his own desires on the back burner, like a true Christian man. But Clara, I miss him and want him to come." Jane bit back tears. "He's my best friend."

Clara rolled towards Jane. "Don't cry. I didn't know it meant so much. Of course I'll go home and come back up later, like you said."

Jane pulled Clara to herself. "*Danki*. You're getting so mature. So proud of you."

~*~

That night, a light shone in the window and Jane, having just dozed off, felt as if in a twilight of sleep. Was she dreaming? She forced her heavy lids to remain open and for sure, a flashlight glow was dancing on the window. And Jane knew it was Jonas, wanting to talk. They'd been distant from each other ever since he threw the box from George at her feet. Clara had been a *gut* distraction, but soon she'd be gone.

They did need to talk, because she needed to set him straight. Give him an answer to his marriage proposal that he didn't have the right to make. How could she be so blind?

Tip toeing out of the room and down the steps, she put on her outer clothing and stepped onto the porch, Jonas right there taking her hand. "Let's take a walk."

"*Nee*, I need to sleep. The snowstorm is over and I work tomorrow."

He bent down and kissed her cheek. "I've missed you. I know you're mad about my immature behavior and I tried to make it up to you by giving Clara a fun visit to the Seneca."

Jane felt the kiss still on her cheek and she feared her resolve towards this man waning. "Jonas, I appreciate you being so kind to Clara. Her life is hard back home and tomorrow's her last day here."

"I'll find a driver to take her wherever she wants. And I'll ask my *mamm* to make a nice supper tomorrow night."

With his eyes on her, Jane felt so defenseless. Why would such a handsome man propose to a plain Jane? "I've been meaning to ask you something, Jonas. Actually, I should have asked when you proposed."

He took her hand. "What is it?"

"Only baptized Amish men can propose to a baptized Amish woman. You're not baptized, so you broke a rule, *jah*?"

"I'm getting baptized, Jane. I thought I told you that."

"But you're not baptized now. Saying 'someday'

doesn't count." She shifted. "Bishop Byler brought it up."

Jonas rubbed her hand with his thumb. "Bishop Byler and I have had differences, but they're getting worked out. He's not too happy about me working for the English weeks at a time and well, that will change once I'm baptized and married." He pulled her to himself. "Honey, have you thought about your answer?"

Jane closed her eyes and prayed for strength to be so near this man who gave her such passionate kisses, something that should have only belonged to her husband. But right there and then, she wanted nothing more than to kiss him. "I need to get inside."

"I love you, Jane, but you don't believe me. Is it because your uncle made you feel so unattractive?"

"I don't know, but it's late. Can we talk tomorrow?"

Jonas leaned his forehead onto hers. "We always get interrupted. And I'm getting mighty insecure. Can't sleep most nights, because I'm afraid I'll lose you."

She looked up, searching his eyes. "Really?"

"Jane, why is Luke coming up?"

"I don't know," Jane whispered. "He has something important to talk about."

Jonas' face contorted. "He'll propose and you'll say yes." His chin quivered and he got so choked up, half crying, half anger.

"I won't say yes to anyone. You have nothing to fear from his visit."

"W-What m-makes you say that?"

Jane gave an encouraging gaze. "Bishop Byler said for me to make no big plans for another month."

"December, too? *Ach, mamm* was hoping to have a Christmas celebration."

Jane tilted her head. "Why can't she?"

He forced a smile. "We'd be celebrating our engagement."

"She'd be celebrating? I don't think Mary Anna is too happy with me."

He kissed her hand. "She told me she regrets accusing you of playing with my heart with that Luke guy. She's a great *mamm* who loves her son."

Jane wanted to say 'babies him' but only nodded. "Rose is becoming like a *mamm* to me. If I don't settle in these parts, I'll miss her something fierce."

He gripped her. "Jane, imagine if we marry, you'll be a member of the Hershberger clan. Don't know how many cousins I have, and we get along real *gut*."

Be a part of a big family. It was a childhood dream. It would be a blessing to be Mary Anna's daughter-in-law and related to Rose.

"Jane, what's going on out here?" Clara's voice called, indignation in her voice.

Jonas released her and Jane gazed like a deer in headlights at her cousin.

"Jane, Luke's coming up in a few days. How could you? I thought you broke this thing off."

Jane wanted to tell Clara to hush. Jonas had just said he was hurting so. She turned to Jonas. "I was upset with you about being jealous over George and proposing when not baptized. Let's talk later."

Jonas grinned and then said, "Clara, Jane's working

tomorrow. Pick the place you want to go and I'll find a driver."

Clara lit up. "Really? *Ach*, I know exactly where I want to go."

Karen Anna Vogel

Chapter 16
A Man of Character

Jane worked the next day, switching between sewing dolls and knitting merino wool blankets, when she wasn't waiting on a customer. She was relieved that her mind was occupied because it was filled with Jonas and Luke's arrival. Jonas revealed his insecurities to her last night, making him more real, more human than just a handsome man full of charm. Was he as insecure as she was? How could he be? He was almost too handsome.

But as the day lingered along, she found her heart feeling so fondly of Luke. *Certain things catch your eye, but pursue only those that capture your heart,* she remembered George saying. She shook her head to clear it.

"What's the matter, Jane?" Stella asked. "Sore neck from too much sewing?"

Embarrassed, Jane blushed and then met Stella's inquiring eyes and laughed. "Have someone on my mind and trying to get him out. Shake him out, I suppose."

Stella chuckled. "Well, finding a nice man at your age is important, but some are waiting to get married in their thirties. I was thirty-five when I got married to Joe. I was more mature, knew my own mind."

Knew her mind? "How do you know your mind? Can it be done?" Jane asked.

"Like anything else. Experience and learning from mistakes, like learning how to do a new craft or sew. You have to undo more than you get done."

Jane knew Stella was right, but this limbo she was in was painful. Deep down, she felt she owed her cousins a Christmas visit, but the more she understood the Hershbergers, she wanted to celebrate Christmas with them. Where did she belong in this world? In Cherry Creek or Punxsutawney?

"Jane, what are you thinking about? You just zoned out."

The voice of her aunt ran like a train through her mind. 'Why do you stare, Jane? Answer my question. Are you daft?' *No she was not.* She was finding she was a very intelligent woman and capable, not clumsy and stupid like she'd been told.

Jane turned to organize the hanks of yarn that customers had misplaced. "I was thinking about back home in Punxsutawney. I don't know where I fit in or where I'll make a permanent home."

"Jane-Girl, you're only twenty. Why are you so hard on yourself? You may live in several places in your lifetime, right? Why try to figure out your whole life out now?" She came near Jane and helped her with the yarn. "You're too serious. If you relax, sometimes you see things more clearly. It's why I do so many crafts. My mind can race at times, but when I sit and knit, my heart rate goes down and my mind settles." She gave Jane a side-hug. "What's your favorite yarn color?"

Jane loved white like the snow outside. "White."

"What shade? Bone white or maybe a hint of cream?"

"Pure white. Why do you ask?"

Stella yanked it off the shelf. "Your job is to knit a

shawl for yourself with this yarn, on me."

Jane embraced Stella. "It's expensive angora yarn. I can't."

"Don't Amish accept presents from us outsiders?" Stella asked in a quirky tone.

Jane laughed. "Of course we do."

"Consider it an early birthday present."

She fingered the soft yarn. "*Danki* so much, Stella. I really love working here."

~*~

When Jane arrived home, Clara rushed at her, a little paper in hand, waving it vigorously. Jonas was close on her heels, but Rose sat at her rocker, knitting, not even looking up to give her usual greeting.

"Guess what I have!" Clara blurted. "*Ach,* Jane, you won't believe it. And it's all because of Jonas." She turned to give him a toothy smile.

"What is it?" Jane asked, making out that Clara had a photograph in her hand. Maybe it was a postcard from the Seneca Museum, but why be so excited?

"Jane, come over and sit in your rocker," Rose said, eyes downcast.

Jane obeyed, her throat tightening. Why was Rose so somber?

"Guess, Jane. Who have you wanted to see a picture of?"

"From the museum? I don't know. Cornplanter's wife?"

Rose let out a long, low groan.

Clara knelt before her. "Jane, I met your uncle. He

gave me this picture of your *mamm*."

Jane grabbed it, stared at the side shot of her *mamm*, apparently taken without her knowledge. She bit back tears. Her *mamm* was carrying a baby in her arms.

"She's carrying you, Jane," Jonas said softly. "What a treasure, *jah*?"

The longing to be held by this dear woman again overpowered her and she could only weep. Pressing the picture to her breast, she rocked back and forth saying '*Danki*'.

It took a bit for her to calm down before reality set in. "Clara, you met my uncle? But the bishop said…" she gazed at the picture. "I'm grateful, but the bishop said not to contact him." Jane looked up at Jonas. "Did you know that?"

"*Jah*, he knew it," Rose blurted. "Has no respect for the bishop or the People."

"I did it for Jane. What could it hurt, *grossmammi*?"

"Jonas, the bishop consults the elders, *jah*?" Rose blurted. "There's safety in a multitude of counsels. There's a reason he forbids it."

"Okay, the man did jail time for fraud, but he's nice now."

"Does he want to talk to me?" Jane probed.

Clara took her hand. "*Nee*, he doesn't. Only offered the picture. He wasn't really that nice either. He said some things about your *mamm* that were upsetting."

"And it's why Bishop Byler thought him a bad influence," Rose snapped.

Clara ignored Rose, which shocked Jane. "He made

fun of her plain ways and ours, but who cares? People make fun all the time, *jah?*"

Jane met Rose's fallen countenance. "Clara, what you did was wrong, but your intensions were *gut. Danki.* Rose, I'm so sorry this upset you. I'll make something extra special for supper tonight."

Rose wiggled a finger, motioning Jane to come near. Reaching up to Jane's face, she cupped her cheeks. "I don't want to see you hurt or be led down the wrong path. Stay away from your uncle."

Jane bent over to embrace the dear woman. "I will. I'd never have gone against the bishop."

"That's my girl," Rose said fondly. "Make me some shepherd's pie. I have a craving for it.

As she made her way into the kitchen, Jonas caught her by the elbow. "Are you sore with me, too?" He was grinning, as if Rose's opinion and feelings didn't matter.

"When you're Amish, you take the vow to obey for *gut* reasons."

"But aren't you glad you have a picture of your *mamm?*" He put an arm around her waist. "I've never seen such tears. Were they tears of joy or sorrow?" He tucked a stray strand of blonde hair back under her *kapp.*

Jane pulled away and headed towards the pantry to retrieve a quart of stew. Clara tip toed in. "Are you done?"

"With supper?" Jane asked. "Just started. Can you peel the potatoes?"

Clara swung her dress around. "I didn't mean that. I mean your thank you kiss to Jonas."

"Didn't get one," Jonas said with a fake pout. "Don't think Jane's happy with me right now."

Jane faced Jonas and then Clara. "How could you disobey the bishop? Bishop Byler of all people? You're Amish."

"I'm on *rumspringa*," Clara chimed. "Not under the thumb of any bishop."

Jane's unflinching glare dared Jonas to cross her. "You're not baptized at twenty-three. Still flirting with the world, Jonas Hershberger. Can't you see that's why your *grossmammi's* upset?"

He lowered his head. "You keep me in line, Jane."

She knocked away his hand as he tried to caress her cheek. "I shouldn't have to. Look to God." Her new favorite saying came out with more force than she intended. She sounded like a sidewalk preacher.

Jonas rolled his eyes and headed towards the door. Jane was too much in shock to even say anything, but Clara ran after him. "Jane, seriously, sometimes you need to lighten up."

Lighten up? An English chastening to not be so serious. But how could she not be serious about her Amish beliefs? She'd have left her uncle's house long ago if she didn't believe what the Bible said was true. Justice would prevail, even if she suffered for a time. Now that she 'grew a backbone' as Emma put it, she would have spoken up, but she was grounded in *gelassenheit*. Humility and putting one's own desires aside for the good of the People. Rose was right. Jonas lacked *gelassenheit*.

Jane pulled the picture of her *mamm* out of her pocket

Lord, I'm so grateful to have this even if was gotten under bad ways. I'll tell Bishop Byler and confess I want to keep it. Lord, am I being too hard on Jonas?

~*~

The next day, Jane awoke early to pray. The picture of her *mamm* had dug up memories buried deep. Abigail Raber was beautiful on the inside and out. Why she was taken when Jane needed her most, going through puberty, having many questions about life, bothered her. She stared at the picture, gulping. *Lord Jesus Christ, Son of God, have mercy on me, a sinner.*

In *The Jesus Prayer,* she'd read that *Lord* meant a good landowner who let poor folks grow wheat for bread on his land for a small price. St. Michael's Day, a day of prayer and fasting every autumn, was an Amish holiday of gratitude, a day her ancestors were grateful to their 'Lords'. They could have been chased off the land, but were given a portion by kind landowners.

Jesus was called Lord, but it always seemed to be someone to fear. After meeting with Bishop Byler, a man who personified kindness, the idea of calling Jesus Lord quieted her soul and made her feel protected. How she hoped the bishop would allow her to keep this photograph. She pressed her lips to it, a kiss to her *mamm* in heaven. *Lord, I don't understand too much about my life, but I trust you. And my prayer for today is to make the best Sister Day possible for Clara. She's suffering, Lord. Help me be a blessing to her.*

~*~

Baking cookies for Clara to take home was mixed with

chatter all day long. They even got into a bit of flour throwing, but by three o'clock, when the driver from Punxsutawney pulled up to collect Clara, Jane wasn't prepared to say good-bye.

"This was a *wunderbar gut* Sister Day," Clara said, biting back tears. "Are you sure you can't come home with me?"

Jane quickly loaded up cookies into a plastic container. "When I'm ready, I'll visit. For now, I-"

"I understand," Clara said, tucking her jeans into her boots. "Sure was fun wearing English clothes for a while."

"You're not going to continue?" Jane asked.

Clara's eyes misted. "*Nee.* Seeing you and having our talks, I know I'm Amish. Was just too tired and depressed back home. I'm going back to serve *Mamm* and others in the community, and maybe take that buggy ride home with Freeman King."

"*Gut* for you," Jane exclaimed, embracing Clara. "Now, I need to run upstairs and get the bag full of presents for Jeremiah, Jacob, Sarah and Aunt Miriam."

"You got my *mamm* something?"

"Of course," Jane forced a smile and ran up the steps. In her room, she heard boots stomping and Clara chattering with the driver. But Luke's voice? *Ach,* she was going batty. She stopped and listened for a spell. "It is Luke!" She grabbed the bag and raced down the steps. "Luke. You came up early!" Running up to him, she stopped shy of giving him a bear hug. "So *gut* to see you."

"Hey, what am I? Chopped liver?" Vinny asked. "Hey,

Babe, tell your sister we need to go right now. Have some other Amish to pick up in Randolph and I'm not driving Route 666 in the dark, no way, no how." He placed a strong hand on Clara's shoulder. "Now have your cry out, say good-bye, and have it done with."

"We already did," Jane laughed, putting her bag near Clara's pile of belongings.

Vinny reached for the bag full of Jane's gifts. "What in the world? What's in here?"

Clara peeked in the large brown bag and gasped. "A Seneca tomahawk! *Ach,* I can scalp you, Vinny, when you drive too fast," Clara snickered.

Vinny's eyes were orbs. "Hey, you wear jeans and stuff, Miss Running-Around-Lady, but Amish are pacifists, right?"

Tears brimmed in Clara's child-like eyes. The same helpless look Clara gave Jane when she was ten. She gripped Clara's hand. "I'll miss you, too."

"*Jah,* but it's not that," she said, her voice trembling. "You got *Mamm* yarn and a knitting book for her nerves, *jah?*"

Jane knew this was a tiny gift, getting the yarn on clearance at the store and the book was given to her by Stella. "It's nothing."

"*Nee,* Jane, it means everything. You believe there's hope for *Mamm* and you care about her bad nerves."

"*Jah,* I do." Jane embraced Clara, not wanting to ever release her, but soon she felt a tap on her shoulder.

"Babe, I don't have all day," Vinny quipped. "You Amish need phones to gab," he chuckled. "Now, let's hit the road."

Luke handed Vinny money and pat him on the back. "Better get going."

Jane released Clara and without thinking intertwined her fingers in Luke's. "Have a safe trip."

Luke squeezed her hand. "*Jah*, drive carefully. Watch out for icy spots." He closed the door and took Jane by the shoulders. "I've missed you. You look better than ever."

Jane had forgotten that look in Luke's eye that said she was the best thing since ice cream. His shaggy sandy bangs framed his dark eyes perfectly and she said, "You look better than ever, too." She cupped her mouth. "I didn't mean that. I mean you look healthy."

He grinned and reddened. "Jane, don't be nervous. It's only me, Luke, come up to see my girl."

Jane felt as if time was suspended and only she and Luke existed. "Am I your girl?"

They neared each other and embraced. He held her head to his chest. "I hope so."

The door blew open and in came Rose followed by Jonas. Confusion etched Rose's face and anger contorted Jonas'.

Jane cleared her throat. "Luke came up with Clara's driver. He's a day early." She wiggled out of Luke's arms. "Clara was rushed out the door. She'll write you, I'm sure."

"You're not staying here," Jonas blurted, nearing Luke and glaring him down, fists clenched.

Rose gawked at her grandson. "This is my house and

you're being rude, Jonas. No way to talk to a friend."

Jane saw a wildness in Jonas' eyes, like a territorial animal. Or was it hurt? She never expected to be so comfortable around Luke, taking his hand and embracing, but it seemed natural. "We'll go over to Bishop Byler's," Jane informed. "He's been expecting Luke."

"You have such *gut* things to say in your letters about him, I'm looking forward to meeting the Man of God," Luke said, picking up his small suitcase.

"You're staying here for a while," Rose insisted. "I want to get to know you better. Jane's told me so much about you."

Jonas spun around and left, slamming the door. Rose shrugged her shoulders. "Sorry about his behavior. My grandson still needs to bend the will, and we're all praying."

"It's alright," Luke said. "We all need prayer, *jah*?"

Luke's humility was so refreshing, Jane wanted to throw her arms around him and pledge her love. What had overcome her? She was considering a life in Cherry Creek with Jonas not long ago, but his behavior lately had been despicable. No, she would only marry a man of character, like Charlotte Bronte's husband.

~*~

A visit with Rose, that was delightful as she got out her best little tea cookies and some specialty teas, went by too fast. Her fancy tea pot and matching cups had been handed down from her *grossmammi* and were a treasure to Rose. And they had roses on them, of all things. Pink roses that seemed to match her completely.

"Rose, we need to walk down to Bishop Byler's, before it gets dark," Jane said.

"We'll take Peanut with us," Luke quipped. "Miss that boy of mine."

"Is it your dog?" Rose asked. "Isn't it Jane's?"

Luke nodded. "Gave him to her as a gift. He's *gut* protection and company."

"*Jah*, he is," Jane said, her face actually hurting from smiling so much.

"Well, come see me again before you leave," Rose insisted. "I'll make cherry rolls."

"*Ach*, I'll be back for sure and certain," Luke said, rubbing his tummy.

Jane and Luke bundled up and were soon on their way to Bishop Bylers, Peanut wagging his tale like a whirligig.

The air was crisp and snow lightly fell like crystals from above. Jane's heart felt full, at peace, and she recalled the Seneca saying: *Follow your heart.*

Luke took her hand. "Jane, before we get to the Bishop's, I want to say something." He stopped under a large maple tree, laden with snow. "I love you, Jane."

She held his gaze. "I think I love you, too."

"So will you marry me?"

"I want to," she began, emotion filling her in places she didn't even know existed. "When I saw you, it just seemed right for us to be together."

"So, is that a yes?"

Jane felt like she was smiling from her eyes and wanted to hide them. "I can tell you in January."

"What? Jane, what's holding you back?" He bit his

lower lip and his eyes grew round with fear. "Are you courting Jonas?"

"*Nee*. Not really. Well, he asked me to marry him and I said I'd tell him in January. You see, Bishop Byler said for me to rest and know my mind, like I've written. I did write that, I believe."

Luke stared at her in disbelief. "So you'll pick between me and Jonas in January, is that it? Jane, please tell me it's not true."

The pain in Luke's voice was unbearable. "I prefer you much more than Jonas. I plan to tell Jonas no very soon. Luke, please be patient. I need time. So much has happened."

Luke threw his hands up. "Love is patient, but I do have my limits, Jane."

"What does that mean?" His tone was one foreign to her. It was as if he had decisions to make of his own. "Is there someone else?"

"Never mind. It's getting cold out here and we better get to the bishop's house." Luke clapped at Peanut who ran out on the road. "Boy, come," he said firmly. When Peanut ran to him he kept walking down the road, not waiting for Jane.

"Luke, I do love you," Jane yelled, catching up. "If I lost you?"

He stopped abruptly and Jane bumped into him, sliding and struggling for balance. He caught her and his soft eyes were hurt. "Jane, I wish I could believe you. There's something keeping you from saying yes to me. As much as it pains me, maybe it's not God's will."

Jane clung to him. "*Nee*, I believe it is, but I'm changing up here. Rose has been like a *mamm* and is mentoring me. Marriage is a big step."

"I know, Jane, and you've known me since we were young teens. Why can't you just say yes and mean it?"

Jane looked away. "I need to come into a marriage whole. And I'm getting there. So many emotions running through me because of the past."

He took her hands. "I can help you. As your husband, I long to cherish you. Maybe more healing will come once we're wed."

Jane hadn't thought of this. "We'll talk to Bishop Byler tomorrow."

"Why, Jane? He's not your bishop permanently, unless you plan to stay here." He shifted. "You'll be coming home for Christmas, *jah*?"

Jane swallowed. She'd promised Jonas she'd have Christmas with the Hershberger clan. A big family she thought she wanted, but seeing Luke, she knew it was him she wanted. How mixed up her mind had become.

"Jane?"

"Luke, I've been so foolish. I have things to confess. You may not want to marry me."

He stepped back. "Don't tell me you and Jonas?"

Heat rose into her face, until she felt on fire. "We only kissed. Nothing more."

Luke visibly shivered. "Maybe we both need time."

"What do you mean?" Jane asked in a panic.

"Well, I have to confess a new girl in town has caught my eye."

"Then why are you proposing to me?" Jane blurted.

"Because I don't love Lauren like I do you."

"But you could?" Pain stabbed Jane's stomach and she doubled over. *Luke had his eye on someone else? How could someone take her place so easily?* Peanut came near and licked her face and started to whimper. She hugged him and let out a sob like no other.

Luke tried to help her up, but she shooed him away. "How could you, Luke?"

"Lauren means nothing to me. Believe me. I love you and was hoping you felt the same."

She plopped down on the wet snow and cried, letting out deep, pent up pain.

Luke knelt down. "Honey, please say yes. You're the only girl I've ever loved."

She looked at him, studying his face. He was serious. *He loved her.* Jane threw her arms around him. "I just realized I could never see you married to anyone but me. I love you. Marry me!"

He pulled her up and held her close. "You're so cold and sopping wet. We need to get you warm."

He picked her up and carried her the distance to the bishop's and Jane felt that horrible feeling of a migraine coming on. *Ach, nee.*

Karen Anna Vogel

Chapter 17
A Broken Wing

Luke kissed Jane's hand. "Martha's here to sit with you."

She grabbed his hand. "Stay. My head."

"Alright," Luke conceded, sitting back in the wooden chair near her bed.

Bishop Byler motioned for his wife, Martha, to sit with Jane and took Luke by the elbow. "Jane, Martha will stay with you. Luke needs to eat."

Jane remained silent and Luke could tell she was bearing the pain of this migraine the best she could. He followed the bishop down the hallway and into the kitchen. "It's hard to see Jane in pain."

"Never knew she had these headaches."

"They started when she left her uncle's house. Too much stress I suppose."

"Well, you must be starving. Cold chicken alright? Could heat it up."

Luke yawned and nodded. "*Danki*. Everything's okay." He leaned against the table, head in his hands. "This is my fault."

"Why'd you say that?"

"I pressed her too hard for an answer to my proposal. She said you told her she needed time to heal, and I took it as another rejection."

Cold chicken and a jar of chow were placed before Luke. "Another rejection? You proposed before?"

"*Jah*. Before she came up and we were courting, sort of." Luke bit into the chicken leg. "My *mamm* wants me to get married and not wait forever for Jane." He offered a faint grin. "Loved Jane since I was fourteen."

Bishop Byler sat back in his chair and pulled his beard. "That's a long time. Never asked her to court when she was sixteen?"

Luke shook his head, his eyes darkening. "Jane wasn't allowed to court. She was like Paul in the Bible, under house arrest." He scoffed. "That uncle of hers was cruel and threatened Jane if she ever told anyone about the abuse. I was the first person she told."

"And how did that come about?" the bishop asked.

"Saw her bandaged hand and asked what was wrong, and she told me. Out of the blue. She always made up an excuse, but she said I pulled it out of her."

"Love pulled out the pain, *jah*?"

Luke's brows furrowed. "I suppose. I take in all kinds of critters and rehabilitate them. It takes time, but they learn to trust and then let me clean wounds even though it hurts. My *daed* thinks I'll get bit hard yet, but never have." The wind shook the house, the windows rattling.

"What was Jane's answer to your proposal this time?"

Joy filled his heart and he brightened. "She said yes. That she couldn't see me married to someone else."

The bishop smiled with satisfaction.

The opened door ushered in frigid air. Jonas appeared, a scowl on his face. "I came to take Jane home. My *grossmammi's* worried to death."

"Jane's sick. She'll be staying here for the night,"

Bishop Byler said evenly. "Now, you go on home before another storm hits."

His icy eyes seemed to cut through Luke. "The dog's missing."

"He's in the room with Jane for now, keeping her calm. We'll give them another few minutes together before Martha will insist he stay in the barn." The bishop took out his pipe and soon a smoke ring appeared. "That dog sure is loyal. People should be so devoted." He eyed Jonas. "It's late. We're shutting the house down."

"Can I see Jane?" Jonas asked, his eyes still on Luke, as if to challenge. "I'm more loyal than that dog."

Luke understood his meaning. He was calling him a dog. *How immature.* The air became so thick, Luke thought he'd choke. How he wanted to tell this Jonas guy what he thought of him, acting so arrogant and dressed Amish. *What a hypocrite.*

The bishop yawned and let out a loud sigh. "I'm bushed. Can you pull the door shut tight and make sure the storm door clicks into place, when you leave, Jonas?"

"*Jah. Gut* night," he spat, giving Luke one last scowl.

When the door banged and the storm door clicked, Bishop Byler groaned. "Sorry for his behavior, Luke. You'd think he was five years old at times. I'll be having a talk with him for how rude he was to you."

Luke put both hands up in surrender. "Don't bother. To overlook an offense is a man's glory, *jah*?"

"That's one Bible verse hard to live out." He clamped Luke on the shoulder as he passed. "Luke, sure am glad you're here. We'll talk about wedding plans in the morning, *jah?*"

Luke only said good-night, but was baffled. Didn't the bishop want Jane to wait? Had he changed his mind? He couldn't help but smile. *Never underestimate the power of a praying mamm.*

He went to sit near Jane, but Martha asked him to take the dog out to the barn, assuring him it was as snug as a bug in a rug. Jane was crying, asking for him, but Martha pointed to the dog. So he took Peanut out and the barn was just like Martha said, and after giving the dog a bear hug, he went back to see Jane. Martha stood in the door frame. "Isn't right for you to stay up with her. Women tend to women, *jah?*"

"Can I say good-night?"

Martha moved aside and Luke heard Jane groaning. Jane's pain had always ripped Luke so deeply, more than he thought normal as a young teen. But now he knew he loved her and seeing her writhing in pain, he wished he could take the pain on himself. He turned to Martha. "Time for more medicine?"

"In an hour."

Jane held her head and sobbed. Luke slid next to her and rocked her, wiping her tears with his bandaged hand. She gripped it and he wanted to howl in pain, but endured it. He'd endure anything for his Jane.

~*~

The next day, Jane felt a little better, but the shades were kept down. Luke, one leg crossed over the other and slouching in the chair, told her he was exhausted. But he kept on reading aloud the Book of Ruth to her from the

Bible. It was Jane's favorite book, filled with loyalty and devotion. The book gave her a keen sense that God was in control.

She realized when in such pain last night, she only felt comfort when Luke was near. When he left it was unbearable. How could she have missed it? She'd always loved him. Why did she feel like she had to stick her head in the outhouse to see if it smelled or not, and that's what she did with Jonas? He flattered her, making her feel pretty, and she'd never experienced such passion. And she felt tainted and unfit for Luke. But even though she confessed it, here he was, by her side, as constant as ever.

"I love you," she whispered, when he read the last line. "Do you still love me?"

He leaned in close. "Of course. You know I do."

Trying to remain calm as to not agitate her mind, she breathed evenly. "Luke, I only kissed Jonas. I told you that, right?"

"*Shh. Jah.* It's okay."

"*Nee,* it's not." Hot tears slid down the sides of her eyes, hitting her pillow. "I wanted such kissing to be only for my husband, but Jonas took me by surprise."

"He kissed you against your will?" Luke blurted.

"*Nee.* He lured me in and I was so stupid. I tried to forget you and I feel wretched about that."

He took her hand. "You were injured, like a bird with a broken wing, and you were trying to fly again."

"What do you mean?"

"Honey, when you left your uncle's house, you were full of self-hate. You didn't even feel worthy enough to

221

stay at our house unless you got up to work. Remember how my *mamm* scolded?"

Jane did remember Ruth telling her to rest and she felt guilty. Here at Bishop Byler's, she let Martha tend to her all night and just rested. So, when she came here she had a wounded spirit and Jonas took advantage of that? "Luke, what's your opinion of Jonas? Is he a wolf in sheep's clothing? Preying on innocent sheep?"

"Well, I don't want to judge him, but in your case, I think he pursued you without knowing you. That's hasty and our human nature, our lower nature, is selfish and impatient."

She reached for his hand. "I see you differently. Maybe it took someone like Jonas to make me appreciate you."

"So you'll marry me? I need to make sure, because if you will, I'll call my *mamm* from the phone shanty and make her day."

"I'll marry you, Luke. I love you so. But your *mamm* barely wrote. I think she'd rather you marry Lauren."

Luke's eyes narrowed. "*Mamm* said she did plenty of times." He slapped his knee. "Did Jonas always get the mail?"

Jane slowly turned to Luke and it dawned on her. "He didn't give me my letters? *Ach*, I was starting to think you didn't care either. But I got Emma's and Clara's…"

"Only the ones from me missing? *Mamm* stuffed her letter in with mine."

"How many did you write?" Jane wanted to know, yet as her anger rose, she was afraid to find out.

"Tried to write three times a week."

Jane bolted up in bed. "Three times?"

Luke gently lowered her head onto the pillow. "Jane, you need to get better so you can have Thanksgiving dinner tomorrow, *jah?*"

She clenched her jaw. How she despised Jonas now. Something akin to hatred ran through her, shocking her. Was this the flip side of lust? *Hatred?*

~*~

Jane awoke to the aroma of sage stuffing. Was it noon? She slid out of bed and slipped on her robe, but dizziness overtook her and she flopped back on the bed. In a flash, Luke was in her room, hovering over her. The pounding in her head had waned, but the dizzy spells and nausea had not.

Luke lay on the bed beside her. "Jane, now what did Martha tell you?"

"Stay in bed, but I smelled something."

"Turkey and all the fixin's. It's Thanksgiving."

Jane pushed back tears. "And I'm supposed to stay in bed all day?"

"The shades are up so that's a *gut* thing, *jah?* No more light sensitivity?"

"No more pounding in my head. Why didn't I get these before, when I was in real stress at my uncle's?"

Luke turned and arched himself up on an elbow. "Too much change. When I change my animal's environment, they get upset and their immune system goes down. Ever see a startled bird? Can't even move."

Jane smiled. "You're always comparing me to an animal."

"It's what I know best," he quipped. "Now, Bishop Byler and Martha invited over some of their *kinner*. Might be noisy." He screwed up his face. "Can your head take the noise?"

"Well, I don't have a choice, *jah*?"

"*Jah*, you do," he teased. "Guess."

Jane heard excitement in Luke's tone. "You turn everything into an adventure, Luke Miller. Remember the scavenger hunt you sent Emma and me on?"

"Never did find the jar of honey," he chuckled.

Jane had gotten the belt that night from her uncle, who used the buckle part that time. As she recalled, it was one of her last excursions with Luke. Could she ever forgive and be whole?

"Jane, you look sad…"

"*Ach*, Luke, my uncle was fierce after I came home." She held her head. "Will I ever be free from that man invading my thoughts?"

He placed his bandaged hand over hers. "Time, Jane, and forgiveness."

Jane knew he was right, but not wanting to talk about it, she asked, "Where can we have a quiet dinner? In the attic?"

"Never thought of that. *Gut* idea. But *nee*. Rose's place, if you can take the sunlight."

Rose. How she missed this dear woman. "Won't she be over at the big farm?"

Luke grinned. "She sent word to the bishop that she wanted to get to know me better before I leave. So, it's only the three of us."

"When you leave? Why can't you stay longer?"

He bent over and kissed her cheek. "No fretting today. When you're up to it, we'll make plans. Now, are you up for a ride to Rose's?"

"I get dizzy," Jane said with a sigh.

"I'll catch you if you fall."

She wrapped her arms around him. "I love you so much, do you know that, Mr. Rochester?"

He backed away. "*Ach, nee.* Not that *Jane Eyre furhoodled* stuff again."

She snickered. "When we wed, I plan to read every book written by the Bronte sisters. Still want me to be your wife?"

"If you stay away from my *Pennsylvania Field & Stream.*"

They embraced again and Jane knew what she was the most thankful for this Thanksgiving Day for sure and certain.

~*~

Rose welcomed Jane with open arms, her eyes filled with concern. "Are you better, Jane?"

Jane clung to Rose. "*Jah,* much better. You should be over at the big house, not fussing over me."

Rose motioned to the chairs in the living room, her eyes dim. Jane noticed great sadness in this dear woman. "Are gatherings hard for you since your husband passed?"

She wrung her hands. "*Nee,* just want a quiet day. It's not an Amish holiday anyhow."

"But it's a *gut* day to feast, *jah?*" Luke prodded.

Rose offered a faint smile. "*Jah.* Of course men like to

eat, so it's a *gut* day for you, Luke." She turned to Jane. "I want you all to myself. Will you be leaving soon?" Her petite chin quivered and tears flooded her eyes and spilled down onto her pink cheeks.

Jane steered Rose towards her rocker and sat at her feet. "Something's wrong. Tell me."

Rose stroked Jane's face. "I'll miss you. Was hoping you could straighten Jonas out, but he's like an unbroken horse."

Jane blinked rapidly and glanced over at Luke, imploring him to help.

"Rose, some men aren't grown up by their twenties. He'll come around, with God's help."

Rose straightened. "He's coddled too much. I got into an argument with Mary Anna about how she makes excuses for his behavior and I decided not to go to dinner. And things will never change with that woman at the helm."

Jane took Rose's wrinkled hand. "I notice you're not visited much. Do you like living back here?"

She pursed her lips. "I keep boarders for a reason. I'm lonely. And Jane, you were *gut* medicine. Never did tell anyone about so many of my woes."

"I helped you? You helped me!" Jane recalled all the talks over cups of tea. Rose opened up like a flower in some parts, others she was as closed as a Venus fly trap. "Rose, tell me what's upsetting you."

"I promised to keep my tears in check, but I'm acting like an old fool."

Luke spoke up. "Would you like to help us plan our

wedding?"

Jane's heart filled with love for Luke, who was ever so sensitive. But she felt dizzy again and made her way over to her chair. "I'd like that," Jane said. "You're not married. Maybe you could be my attendant."

Rose stared hard and then snickered. "An old woman like me..."

"You'll come to the wedding, *jah*?" Luke prodded.

"When is it?"

Rose's question hung in the air, silent as a windless summer day. She inspected Jane and then Luke. "No plans?"

"Well, since I've been sick since Luke came, we haven't had time to plan anything." The room began to spin and Jane gripped her head. "*Ach, nee.*"

Luke ran to her. "Dizzy?"

"*Jah.* I spoil everything."

"I'll make some peppermint tea," Rose offered, rising. "*Gut* for the nerves. Too much change for my Jane all at once."

Luke held her tight. "Is she right? Moving back home is making you sick?"

"I don't know. I like Cherry Creek. And my uncle's far from here."

"Then you stay here until you're at peace about where to live."

She leaned into him. "I'll live with you."

"And I'll live with you."

Jane managed to look up into his eyes. "What are you saying?"

"I can make a life up here if it makes you happy."

Jane could not believe the depths of Luke's love. He'd read the Book of Ruth to her, a story of sacrifice and love. Ruth wouldn't let her widowed mother-in-law live alone and went into a country where she was not welcome, not being Jewish. Luke would do that for her. It was too much. She'd have to gain the courage somehow to live back in Punxsutawney and run the risk of seeing her Uncle Malachi.

Chapter 18
Charm is Deceitful

Luke had kept Peanut's disappearance from Jane, hoping the dog would show up. When Thanksgiving dinner was over, and Jane and Rose were sipping tea and planning their wedding cake, Luke slipped over to the barn to see if Peanut by some chance went to his old camp out

The azure blue sky awestruck him. Everything in Cherry Creek was more vivid and intense, the colors, weather and some of the people, namely Jonas. How could such a hypocrite be the grandson of Rose? The child-like man worried his dear *grossmammi* and Luke hoped he'd straighten out for her sake.

He yelled the dog's name into the massive red barn, air tight and well made, and amazingly warm. Pigs snorting and the usual animal sounds could be heard, but not a bark. He yelled again as he walked through the barn, but to no avail. He hoped Bishop Byler had greater success as he was out looking for the gentle dog, too. Peanut, although bruised in body and mind, had learned to trust again. Fear grasped him that he'd been stolen. Peanut wasn't a roamer. Had he learned more trust in a foreign place? Did he miss Rose and try to find his way back to the Hershberger place?

Luke waited a while, but the dog didn't show up. Jane's questions about him and her need to see her canine comforter brought him to the end of his rope. *Lord, lead the bishop and watch over my dog. Jane's dog. Our dog, when we wed.*

He headed over to the Hershberger farmhouse to inquire if they'd taken Peanut in. He rapped on the back door, and Jonas' *mamm* that he'd met briefly, oddly was happy to see him. "Have you found Jonas?"

"Found Jonas? Is he missing?"

Mary Anna wrung her hands. "He left early this morning and hasn't been seen. Missed Thanksgiving dinner, but then again, his *grossmammi* had words with him and may have upset him." She sighed. "You'll have a mother-in-law someday and just pray she's not meddlesome."

Luke was too stunned to speak. Such disrespect to an elderly woman was not common among the Amish, or if they quarreled, they worked it out, but here he was a near stranger and she was telling him her woes about Rose. "I, ah, won't have a mother-in-law. Jane's *mamm* died years ago when she was fourteen."

"Well, count yourself blessed."

Luke measured his breathing as his heart raced. "The weather's milder in Punxsy. If Rose wants to make a home with Jane and me, we'd be happy to have her."

Mary Anna shook her head. "You and Jane getting married? Are you hoping or telling me?"

"I'm telling you. She said yes. Rose and Jane are over there talking about the cake Rose is making," he said, motioning towards the little *dawdyhaus.*

Mary Anna's cheeks ballooned out, her eyes grew so big they looked like they'd pop out. "Rose is on your side, against my Jonas? How despicable."

Pity for Rose enveloped Luke's soul. He tipped the rim of his black wool hat. "I think more words will only add fuel to the fire. I best get going."

"Wait. Why'd you come over? To gloat?"

"Gloat? *Nee*, it's not in my Amish upbringing to gloat. My dog's missing. Thought you might have Peanut in your house."

She shook her head. "*Nee*. You took him over to Bishop Byler's and it's the last I've seen him."

"*Danki*," Luke said, forcing a smile.

Mary Anna let out a humph and slammed the door.

Sorrow filled Luke for Rose's sake. Maybe she could come down to Punxsutawney and stay until the wedding or a long vacation. He'd be telling Bishop Byler about this matter.

~*~

That night, Jane kept asking about Peanut, but Bishop Byler and Luke tried to put her questions off and it got awkward. "Is he hurt? Tell me."

"*Ach*, he's a hunting dog and it's hunting season up here. Maybe a nice female went by and he followed," the bishop said lamely.

"Hunting season can make a dog restless, especially if they're bred for it, like Peanut," Luke added.

"Well, I'm going out to look for him," Jane insisted.

Bishop Byler stroked his gray beard. "We'd need to hook up the sleigh runners, and I'm awful tuckered out. Can we wait to see if he shows up?"

Jane, although suspicious, nodded in agreement.

Martha brought stiff laundry into the utility room off the kitchen and Jane ran to the coffee pot. "Here's some piping hot coffee, Martha. You should have asked for help."

She unloaded the clothing and entered the kitchen, gratefully taking the coffee from Jane. "I enjoy the winter. Everything's so crisp and quiet. I hang clothes and watch the birds and thank God for battery operated socks," she said with a grin.

"Never seen those before," Luke quipped. "I'm buying some." He cleared his throat. "Can I speak to *yinz* about something?"

"Who's *yinz*?" Martha asked. "Never heard of anyone by that name."

Jane burst into laughter. "It's slang in Western Pennsylvania. It means 'you all'."

A round of hoots and chuckles echoed around the room.

"*Jah*, you can talk to yen."

"*Yinz*," Jane corrected. "Luke, what's this about? You look worried."

Martha went to her white cookie jar and just set the whole thing on the table. "Cookies are the cure for worry."

Luke grinned. "*Danki*. It's about Rose. Is she treated well by her *kinner*?"

"Well, it's a long story. *Jah*, by some, but others think she's too opinionated."

"No excuse though," Martha interjected.

Jane spoke up, hoping to distill Luke's fears. "She

doesn't get along with Mary Anna. I know that. Her first husband was 'cruel' as she put it, and the *kinner* she had with him defend him, saying Rose didn't submit like a *gut* wife. I don't think they ever saw her bruises."

"Bruises?" the bishop asked, aghast. "That was before my time as bishop. Was there a warning? Church discipline?"

Jane realized why Rose revealed so much to her. She understood. "Women who are hit feel like it's their fault and they're embarrassed. Lots of fear involved and threats to keep quiet."

Martha reached across the table, taking Jane's hand. "You're talking from experience, *jah*?"

Jane nodded and turned to Luke. "Are you saying she's not treated *gut* now? Jonas checks in on her. I think he looks out for her."

"*Jah*, I'm sure he does," Bishop Byler agreed. "If there's any hope for that man, it's Rose."

Jane didn't know if she should say what was on her mind, but she knew holding back information, keeping things under wraps, never came to any good. Problems were solved in community. "Rose cries about Jonas quite a bit. She sees in him her husband, Matthew, and keeps hoping he turns the bend and gets baptized. She confessed to putting pressure on me to reform him. I did feel a little bit manipulated over there, but all's forgiven."

"Can Rose live with us?" Luke blurted. All eyes, round as buttons, landed on him. "The weather's warmer back home and she's attached to Jane. Or, maybe she could come for a while and help with the wedding."

"*Ach,* Luke," Jane said softly. "You have a heart of gold. But where would she stay?"

Luke grabbed a cookie. "My house. I'm sure *Mamm* and *Daed* would welcome help with the wedding."

Martha rose to replenish coffee cups. "Do you think Rose would go?"

"For a vacation? *Jah,*" Jane said, gripping the hot mug.

"Well, let me pray on that. Don't want to be accusing the Hershbergers with neglect," Bishop Byler said, "because her son loves his *mamm*. It's the tension between his wife and *mamm* that makes him want to pull what hair he has left out. But a vacation?"

Jane stared at Luke across the table, his eyes full of concern for her dear Rose, and love filled her heart to near bursting.

~*~

As the weekend progressed, Peanut still didn't show up, even though Luke put up 'Dog Missing" signs all over town and Englishers offered to take them to neighboring towns. Luke called Vinny to leave a message for his parents. In a few hours they were calling the phone in Bishop Byler's barn.

"Hello?"

"Hello, Son," Moses said warmly. "So, glad to know we have a wedding to plan for *yinz*. Nice of you to call your *mamm*. She was pulling her hair out with worry."

Luke chuckled. "*Daed,* I've never heard you so sing-songy."

"My youngest son never got engaged before. Now, is something wrong that you called? Hand alright?"

"*Jah, Daed,* Got the stitches out this morning. Peanut's missing. Put fliers up in our neck of the woods, but I'd like to stay for a while."

Silence and then a 'hmm' and then, "Sorry, Luke. I just can't take care of these animals you have. Don't have the knack for it. Some are getting skittish. Best come home." Luke's eyes misted. He needed to find his kind hearted dog. "Okay, *Daed.* I'll be home by tomorrow morning."

"Tell Vinny not to speed. I know he's afraid of that Route 666 and speeds through it, but there's snow on the ground here. Okey Dokey?"

"Okey dokey, *Daed.*"

He hung up the phone and leaned on the old-fashioned wall phone. He shed tears right there in private. "Peanut, my *gut* dog. Where are ya?"

~*~

That night, Jane and Luke had supper with Rose in her little house, cozy and warm as the wind howled. Rose was all abuzz with talk of not only the wedding cake, but cookies and other candy she'd be making for favors. "This will take time, so maybe you can come home with me," Jane suggested.

"I'd like that. And, Jane, maybe I can help mend things between you and your aunt. She's suffered as I did with that wretched first husband, as you know."

Luke sipped his coffee. "Do you talk about your first husband like that in front of your *kinner?*"

A shadow crossed Rose's petite features. "They don't believe me. Now, Jane does and it's been a balm to my heart." Her light blue eyes landed on Jane fondly. "Maybe that's what created our bond."

Jane's heart warmed. "We helped each other, *jah?*"

"*Jah,* for sure and certain."

The door swung open and Jonas stepped in, his face covered with his scarf. His eyes met Jane's, sorrow mixed with confusion. Pulling down the scarf, he glowered. "What's this, *Grossmammi?*"

"Making a farewell dinner for Luke, if it's any of your business. Now, you go on home. We'll talk tomorrow."

Jonas eyed Luke with contempt, but he quickly brightened. "Jane, I can pick you up for church. Can put the sleigh runners on and we can be real snug under the buggy robe."

"What about me?" Rose blurted.

"I want to talk to Jane in private."

Jane straightened, clenching her left hand from trembling. "I'm engaged to Luke."

He rolled his eyes. "My *mamm* told me something like that, but didn't believe it. That's what we need to talk about."

Luke shot up, his chair toppling over. "There's nothing to say except congratulations."

Jonas ignored him completely. "Jane, what time can I pick you up?"

"Are you *furhoodled,* Jonas," Rose snapped. "Or are you deaf? Jane's marrying Luke and I'm sure glad of it. He's a *faithful* Amish man."

"Jane, can we talk?" he pressed, as if it were just the two of them in the room.

Rose clenched her chest and started to pant. Jane ran

to get water and held it to Rose's lips. "What is it?"

"My heart's jumping."

Luke checked her pulse, pressing two fingers to her palm.

"I'm fine. Happens when I get upset," Rose panted. "Get worked up. Tired."

"She needs to see a doctor," Luke insisted. "Jonas, get a driver."

Jonas stood there, his arms crossed. "You tired her out, Luke. Glad you're leaving."

Jane gawked. "Jonas, how can you be so selfish? Your *grossmammi* needs help. Now get a driver. Now!"

Jonas' face turned cold. "Okay, but I'm not paying."

~*~

Late that night, after the doctor had examined Rose, Bishop Byler sat at the foot of her bed, Jane on the other side. "How long have you had these panic attacks?"

"Never had one. I was just upset." She protruded up her chin in defiance.

Bishop Byler stifled a laugh. "You're a woman of grit, for sure, Rose. I've watched you over the years as a young man. Can you keep a secret?"

"*Jah.* Always have."

"I always wished we were related. That you were my aunt. You would have spoiled me rotten and I would have enjoyed that."

Tears pooled in Rose's eyes. "Really? I remember when you first courted Martha. I could have made your wedding cake."

Jane never knew how much Rose loved to bake, but

was told her help wasn't needed over at the big farm, as if she was too old, an old cow put out to pasture.

The Bishop rose and paced the floor. "Rose, I'm going to ask you something and I want an honest answer. Nothing will leave this room unless someone has not abided by the *Ordnung*."

"Go on," Rose prodded. "You know me; I tell it like it is."

He shifted his weight and wiped his forehead with his large handkerchief. "Do they treat you right over at the big farm? It's our culture to not just provide a house for aged parents, but visit them and make sure they're not lonely."

Rose stared ahead at the wall. "Jonas stops over. Has been here more since Jane's been here."

"And before that?"

"*Ach*, they get my mail. I see someone every day."

"Do they stay or just throw the mail on the table?"

She bit her lower lip as if he could pull no more words out of her.

Jane noticed ice was pelting the window and wondered if Luke should be traveling in the morning if this ice storm kept up.

"Rose, Jane and Luke are real fond of you. Jane doesn't have a *mamm*. And like I said, I always wanted you to be mine."

Rose frowned. "You said aunt."

"I was too embarrassed to say *mamm*. Mine was a hard woman, as you can probably remember?"

Tears pooled in her eyes... "I prayed for you, but

didn't know how to help. I've learned to be more outspoken after my first husband died. Good bye and good riddance to him."

Jane covered her mouth to hide a laugh. Rose sure had learned to speak up.

"Do you want to live with Jane, when she's married to Luke? Punxsutawney has milder weather."

Sorrow filled her eyes. "I have a mission here."

"Which is?" Jane nudged.

"To see Jonas turn out to be like my dear Matthew. They look alike, and deep down, they're the same."

Jane's eyes met the Bishops' and could see the frustration in them. "Rose is coming down for a vacation to help me with my wedding."

"*Jah*, only a visit," Rose repeated.

Karen Anna Vogel

Chapter 19
Truth Comes Out

"*H*urry it up, Amish buddy," Vinny said, snapping his fingers. "Promised your dad I'd get you home early. Your old man's dragging, taking care of all those critters you have."

Jane's heart sunk to her toes but was sure she could keep her tears at bay. She'd done it for six years while living in her uncle's house. But when Luke took her hand and kissed it, she was undone and the tears ran. He led her into the living room, telling Vinny to have another cup of coffee with Rose.

"Jane, you can come back with me. I think Stella will understand."

She hugged him around the middle and leaned into him, sobbing. She knew she could, Stella being so understanding and weekly someone came in inquiring about a job. But Rose needed to pack and help her family understand she needed a vacation for a season. And Rose seemed to cower under their influence. And what if Peanut showed up? No, she had to find her dog somehow.

"I hate being apart from you," Luke moaned.

"Me, too," was all she was able to get out.

"So, we'll write about wedding plans. When are you thinking we can tie the knot?" Luke asked, kissing the top of her head.

"I'd marry you today if I could."

He held her back at arm's length. "Are you serious?"

She forced a smile. "Rose can't make a cake in one day, *jah?*"

Luke's brows furrowed. "I want you to promise me something. Don't go anywhere alone with Jonas."

Jane cupped his cheeks. "You have no reason to be jealous. He can't lure me like he used to." She pulled him down and kissed his cheek. "I love you."

"It's not that. I'm afraid for your safety."

"My safety? You think he'd hurt me?"

Luke chewed on his bottom lip. "Don't like how he looks at you and he's too short tempered. Promise?"

She embraced him again. "I promise, Luke. Please don't worry."

"And you'll try to get Rose to have a Punxsutawney Christmas?" he asked.

"If you write her that you want her to make plum pudding. She loves a challenge."

"Hey, Lover Boy," Vinny said, clapping his hands. "We gotta hit the road, Bub."

Jane didn't let him go, no matter how much Vinny teased. "I'll write you every day."

"Finish up your work here and I'll talk to my *daed* about where you can live, now that Rose is coming."

Vinny took Luke by the elbow. "Hey, Romeo, do I have to drag you away or what?"

Jane felt ridiculous being so clingy to Luke, but he indeed held her heart. He loved her, but she couldn't receive it until she'd opened her heart. Life here in Cherry Creek had changed her. Waiting on God to make everything beautiful in his time had changed her. In time, she'd be Mrs. Luke Miller, she just needed patience. "Drive carefully, Vinny," she blurted.

"Once I get through Route 666, I'm okey dokey." He winked and blew Jane a kiss. "Bye, Juliet."

Juliet? She was Jane. Well, he must drive for lots of people and get them mixed up.

Luke looked back at her and his loving gaze gave her strength.

~*~

Jane spent the day in her room writing letters and reading since it was an off Sunday with no services, and Rose was tuckered out. So fascinated by Charlotte Bronte's family, she'd taken *Agnes Grey* out of the library, since Anne Bronte wrote it and it had the same flavor: a governess mistreated and in those parts of the book, she let memories of injustice surface, so she could forgive. Bishop Byler said to look back only to forgive and be free. Jane was linked to her uncle by unforgiveness and it could only be broken by her.

But her eyes could only take so much reading, so she wrote to Clara.

Clara,

I'm so glad we became like sisters when you were here. We can have another Sister Day, when I come home for Christmas. I hope I'm coming home for Christmas, if I can get Rose to come. We're having the hardest time parting and she told Bishop Byler she was happier with me. So she's coming down to help plan my wedding.

Oh, Clara, how could I have missed it? Luke was made for me. We're engaged, but please keep it a secret, until it's published. When I come home, it will be for good. I just don't know where we can live. Any empty dawdyhaus' for rent? Let me know if you hear of anything opening up. Luke's looking, too.

Clara, tell me more about Freeman King. Please don't let your parent's marriage make you afraid to love someone. I think I've found a real key in finding the right mate. First of all, you have this odd peace that you've come home or are settled. And if you can't imagine life without him. When Luke told me he'd move on with Lauren King, I never cried so hard. I can't describe the pain. I got physically ill. Also, love is patient, like the Bible says, and it doesn't seek its own way. It's gentle and kind. Read 1 Corinthians 13 and think about all that's said about love. It is real, Clara. Like I said, your parent's marriage wasn't a gut example.

Jane

Jane yawned and lowered her head onto her desk as sleep overtook her.

~*~

Jane awoke to flashing lights. Lightning in winter? How odd. When she realized she'd fallen asleep at her desk, she chided herself for not checking on Rose more that day. But when Luke left, so did her energy.

She got up and smoothed the wrinkles on her apron. A flash lightened the room and she jumped. *How odd.* The only time she'd seen such a bright light in winter was when she was watching the fire department put out the house fire that took her parents. She barely had any recollection, but a fire fighter came in to rescue her and she was taken to an ambulance.

Jane's heart jumped and she ran to the window. Was there a fire? She peered out, but saw nothing, but then that bright light played against the window again. She opened the window and heard Jonas' voice calling her name.

"Jane, hey, I got this high powered flashlight."

"Jonas, go away. I'm engaged to Luke and you know it. So leave."

She shut the window and made her way across the hall to check on Rose, but she wasn't in her room. So, she crept down the steps and with no lights on, she fumbled into the living room. "Rose, are you in here?"

"*Ach,* Jane, I fell asleep knitting. I was more tired than I thought."

Jane's eyes adjusted to the room, and she went to Rose. "Are you feeling alright?"

"*Jah.* Fine. Embarrassed I fell asleep in my clothes."

"I did, too. One minute writing a letter and the next waking up with my face on it, snoozing."

The flickering of Jonas' flashlight was on the living room windows. "What in the world?" Rose asked.

"It's Jonas. He flickers a light to signal for me to come out and talk. I promised Luke I wouldn't be alone with him."

"Did you tell Jonas?"

"*Jah,*" Jane groaned, "but he's not getting the hint."

The front door opened. "*Grossmammi,* are you alright?"

"*Ach,* Jonas, you know I am, and you want to see Jane.

Now she told you to leave, so skedaddle."

As if he didn't hear his *grossmammi*, Jonas came in and lit an oil lamp. "Will you kick your favorite grandson out?"

Rose leaned her head back and pressed a hand over her heart. "Please, Jonas, go."

Feeling furious at Jonas' impertinence and fearing Rose was having another panic attack, Jane flew at Jonas, pushing him towards the door. "Leave. She said to leave, so go."

"Don't shove me like that, Jane."

"Rose has had a hard day and needs rest. It's late, so leave." She poked him with her finger and he grabbed her wrist and wrenched it. Pain shot up her arm and she screamed.

"Jonas, you fool. Look what you've done," Rose snapped, her voice faint.

He stomped his foot near Jane as if to shoo her like a cat. Although her wrist arm was throbbing, memories of her uncle shooing her came to the surface and she backed away, trembling, but she got out, "You hurt my arm."

"You pushed me and I stopped you."

"Go home, Jonas," Rose near begged.

He spun around and headed towards the door, slamming it so violently, it was a wonder he didn't break the windowpane. Jane ran to Rose. "Are you alright?"

"My heart fluttered a bit, but not out of fear, but of disappointment. Jonas is nothing like my Matthew, Jane. Did he hurt you?"

The sorrow in Rose's eyes was unbearable. "He's

stronger than he thinks and I did push him."

"I saw his face, when he grabbed your hand. He was furious."

Old feelings of low self-worth, that she deserved what she got, overtook Jane, but she collected herself and recognized it. No, God loved and cherished her. "Rose, can we make plans to leave for Punxsy soon? He scares me."

She put a hand to Jane's cheek. "*Jah*, for you honey."

~*~

As the next few days went by, Jane realized how painful it was to use her right wrist. Stella asked her if she was upset that she was asked to cut so many felt reindeer for a kids' craft project, but Jane told her the truth, not hiding the pain or abuse anymore. Her arm ached. Stella said there was a bad apple in every bushel, a saying Jane was used to hearing. *A bad apple can ruin a whole bushel* was another saying, and how much damage her uncle and Jonas were creating. Rose was so shaken after Jonas left, but she tried to hide it. Today, she was going to be talking to Rose's *kinner* about her visit to Punxsutawney. Not their permission, but her decision to go. Matthew had left her enough money to last a lifetime and she had Bishop Byler's blessing.

When Jane got home from work at five, she was startled to see a car in the driveway. A car with a Seneca decal on it. "What on earth?" She swiftly took her horse to the barn, not bothering to unhitch the buggy until later. Was George visiting her? *Ach*, she did not need this. What would the Hershbergers think? That she had a secret romance with George?

She half slid and half ran up the steps to the *dawdyhaus*. Upon entering, she was toppled over by a dog licking her face. *Peanut!* Struggling to get up, Peanut lathering her face with kisses, George pulled the dog back with a hardy laugh.

"You found my dog?"

George's face fell. "I got it back." He glanced over at Rose. "Can we talk in private?"

"Rose, do you mind?" Jane asked.

She wagged a finger. "You're engaged."

George raised a hand. "Ma'am, I'm married with two kids."

"You are?" Jane asked, astonished. "I didn't know that."

Rose scooted up to George, being half his size. "Were you making romantic advances towards Jane as a married man? We Hershbergers had our suspicions."

Jane placed a hand on Rose's shoulder, laughing. "George has only been a *gut* friend. I'm just so surprised at how young you look, George. I thought you were in your twenties."

"We Natives age well, like a fine wine, we've been told. I'm forty. My kids are twelve and ten."

Jane felt laughter keep bubbling up in her and she got the giggles. For the first time in her life, she couldn't stop laughing. The Hershbergers made such a fuss about George bringing her home, thinking she was dating him. And seeing Peanut was safe and sound, her joy overflowed a little too much.

He bowed to Rose. "Can I speak to Jane in private as a happily married man?"

A smile slid across Rose's face. "I suppose."

"Let's take a walk outside, Jane. Peanut has energy to run off."

Jane hadn't even taken off her cape, outer bonnet and boots, so they were soon off to take a walk. "I think I'll slip my hand through your arm, George. I see Mary Anna peeking through the window. Let's give them all something to talk about."

George didn't laugh, but became somber. "Jane, you're such a nice girl, and I need to be honest with you." He knelt down and pet Peanut, who seemed to stay very near them. "Jonas took your dog. He's a gambler. Goes to the casino often and had a debt and paid it with Peanut, since he's a hunting dog."

Jane could only stare ahead in disbelief.

"Remember when I met you and asked why Jonas was dressed like an Amish man?"

She nodded, it all coming back to her.

"Well, he comes dressed in regular clothes to Salamanca a lot. I think he's had girlfriends there; seen him with a few. But when I met you, I thought well, maybe this Amish woman could straighten him out. I'm sorry, Jane, but I thought you should know, especially since you're engaged."

"I'm engaged to Luke," Jane blurted.

"Your friend from back home?" He asked, his face split by a smile.

"*Jah.* I was going to stay here for a bit longer, but

knowing how despicable Jonas is, I'm leaving as soon as I can convince Rose to pack."

Jonas came around the side of the big farm and George whispered to Jane to say nothing. "Peanut, old boy. So you've been found. George, how'd you find him?"

"I saw posters up in Salamanca and recognized the name."

"*Jah*, I did it for Jane. Put my name on the fliers, since people know me around these parts."

George crossed his arms. "And they'd return the dog to you even though it's not yours."

Jonas nodded. "I'd give him back to Jane, of course."

"Well, I'm returning the dog for River Jones. You still owe him five hundred in gambling debts, but he said he's open to a payment plan if you're that hard up you'd steal a dog." George clenched his fist. "You need to stop riding the fence. Be a Christian or not, but don't come into my town trying to be a holy man and acting like the devil."

Jonas growled and jutted out his jaw. "Don't judge me."

"Would you rather I call the police and let them judge? I'm showing mercy, young man, and hoping you'll repent and change your ways."

Jonas' eyes met Jane's with contempt. "You provoked me. You led me to think you'd be my wife and then Luke shows up and you announce you're engaged. Anyhow, I pay for Peanut's food and I figured he was half mine, since we were supposed to be engaged."

George went over to Jonas, took him by two strong arms and held him up in mid-air. "Pick on someone your own size."

Jonas tried to wiggle free, swearing up a storm, but George was too tall and strong.

"Now, apologize to Jane."

"Never."

"Well, you asked for it." He let Jonas down, but held him in a head lock. "Say it."

"I'm a pacifist," he grunted.

"I come from a long line of warriors," George said evenly.

Mary Anna came running out of the house. "Let go of my boy."

After a few tense seconds, George released Jonas. "Boy! That's exactly what he is. A little boy who needs to grow up."

Mary Anna hovered over Jonas, who sat in wet snow. "Are you alright?"

"*Jah, mamm*, I'm fine."

Mary Anna darted a glare at Jane. "You flirt. Making my son upset over Luke and now this man?"

"He stole Peanut to pay off gambling debts," George said evenly, stepping in front of Jane. "And I'm a happily married man. Just came to return the dog."

Mary Anna was visibly shaken now. She looked down at Jonas. "Gambling?"

"*Ach, mamm*, I'm still in *rumspringa* and do it for fun."

"Owing five hundred bucks isn't just having fun. You're lucky you didn't owe someone else that money,"

George groaned. "You need help for your gambling addiction."

Mary Anna put a hand up. "We handle our problems among the People."

"Hope you all the best, ma'am. Meant no harm, but needed to return the dog. Almost got sold to someone in Canada."

Upon hearing this, Jane hugged Peanut around the neck and wished she could be transported right now back to Punxsutawney.

Chapter 20
Amish Forgiveness

Dear Luke,

I can't give all the details in this letter. Peanut was returned.
Jonas sold him to pay off gambling debts. Rose is so upset over
his behavior and said it's high time for her to take a vacation.
The only problem is, I don't know where we can stay. I wrote to
Clara the other day and asked her to look for a dawdyhaus we
could stay in or a house for rent. We can't stay in the same
house being engaged, but how I'd love it.
I called Vinny and he said he could pick us up in a week.
Please ask your daed and the elders and bishop for advice for
me. I don't want to live in my Aunt Miriam's house. I fear I'll
turn back into my old scared self and be a bad wife to you. I've
made such progress up here and reading Jane Eyre. Haha. I
have to keep needling you about my love for the Bronte sisters.
Agnes Grey was a great book.
I love you with all my heart!
Jane

Luke let out a "Yippy". His *daed* put down his hammer
and all his co-workers stared at him. "Peanut's been
found and she's coming home next week!"

Cheers went up. "Best get to work, men," Moses
commanded in a firm tone and then they all broke out
into laughter and started to sing another song.

~*~

December's glistening snow lured Jane to the

window to daydream. How she'd been chided for doing this by her aunt. Her aunt she would be seeing all too soon. Bishop Byler had smoothed out Rose's 'vacation' to Punxsutawney by saying she could do some good to an ailing woman. Rose would help Aunt Miriam get past a bad marriage. It was to be a short stay, so the Hershberger clan was even happy for her to be able to travel, something Rose had wanted to do.

As the days of packing and cleaning the little house blurred into each other, Jane took small intervals of rest, for contemplation. Her mind always wandering to Luke and being Mrs. Luke Miller.

But deep in her heart, only Bishop Byler and Rose knew the struggle inside her to forgive not only her aunt and uncle, but the entire church district for turning a blind eye to the abuse that she endured. Not her peers, but the ones who could have some influence, the older members of the *Gmay* who's accusations would have been taken more seriously.

But one thing she learned here in Cherry Creek in the most unsuspected way was from the Seneca's. They had their share of troubles, differences and hurdles to jump, but they were in it together as a people. George's devotion to his heritage was admirable. Their sayings, proverbs of sorts, were to keep the next generation in step with their customs, much like the Amish.

And then Jonas' acting like he was free, almost boasting about it. He wasn't free. He was a slave to gambling and materialism, never content. Jane had seen a life of rigid rules with no love enforcing them, and here in

Cherry Creek, rules given out by her dear bishop with such love, she knew he had her best interests at heart, so she didn't feel caged in. She never thought much about meeting her *mamm's* brother. If Bishop Byler knew it would hurt her, she trusted him and somehow, there was healing in that. How kind he was to allow her to keep the picture of her *mamm* holding her, a treasure for sure and certain. Yes, she trusted a man. Jane could barely remember the bond she had with her father, but it gave her a sense of security. He was stable and kind and not moody. Maybe this was the quality she loved so much in Luke.

But to see her aunt again, it made her head tighten, but only mild stress headaches had come on her throughout the week.

Jane glanced around the little bedroom, everything packed up, and thought of her future. Bishop Byler had read Ecclesiastes 3 to her and yes, there was a time to embrace and a time to refrain from embracing. A time of war and a time of peace. But in the end, He made all things beautiful, in His time. It was time for her to leave this beautiful place and move back to Punxsutawney again. But she had someone with her at all times, the Lord above and Rose. *Lord, thank you for this dear woman, who loves me like a daughter.*

~*~

Rose held her embroidered handkerchief up to her nose nearly the entire three-hour drive to Punxsutawney. She made comments on the beautiful scenery and the change in altitude, her ears popping and such, as her handkerchief muffled the sound of her voice. Jane had given Peanut a bath before leaving, but to Rose's delicate senses, he smelled horrible and his dander was giving her the sniffles.

When they passed Route 80, Vinny yelled out, "Told ya so. No snow, and you didn't believe me."

Jane couldn't believe him, since at least six inches of snow had fallen last night in Cherry Creek.

"Will you miss the snow belt, Babe?"

"Her name is Jane," Rose informed. "Why do you keep calling her Babe?"

Vinny chuckled. "Because she is one. But taken, I hear. Luke Miller's on lucky fellow. Am I right?"

"*Jah*," Jane said.

"And you owe it all to me, Jane, who drove up your hunk of a man to see you, the excuse being the dog."

"Excuse?" Jane laughed. "*Nee*, he was keeping his promise. Luke gave Peanut to me as a gift before I left home."

Vinny shifted gears and soon the car jerked and sputtered. "Aw, no. Come on, girl, you can make it. Don't get us stuck in Alaska!"

Rose leaned towards Jane. "He thinks we're that dumb? Alaska?"

"There's an Alaska, Pennsylvania," she told Rose, gripping her hand.

Vinny coasted the car into a hotel, of all places. "Well, she needs fixed up. We'll need to stay here overnight."

"What?" Jane and Rose crowed in unison.

Vinny threw his hands up as if under arrest. "It's not

safe to drive. And I'm tired, so I'll check it out in the morning."

"It's only one o'clock in the afternoon," Jane blurted. "Can't you find help now?"

He rubbed his eyes and gave the loudest yawn. "I'm too tired. Have been driving too much lately. Being an Amish taxi man tires me out. You people get up too early."

Flabbergasted, Jane stared at him hard. "We'll have to pay for a hotel stay."

"Not to worry, Babe. Luke gave me some extra dough to pay for any extra expenses."

"Her name is Jane and you can't buy anything with dough!" Rose growled.

~*~

Their stay in Alaska, Pennsylvania ended up really being the outskirts of the quaint town of Brookville. Jane had dreamt of coming here to see the historic houses. As odd as their breakdown was, Vinny gave Jane twenty dollars to spend at the craft store.

After they secured their rooms at the hotel, they were soon puttering down the main street, and Jane cooed. "These houses are so pretty. All the gingerbread trim and colors look so cozy."

"And with the Christmas lights up, seems magical, huh, Babe."

Jane stopped correcting Vinny about her name but only agreed.

"Luke said you like the Victorian houses. Can you

Amish have anything fancy on your houses?" he asked, looking back at her.

"We can have some little touches like lattice or a simple little gable, but nothing that would stand out too much, bringing attention to itself."

"Does it have to be painted white like the rest of the houses?" he continued to probe.

Jane was getting more confused by the minute. Their break down, the money to buy crafts and now wanting to know her taste in houses. "I'm not leaving the Amish, Vinny," she sputtered.

He glided into a parking space along the tree lined sidewalk. "Babe, where did that come from?"

Rose had fallen asleep beside her, so she lowered her voice. "Why are we here? I want to go home."

"My car needs looked at," he exclaimed.

Jane pointed to a mechanic shop down the road. "Go there now and get it looked at," she insisted, surprising herself at her commanding tone.

"I'm too tired to drive any further."

Jane's dander went way up. "There're signs everywhere saying 19 miles to the Home of Punxsutawney Phil!"

Vinny smirked. "Trust me, kid, I just can't drive anymore today. You'll see the Land of Phil tomorrow."

Jane clenched her jaw and mutely nudged Rose. "What? Where are we?" she asked.

"At a craft store to buy yarn. Why? I don't know."

~*~

Jane barely slept that night as Rose snored so loud, it seemed impossible for such a sound to come out of such a small woman. And she also talked in her sleep, mentioning Matthew. Jane's droopy eyes barely made out the Miller house as snow gently glided from the sky. But Peanut recognized his old home and wagged his tail, hitting Rose in the face. But Rose had grown fond of Peanut and only ruffled his fur.

"Jane, is this where we're staying?"

Jane's heart filled, when Luke ran to the car. "*Jah*, this is Luke's place. But we can't stay here."

The car door opened as soon as the car stopped and Luke and Jane clung to each other, and he twirled her around, pulling her in for a kiss. But out of the corner of her eye, she noticed many people, all in black coats and capes. So many from the *Gmay* were here to greet her?

Ruth ran up to her. "Jane, I'm so excited."

Emma bounded after her. "*Ach*, Jane, you deserve this."

Clara, Sarah, Jeremiah and Jacob nearly toppled her over, but her Aunt Miriam was nowhere in sight.

Jane looked back to see Rose holding on to Vinny, who wore a smug grin. What was all this about?

A bon-fire with containers full of hot chocolate and trays of cookies welcomed them. A hundred people or more were in the Miller's back yard. Jane was truly perplexed. Had Luke announced their engagement? Custom had it that it would be told to the People only two weeks before the wedding.

Moses came near Jane. "Jane, I'm so happy for you."

Jane took his hand. "Why? I don't understand."

"You will. You will." He pulled his long beard with

satisfaction.

Vinny handed a box to Luke and the whole lot of them proceeded to a new pathway Jane had never noticed before. A stone walkway that she could see through the bare maples and birches led to a tiny house. Her eyes misted as they drew nearer and Luke asked her what she thought.

Luke took Jane's hand along with the box and led her up the steps to the tiny porch. He ripped open the box to show Jane two pieces of gingerbread trim that were plain, but fitting. "We'll put them on the edges of the porch."

Jane was still speechless. The Bishop soon met them on the porch and a hush fell over the crowd.

"Jane, we're here to welcome you back to Punxsutawney, but also to ask forgiveness for not helping you sooner. As Amish, we strive to see the best in people, but in your case, we were blinded. This house was built not only with love, but with money collected by our *Gmay* as a gift. You and your friend from New York can live here until, well…"

Luke whispered something into the bishop's ear and he stepped back. "*Danki*, bishop." He took Jane's hand as she faced the people. All eyes on her were earnest and filled with hope of putting the past behind and looking to the future. "I forgive you all, even though I never spoke up like I should have."

As they lined up one by one to kiss her cheek, Jane was enveloped not only by the People, but the love of God in them. As snow fell on patches of muddy ground, Jane recalled the scripture, 'though our sin be as red as crimson, they shall be white as snow.' The dear Amish of Punxsutawney that day etched a permanent mark into her heart.

The last to greet her were Vinny and Rose, who were chuckling. Rose put a handkerchief to her nose. "I knew all about Luke's plan. I hid my face half the way home, so you wouldn't see me grinning from ear to ear."

Jane's lips parted. She pointed to Rose and then Luke and then burst into laughter.

Luke kissed her cheek. "Vinny delayed you. We've been working around the clock here. You and Rose will live here, until we finish *the* house."

"*The* house?" Jane asked, puzzled. "Not this one? A sweet little house is what I want."

Luke drew her near. "This is a *dawdyhaus* for Rose to live in while she's on 'vacation', which I suspect will be a long while." He kissed her and then led her into the house where the layout was exactly like Rose's in Cherry Creek. "Do you think Rose will feel at home here?"

"Luke, it's perfect. Even furnished in traditional furniture and white curtains." A braided rag rug nearly covered the entire living room and Jane was too stunned to ask where it all came from. She laced her fingers behind his neck and pulled him into an embrace. "I want to cry, but can't. It's too much."

"Too happy?" he inquired.

As if he could read her mind, she nodded. "*Jah*, too happy."

~*~

But Jane's happiness was short-lived when Aunt

Miriam stopped to pay her a visit the next day. With a pie in hand, a vinegar pie no less. A delicious pie, but Jane wondered if it had a hidden meaning. Vinegar was used to clean things. Did her aunt think she needed a cleansing? Rose took the offered pie with a smile and introduced herself, while Jane stood there, tongue-tied like she used to be when under her aunt's thumb. Miriam looked older, gray hair peeking from her prayer *kapp*. Wrinkles creased her brow and no color graced her cheeks. She appeared sallow, her cheek bones protruding from a sunk-in face.

Rose tied on a baking apron. "Jane and I are making Christmas cookies. This house came fully furnished, even the kitchen has everything a person could want for baking. Do you bake, Miriam?"

She shrugged, eyes avoiding contact. "*Jah*, sometimes. But I came here to ask Jane for forgiveness." Her rigid jaw was set, not a softened look that would accompany an apology.

Rose scooped cookie dough onto a pan, glancing over at Jane to break the silence, but she didn't. Anger burned in Jane and she needed some air. A walk with her dog or a run? A 'jog', like the English called it.

"Sit down, Miriam," Rose near demanded. "Now, honesty is the best policy, as my English friend says. What are you asking forgiveness for?"

Jane's eyes rounded and she wanted to clap her hands to applaud her dear Rose. Aunt Miriam was a hypocrite to her core.

"I, ah, wasn't kind, when Jane lived with us."

"And?" Rose prodded.

"Never told anyone about Malachi's behavior."

"Why?" Rose asked, patting the chair. When Miriam just stood there like a wooden carving, hollow inside, Rose put a cup of tea on the table. "Now, take a seat and sip some tea."

Miriam obeyed this time, seeming to be afraid of Rose. "What has Jane told you?"

Rose took a seat across from her and clasped her hands on the table. "I don't beat around the bush. My first husband was an idiot. Abusive and mean. It took a toll on me, until he finally died. But when married to him, I hid all kinds of things. A *gut* friend and our bishop slowly pulled the truth out of me and it was like releasing a poison. I'd like to help you."

Miriam lowered her head in shame. "Your kind, but I don't deserve it."

"None of us deserve forgiveness. Now, I'm going to make as many Christmas cookies as possible to sell to the English. Do you want to join me?"

Jane scooted behind Aunt Miriam and shook her head. *N-O* she wanted to scream.

"And Jane will be here helping and maybe over time, you'll know why you're sorry and need forgiveness. God needs time to work on a human heart." She raised an eyebrow to Jane. "Jane learned in New York that God makes all things beautiful in his time, but it does take time."

"I'm willing," Miriam croaked out, her voice breaking.

Rose's eyes told her she should do the same, but Jane turned and left the house, not even taking her cape.

Karen Anna Vogel

Chapter 21
White as Snow

*J*ane burst into Luke and Moses's clock shop. "Can I help in here?"

Luke frowned. "You look pale. What's wrong?"

"My aunt came over to so-call ask for forgiveness and Rose offered to include her in our Christmas cookie sale," she fumed. "Without asking me!"

Luke looked over at his *daed* as if asking permission to leave, and Moses nodded. "Jane, let's take a ride over to Yoder's. Haven't done any Christmas shopping yet." He slid his arm through hers, leading her from the workshop. "Please calm down. I don't want you getting a migraine."

"I'm trying," Jane snapped. "I just thought the little house could be my haven, but not with Aunt Miriam coming and going."

"I agree that Rose spoke too hastily. But didn't you say Rose had a hard marriage?"

An icy spot under the newly fallen snow made Jane slip, so she clung on to Luke. "*Jah*, her first husband."

"Well, maybe Rose was moved with compassion, just like Jesus was."

Jane hadn't considered that. Her aunt looked simply horrible and knowing Rose's giving heart, she was reaching out already in her new community while on vacation.

"My *mamm's* so excited about us getting hitched and I think a little jealous of Rose. Why not bake with her?"

She pulled Luke near. "I'd like that." They went towards the little *dawdyhaus* so Jane could get her outer bonnet and cape. She noticed Ruth's bird feeders were filled, and peanuts were put out for squirrels, but starlings bullied away all the songbirds and even squirrels. Aunt Miriam was a starling and although she could molt and grow new feathers, she was still the same nasty woman deep down.

~*~

After shopping at Yoder's, Luke hauled bag after bag of baking supplies onto his *mamm's* table. "A gift from Jane."

Ruth ran to embrace her. "I don't need all this."

"*Jah*, we do. I'd love to have a baking frolic with my future *mamm-in-law*."

Ruth's eyes misted. "Jane, I'm so happy for you and Luke, but do you forgive me for pushing too hard?"

Jane, feeling at home, slid onto the table's bench. "I don't understand. Pushed too hard?"

Ruth sat across from Jane. "I told Luke to get over it with you up there in New York. I thought you'd say no, and I was kind of pushing Luke towards Lauren King. But I always hoped you would be my daughter."

Jane soaked in this confession, which she found refreshing with no barriers between them. "I'm glad you did push him to propose and consider Lauren. That's what broke me or woke me up. Losing Luke, just the thought of it made me realize I wanted to spend my life with him."

Ruth wiped her brow with a handkerchief. "I'm glad."

She peered up at Luke. "So, son, you have me to thank, *jah*?"

Luke put a hand on Jane's shoulder. "There was never anything between Lauren and me. Jane's the only girl for me, ever since I was fourteen."

"*Ach*, that's so sweet," Ruth gushed. "When's the wedding?"

"Maybe we can plan it while we bake?" Jane suggested.

"But what date? Do *yinz* want to get married soon or wait until spring or wait a year?"

"Wait a year?" Jane and Luke both blurted, and then stared at each other.

"I think you two need a wedding sooner than later," Ruth suspected.

"*Jah*," Luke said, "but where can we live if we have a winter wedding?"

"*Ach*, a winter wedding. I always dreamed of a winter wedding," Jane said, her hands pressed to her heart.

Ruth's face split with a smile. "Jane, you of all people deserve to have some dreams come true. A winter wedding you will have."

"*But where will we live?*" Luke asked again. "We have to wait until February to dig out the foundation on the house. Ground's frozen solid."

Ruth put up both hands as if she wasn't listening to her son. "Leave it to Jane and me."

When Jane's eyes met Ruth's, she remembered coming to this house, sitting at this table, wishing that she could have Ruth as a *mamm*, and it was happening. Who cared when the wedding was? Spring was just as good. It was a trifle compared to what she'd gain. But then reality set in; the bride's family paid for the wedding. "I can't get married," she blurted.

"What?" Luke and Ruth asked, aghast in unison.

"I still don't have any money. I don't even have a hope chest. Who will host it?"

Ruth let out a loud sigh of relief. "Jane, you near gave me heart failure."

"Jane, the *Gmay* furnished the little house. It's all yours," Luke informed.

"It's not Rose's too?" she asked, bewildered.

"She's only here on vacation, *jah?*" Ruth quipped.

"I don't know. She talks as if she's here for a long while."

"Well, that house is yours and you and Luke can live in it when wed."

"Where will Rose live?" Jane asked, looking to Luke for an answer.

Luke cocked an eyebrow at his *mamm*. "With you?"

Ruth glanced around her large kitchen. "This kitchen is my domain, but I can share it for a little while if it makes you both happy to wed."

"And we can get married here in this house?" Luke asked.

Ruth's face was aglow. "I was hoping so."

~*~

That night as Jane lay reading *Jane Eyre* again, a light flashed on her bedroom window. *Jonas? It couldn't be!* Her heart in her throat, she crossed the room to look outside. Luke? Had they always done this in Punxsutawney, but she didn't know it? Well, she was never courted, so she didn't know. She quickly tied her hair into a bun at the nape of her neck, followed by a black bandana, and grabbed a long robe that covered everything.

She tip toed down the steps, actually thankful for Rose's snoring, and let Luke in. "Is something wrong?"

He scooped her into his arms. "You tell me. You're skittish."

"Skittish? How do you mean?" Jane was trying her best to adapt back to Punxsutawney and thought she was doing quite well.

"I see fear in your eyes, or is it doubt?"

She led him by the hand into the living room, landing on the loveseat. "Luke, I have no doubts about marrying you."

He studied her in the dim room as his eyes adjusted. "Then what's wrong? I'm afraid..."

"Of what?" she asked, taking his hand and kissing it.

He scratched the back of his neck. "I don't know. But I see fear in you and you could fight or fly."

She cocked her head. "Meaning?"

"Well, when an animal is afraid, they either fight or fly away. It's called the fight or flight syndrome and I see it in you and it scares me."

That he would care so much about the inner turmoil that she was desperately trying to hide, melted her heart. "I'm nervous about many things. Rose talks about the wedding cake so much, and I don't want a big wedding. If I had it my way, it would be thirty people or less."

"Because you're afraid of burdening my parents and

embarrassed that your family isn't contributing?" he inquired.

"*Nee.* I don't want my Aunt Miriam there. She still unnerves me. I hear her talking to Rose and its bringing back bad feelings"

"And?"

"You'll laugh if I tell you." She felt heat rise in her face even though there was a chill in the room, the woodstove needing a log thrown in.

"I promise not to laugh," he said, concern heard in his voice.

"Jane Eyre only had four people at her wedding. There, I said it."

Luke chuckled. "But the wedding was called off."

She pinched his cheek playfully. "How do you know?"

He leaned down and kissed the side of her prayer *kapp*. "I read the book when you were in New York. Thought it might help me understand you."

Jane twisted up her mouth to stifle a laugh, but it soon came out. "And what did you learn?"

He rubbed his eyes. "Not much."

She pulled away, in disbelief. "You didn't read the whole thing."

"*Jah*, I did." Luke hit his knee. "*Ach*, one thing. I know that you're not plain, Jane. You're beautiful on the inside and out, and I can't wait to make you my bride. I'm as impatient as Mr. Rochester, dragging Jane to the little chapel."

She laughed. "I feel the same. I can't wait to marry you, but I won't be getting over my feelings for my Aunt

Miriam anytime soon. If she's there, the day will have a dark cloud over it."

"So put me and my *mamm*'s mind at rest, and let's set a date."

"I love snow. Would January be too soon?"

"Can't wait 'til February or we'll run into Groundhog Day crowds."

"Can't have it on January sixth, since it's a day of fasting, being Old Christmas."

"Can I tell *Mamm* January and we can get all the details down pat tomorrow?"

Jane stared at the rag rug. "What about my Aunt Miriam? I want my cousins there, but not her."

Luke held her tight. "Let's trust the Lord on that one."

~*~

Over the next few days, Jane tried to bake Christmas cookies at her aunt's house, the setting of her nightmares. Rose was challenging her at every turn to walk towards forgiveness, but why? She still talked about her first husband with contempt etched into her tone. Was there something about Aunt Miriam she could identify with? Or did Aunt Miriam tell her a falsehood about Jane, making Rose more compassionate towards her? Her aunt had fooled the community for ages, she could turn Rose on her!

Jane cranked the handle of the sifter faster, watching flour and baking powder explode into the bowl, making a puff cloud.

Clara, right next to her for support, flung some flour at Jane. "Are you getting me back?"

"What?" Jane asked, coming out of her daydreaming.

"On Sister Day, when we baked and threw flour." Clara leaned towards Jane and whispered, "Don't think *Mamm* will allow us."

Of course her Aunt Miriam wouldn't allow anything fun or that included cleaning up afterwards. She was a joy killer, for sure and certain.

Sarah scooted over. "Let's try. Flour's easy to clean up." Before anyone could stop her, Sarah took a heaping scoop of flour in a tablespoon and hurled it into Clara's face.

"Sarah!" Clara screamed. "Freeman is coming over. Look at me!"

Rose snuck up behind Sarah and soon it was 'snowing' flour onto her black scarf tied at the nape of her neck. "What's *gut* for the goose is *gut* for the gander."

"Stop," Miriam commanded with clenched fists. "We can't afford to waste flour."

"Come, come, now, Miriam," Rose said, a lilt in her voice as if to raise Miriam's mood. "A little fun never hurt anyone." She confidently crossed the kitchen, a bag of white flour in tow. "I dare you to throw a fistful of flour at me."

Miriam stomped a foot. "Rose, grow up!"

"Why?" Rose opened the bag and took a pinch of flour. "I'm still quite a *kinner* inside and it keeps me young."

Miriam looked past Rose, straight at Jane, contempt written all over her face. She ran towards the utility room and the back door banged shut.

"I better check on her," Clara insisted. "She can't be alone."

"Jane, you go," Rose said, sympathetically.

"Why me? *Nee*, how about Sarah? She's the *boppli* of the family and doesn't get whipped."

Rose's eyes narrowed. "Jane, you're going to be twenty-one in January and you're still afraid of a spanking?"

She wanted to scream '*Whipping! Not a spanking!*' But she had learned to read Rose. It was as if she did know something and wanted Jane to know, too. *What?* "Okay, Rose, if you insist." She exited the house through the utility room, grabbing her cape but no outer bonnet, since the weather was mild compared to New York. She heard Peanut whimpering and picked up her pace. Had her aunt kicked him? Why did she bring him to this awful place, too afraid her uncle would show up?

But when she got within a few yards, she recognized Peanut wasn't crying but romping about, playing. She peeked through the crack in the barn door, and was not prepared for what she saw: Aunt Miriam crying while holding Peanut's neck. She backed away and held her thumping heart. What should she do?

"God, ah, God, I'm a wretched woman. Please forgive me for all my sins. All the hurt I see in Jane, was my fault. I didn't speak up. I was afraid. Danki for Rose being put into Jane's life. Jane deserved an aunt like her, bold and not a woman beat down to think she was no better than a worm."

Like the melting snow under her feet, Jane's heart did

the same. She ran into the barn. "Aunt Miriam, you were like a prisoner, too."

Jane held out her arms, but her aunt lowered her head. "I don't deserve forgiveness."

Jane remembered *The Jesus Prayer* book and the short ancient prayer broken down word by word. She went to pet Peanut, the big lug of a dog being common ground. "I've changed, too. I know I'm a sinner. And I've held such hatred towards you. Will you forgive me?"

Aunt Miriam buried her face into Peanut's neck.

"I learned a prayer that helped me see this. When I lived in Cherry Creek, I was exposed to temptations I never knew existed. I prayed a prayer, 'Lord Jesus Christ, Son of God, have mercy on me, a sinner.' And every time I prayed it, I felt a mix of sorrow for my sin and love from God; gratitude for forgiving me."

By the shaking shoulders, Jane could tell her aunt was now sobbing, trying to hide her tears.

"We've all sinned and fallen short of the glory of God," Jane said, putting a hand on her aunt's shoulder, trying to soothe her. "That's in the Bible for all of us."

Aunt Miriam turned to Jane and clung to her. "Can God forgive me?"

Shocked at the love that poured out of her heart towards her aunt, she knew it was a miracle. This love came from God, who lived in her heart. "I'm sure he forgives you. He takes our sins and makes them white as snow."

Her aunt could not speak, so Jane just held her, letting this woman she now saw with new eyes cry out all the sorrow pent up deep.

Karen Anna Vogel

Chapter 22
Not Plain!

Jane flew into the clock shop the next morning. "Luke!"

He looked up, his safety glasses making his eyes appear much larger.

"Can we talk?" She glanced over at Moses. "Only a minute."

Moses nodded with a grin.

After dusting off wood chips, Luke put on his coat and stepped outside with Jane. She threw her arms around him. "It works!"

He stared at her, dumbstruck. "What works?"

"Prayer! Looking to God, as Jane Eyre always said. And we can have a wedding with Aunt Miriam seated right up front with me."

"What? You mean Rose?"

Jane let out a laugh, even to herself sounding a bit giddy, but she was overjoyed. "Remember when we prayed for our wedding? Giving it to God? Well, the only obstacle was my feelings for Aunt Miriam, who I knew had to be invited."

Luke cupped her cheeks. "Jane, we need to talk about this when I have time. Lots of clock orders, but I'm so happy for you. So, are you saying you want a big wedding after all?"

She kissed his cheek. "Do you know Peanut helped us reconcile?"

Luke erupted in laughter. "Seems like you have a lot to say."

She jumped up on him, hugging his neck. "Luke, I feel so free. Maybe too free, but I never knew how bitterness weighed me down."

He squeezed her tight. "Coming over for supper tonight?"

"Rose is having a dinner just for Aunt Miriam and me. But I can ask if you can come. Truth be told, I'm a little nervous."

"Just give me a holler, neighbor for now."

They fell into a mutual kiss that lingered a little too long. Jane, feeling shy afterwards, said, "Maybe I'm a little too free?"

He leaned to kiss her again. "I can finally say I'm glad you read that Jane Eyre book if it made you so free."

~*~

That night the wind kicked up and spit snow on the windows of the *dawdyhaus*, but there was only warmth inside among Jane and her Aunt Miriam. As Rose served dessert after a delicious meal of stew and biscuits, Miriam finally unveiled what was in the contents of the present placed on the China closet.

When Jane saw the small quilt her aunt lifted up, she tried to be surprised, but she'd helped place sheets of paper between the many antique quilts stored in a cedar chest in the attic.

"Read what it says, Jane," Aunt Miriam said, showing her the embroidered message on a corner. Jane held it up and read:

Joanna, the grace and mercy of God.

"Joanna? Who's she?" Jane asked, fingering the threads, so skillfully stitched.

Aunt Miriam placed a hand on Jane's shoulder. "It's your *grossmammi's* baby blanket." Her hand started to tremble. "We should have given it to you earlier, but..."

"Why me?" Jane asked.

"Well, Jane is short for Joanna. Joanna was your *grossmammi's* name and you were named after her."

She gulped, willing back tears. "I think my *mamm* told me this as a *kinner*. So long ago."

"Well, your *grossmammi* died giving birth to your *daed*, poor woman. She had diabetes and there were complications."

Rose sat a cup of tea on the table in front of Jane. "I'm still calling you Jane," she quipped. "It fits you."

Jane just couldn't stop staring at the stitching and then the green and white patchwork quilt. Her *grossmammi* stitched these? She felt close to this woman who was never talked about. "What was she like?" she near whispered.

"Malachi said her name fit her," Aunt Miriam informed, settling back in her chair. "But he was only five when she passed and his memories were limited."

"What do you mean, limited?" Rose asked, sipping her tea.

"Well, he was sent off to live with neighbors after her death. They near raised him. Malachi would go live with his *daed* and new *bruder* on weekends, but his *daed* had a farm to run, so over the years the boys were raised by half at home and half on the farm."

Jane's head spun.

Miriam took a handkerchief from her apron pocket and dotted the tears from her eyes. "Malachi favored your *daed*, but his name wasn't in the will. Hurt him deeply, so when fire took the house, Malachi took you and the money from the auction. Lots of land and outbuilding fetched quite a bit."

Feeling sympathy for her uncle for the first time was so foreign to Jane, she fought it. Maybe her uncle was cruel to her *daed* and *grossdaddi*. Her *daed's* father was someone she never even thought about. "When did my *grossdaddi* die?"

Miriam pressed her index finger around the rim of the tiny tea cup. "When the boys were old enough to marry. I remember him. He was a lot like your *daed*. Malachi was the odd one in the bunch and I felt sorry for him, not being his *daed's* favorite." She paused to sip her tea. "Your *daed* was all set with a farm and all when he wed, but Malachi and I struggled."

The front door opened, ushering in wind and a chill. "Luke!" Jane exclaimed, putting a hand out to him. This was too much to take in, as sympathy for her uncle grew and she tried to squelch it.

He gripped her hand and took a seat. "Jane…you're so…. you're blushing. Everything alright?"

"Call her Joanna," Rose quipped. "She just learned she was named after her *grossmammi* and is in a flutter."

Luke smashed his lips together, and Jane could see he was trying to bite down a hardy laugh. "What's so funny?"

He exhaled, having held his breath. "After you feeling like a plain Jane and your obsession with *Jane Eyre*, I'll call you Joanna from now on."

"Plain Jane?" Rose gawked. "She's not plain at all."

Luke put a hand up. "Tell her that. Someday she'll actually believe she's a beauty."

~*~

Dear Bishop Byler,

My wedding date has been set. It's the third Tues. of January, the 19th my birthday. The best present I could receive is for you and Martha to attend the wedding. Actually, I'd like for you to perform the ceremony. My bishop here understands.

Thank you for praying for me and thank you for encouraging me to forgive my aunt and uncle. I understand my aunt much more, and maybe my uncle, too. He was compared to my daed and not the favorite. He also might have blamed my daed for his mamm's death, since she died in childbirth.

No sign of Uncle Malachi, but I'm no longer afraid of him showing up in town. I can't explain why. Maybe it's because I'll be Mrs. Luke Miller soon.

Please tell the Hershbergers hello for me, even Jonas. Rose and I pray for him.

Speaking of Rose, she loves it down here and will have a longer vacation than she thought.

Let me know if you can come to the wedding when you or Martha write back.

Jane

~*~

Jane, feeling freer to be at her aunt's house, went over often to bake cookies over the next week. Rose also had a cake recipe to try—gingerbread cake. Jane wanted a gingerbread cake with snow icing to match the season and many gingerbread men and women without faces were made to add to not only the Christmas feast, but also her wedding.

One day, she decided to go into her old bedroom and see how she'd react to her former prison cell. But when she entered, memories of running and bolting the door didn't rush at her, like she feared. This little room held no nightmarish memories at all upon first seeing it.

So, she sat on the small thin bed, waiting for anger, rage and other feelings she'd harbored to surface, but they didn't. She was calm. How odd, she thought.

She picked up the candlestick that still lived on the little table. No envious thoughts of others having oil lamps bombarded her.

Stumped, she wondered if she was just too happy to be married for these horrid feelings to flee so quickly. But then she remembered Luke saying, *Jane isn't plain but beautiful on the outside and inside*, and she felt beautiful on the inside for the first time. No mental images haunting her, or bitterness, but the peace she'd always craved after. *Lord Jesus Christ, Son of God, have mercy on me, a sinner,* she prayed. Yes, all have sinned, no one was perfect except God. And as the days led to Christmas, she was ever so joyful that His son came into the world to take our sin and make us clean, white as snow. This is how she now felt: clean, white as snow.

Elated that her past couldn't disturb her anymore, she left the room and went up the narrow stairs into the attic. Now that she knew her *grossmammi's* signature, she wanted to go through the quilts. Did she make a one for her uncle? Did the dear woman make a quilt for her newborn baby, her *daed*?

As Jane neared the cedar chest that held these treasures, it was open and empty. Empty? Had someone who came to help her aunt wash them, not knowing they were old and needed special care? Jane near flew down the attic steps and then downstairs to the first floor.

Jeremiah and Jacob had cookies in their hands, held up in mid-air, staring at her. "Did you see a ghost or something?" Jacob joked.

Aunt Miriam crossed the kitchen. "Jane, you're as white as a ghost. Not that we believe in them," she turned to eye Jacob with squinted eyes.

"The quilts in the attic. Who took them?"

Clara, who was rolling out gingerbread, had concern carved onto her face. "No one took them. I made sure no one was allowed up there."

Sarah stepped forward sheepishly. "I went up there after *Mamm* showed me *grossmammi*'s blanket. There was mud on the floor."

Clara turned Sarah, making her face her. "Mud? What are you talking about?"

"Don't get mad at me. I didn't track mud through the house." Her chin quivered. "I cleaned all the footprints upstairs and downstairs, too."

Aunt Miriam paced the floor. "Where did the muddy

footprints start, Sarah?"

"From the front door."

Jane knew the Amish didn't use their front doors. "Have we been robbed?"

Aunt Miriam took a seat. "They know how much an antique quilt can fetch, too, most likely."

Rose, who'd been as quiet as a mouse, spoke up. "We can ask around the *Gmay*. Maybe someone did take them to be cleaned and maybe someone did come in leaving muddy tracks."

The room was silent, only the faint sound of blue jays and cardinals fighting at the birdfeeder could be heard. They all looked at each other and went back to baking and the boys back to eating.

Chapter 23
A Christmas Confession

The one-room schoolhouse was decked with paper chains, strung popcorn and branches of pine on the window sills and it made a perfect setting for the annual Christmas Eve program. Jane sat next to Sarah, who was anxious about reciting a poem she'd written and she clung to Jane for support.

The smell of cookies and hot chocolate wafted to the rafters and Jane thought she'd be battling envy, since she never was invited to the school program, but if a sliver of envy came near, she gave thanks for what she did that day instead; she read the entire Gospel of Luke. She twisted up her lips. And now she was marrying Luke. Too many things to be thankful for to let self-pity rob her.

But as the program continued, Jane felt as if someone was staring at her. She turned, and the *Englisher* man quickly turned his head. He was seated next to Vinny, who shot her a wink and mouthed a 'Hi, Babe'. Jane knew her eyelid was starting to twitch. Surely Jonas hadn't come down to see her. *Ach, Lord, just when things were going so smoothly.* She kept her eyes on the man, who had on a knitted cap, waiting for Jonas to look up, but he appeared to be talking to Vinny, who had a smirk on his face.

After the program, she'd find Jonas and tell him to go right back to Cherry Creek. He'd probably give a sob story about how he missed his *grossmammi,* but Rose was not ready to see her wayward grandson.

285

Much to Jane's dismay, a very large woman took a seat on the bench, blocking Jane's view of nearly half the audience. She turned around and started to grind her teeth.

Luke leaned towards her. "What is it?"

Not wanting to unnerve Luke on this blessed day, but curious as ever, she just said she forgot something and made her way out of the rows of benches and looked over to where Vinny sat. But the man was no longer there. She ran outside and saw the image of a man walking briskly down the road. Headed in the direction of their *dawdyhaus*. "Jonas!" she yelled, but he broke into a run.

Flustered, she entered the schoolroom again and through the flickering candlelight, she saw Vinny, for the first time concern on his face. He put up both hands as if under arrest.

~*~

"How *furhoodled* I acted last night," Jane said to Rose as they placed hot side dishes in boxes, soon to be delivered to the Miller's Christmas dinner.

"*Jah*, to think Jonas would care so much about his *grossmammi* is *furhoodled*."

Jane sighed. "*Ach*, Rose, he loves you. He just needs to grow up."

Rose was as chipper as a little bird. "Jane, I'm just being sarcastic, which I need to work on."

"Work on? I like your spunk," Jane quipped as they took their boxes and stood on the little porch.

"Well, Bishop Byler said I need to work on it," Rose

said, a lilt in her voice.

"*Ach,* you're pulling my leg."

Rose snickered. "You didn't ask me which Bishop Byler."

Jane stared at Rose. "You sound like a school girl with a crush. Do you mean the widower, Daniel Byler, the senior bishop?"

She looked as startled as a deer in headlights. "Jane. You know better."

"I know what better?"

Chin up, Rose padded down the porch steps. "Courting is done in secret."

~*~

An extra table was placed up against the long oak one, a long table cloth covering them both. A large stuffed turkey was the centerpiece, bowls of mashed potatoes, gravy boats filled to the brim, bread rolls, and green beans and asparagus matched the green leaves on Ruth's China plates. Jane opened the tureen of soup and took in the aroma of pumpkin soup. Joy filled her as the voices of her cousins were heard from the back door and her aunt, cheeks red from the frosty cold. She did have a family and once wed, they'd gather like this often. All but her uncle, which Jane still feared might show up at any time.

The thought escaped her mind when she felt the firm hand of Luke's taking hers, leading her into the living room. "Happy?"

"*Jah,*" she said, her lips slipping into a smile.

"You'll meet my *bruder* tomorrow on Second Christmas. *Mamm* and *Daed* seem a little disappointed the storm's keeping them in Smicksburg."

Jane had wondered why Ruth seemed a bit down in the mouth, but figured it was fatigue at making such a feast. "Well, we'll have to play plenty of board games, sing and make snow ice cream after dinner. Help keep their minds off their other *kinner.*"

Soon Ruth announced dinner was ready and Jane headed towards the coffee pot to serve the hot beverage but Luke didn't let her hand go. He pulled her into an embrace and kissed her forehead. "I love you, Jane. And you'll be Jane Miller in three weeks, *jah?*"

His eyes on her, filled with a deep down settled love and satisfaction, gave her a glimpse into what her life would be like as man and wife. It was something she noticed in Ruth and Moses' marriage and she was so grateful to be kin to this family, where love ruled supreme.

When they entered the kitchen, all eyes were fixed on them and they quickly took their seats. Moses sat at the head of the table and bowed his head, and they all followed suit, silently thanking God for the bounty before them. Jane reached for Luke's hand and squeezed it. He was her Christmas present.

After the prayer, all dug in to eat and Ruth stood behind Moses, clearing her throat. "We'd like to make an announcement." Her eyes pooled with tears. "The China on this table was given to me by my *grossmammi.*" She put her hand to a trembling chin. "Merry Christmas, Luke and Jane. It's yours now."

Jane gawked. "*Ach,* Ruth, we can't. It's too hard for

you to part with."

"*Jah, Mamm*, you're crying." He quickly made his way to her. "Don't cry."

"I-I'm happy," Ruth said, pushing Luke away playfully. "Thought you two would never get together, and I'm mighty happy. Can't a body be too happy?"

Jane ran to her and they embraced. "I always wanted you as a *mamm*," Jane blurted.

"*Danki*, and I've wanted you to be my *dochder*."

~*~

As the women cleared the table and made an assembly line to wash dishes, Jane kept noticing Ruth's uneasiness and left her position of dish drier and offered to wash dishes, telling Ruth to sit down and take a break. Ruth was determined to scrub the pans as well as the dishes, fiercely scrubbing the bottom of a stock pot.

Jane returned to drying dishes and made small talk with Clara. "How's Freeman?"

Clara's cheeks turned pink. "He's *wunderbar* to me. Some of his kin from Lancaster may be moving out this way, since land prices are cheaper."

"Where is he spending Christmas?"

"The Weavers had them over. You know, Jane, our *Gmay* seems so much closer. The tension is gone."

Jane knew her uncle was gone, someone who made everyone uneasy, but Clara didn't recognize it. "Are you missing your *daed*, today?" she dared to ask.

Clara shrugged. "Not really. It's nice to have a big dinner without fear of him exploding or criticizing. Jane, I've been wanting to say how sorry I am that I didn't speak up sooner, but I took the 'honor your *mamm* and *daed'* to an extreme. I know better now."

"*Ach,* Clara, he had us all tied up in knots. Do you really think you could have stood up to him?"

Clara wiped the delicate China plate and stacked it ever so carefully on the table. "We had a counselor come talk to us from the state. We almost had to go to different houses unless we could show things were stable. Luke stepped in along with Emma and other church members. The counselor said she was touched by all the community help and, well, we're all closer now. And there're no more secrets, and if anyone else in the *Gmay* suspects abuse, they're to speak up."

Jane pondered this knowledge for a while. Maybe by her leaving, it affected the whole community and they all changed, not being told to keep mum. How often she'd thought of her uncle's place as a white washed tomb, clean and sparkling on the outside, but just the opposite on the inside. Had following in the steps of Jane Eyre, even though a fictitious character, changed the whole *Gmay?*

Aunt Miriam brought a stack of wet dessert plates over. "Are you girls having a *gut* Christmas?"

"*Jah, Mamm,*" Clara chimed. "Are you okay?"

"*Ach,* why wouldn't I be okay? Do I look, you know, sick?"

Jane knew how embarrassed her aunt was about her mental breakdown. "You look just fine."

Miriam's face lifted into a merry look that Jane had never seen. "*Danki.* Feeling mighty fine."

~*~

As the day continued, Rose had everyone making snow ice cream, scoops of snow being brought in by the men. Luke kept reminding everyone to collect only white snow in front of the house, where none of his critters were allowed to wander.

Rose seemed so chipper and Jane took her mug of coffee over and settled in next to her as ice cream was shoveled down in the kitchen. "What are you knitting? And when did you go out in this storm to get your yarn?"

She held up a little white blanket. "A *boppli* blanket for charity and I walked back to the house myself. Not as old as the hills, you know."

Jane sipped the coffee. "But it's pelting down snow something fierce. You could have slipped."

Rose chuckled. "This is nothing compared to New York snow. Speaking of, did Bishop Byler say he's coming to your wedding?"

Jane nudged Rose. "Which Bishop Byler? Mine or yours here in Punxsutawney?"

Rose cackled. "You know which one I mean."

Jane did know who she meant. "*Jah*, he and Martha will come if the roads are *gut*."

The men came into the large living room, bowls of ice cream in tow. Moses asked everyone to sit down and Jane knew this was the special time to read from the Bible the Christmas story.

He stood in the circle of family and friends, licking his lips, eyes wide. "I have a Christmas present." He darted a gaze over at Ruth, who seemed to be encouraging him by her expression. "But I need to talk to *yinz* first. You see, Malachi has come back to the area, a very changed man. He's been living in Ohio after being a truck driver for a while."

Murmurs and groans echoed off the walls. Jane took Rose's hand, feeling ill.

"He came to the end of his rope and as the saying goes, that's where God finds some of us. So, while driving out in Ohio he met some Beachy Amish, and they took him in, and he got much needed counseling. He'd like to come in and tell his story and confess, but don't know if it would spoil your day."

Sarah jumped up. "God answered my prayers: see *Daed* on Christmas."

A hush fell over the room, but then Aunt Miriam said, "I'm willing, only if you are, Jane."

Luke crossed the room and sat at her feet. "You don't have to see him today or any other day."

"What about forgiveness that sets us free?" Rose near whispered to Jane and Luke.

Jane felt her heart jump into her throat. Not able to speak, she nodded to Moses.

Moses swiftly left the room and Jane looked out the window, not noticing an additional buggy had pulled up. Moses ran to it and soon she saw her uncle, hitching his horse to the post. *Lord, have mercy.*

Jane bit her fist, and Luke scooted on the couch next to her, placing a protective arm around her. When Malachi ambled into the room, Sarah ran to him, hugging him and crying up a storm of tears, but other family members had their faces set like cold marble.

"I came here to ask for forgiveness," Malachi started, being alone in the circle as Moses took a seat as well as Sarah.

"I'm a changed man, but I don't reckon you should believe me just by me saying it. I'll prove by my actions." He pulled at his black beard. "Well, I've been a bitter man most of my life. I was five when my *bruder* John was born, taking my *mamm's* life. I blamed John. And then as my *daed* seemed to favor John, my anger grew and I turned into Cain in the Bible. I was jealous of him. When he got the family farm, being the youngest, I was seething mad. My rage turned to him and his wife, long passed son, and Sammy and Jane." He turned meekly to Jane. "I'm so sorry. When you needed a family after yours was gone, I felt too guilty to look you in the eye. I hated my *bruder* but when he passed on, I realized I'd never have the chance to make things right. Jane, I just couldn't look you in the eye, because I saw my shame and hatred, you being so *gut* like your *daed* and *mamm.*"

Jane gulped and wiped perspiration forming above her lips. What had Jane Eyre done? She forgave her aunt. "I forgive you," she said mechanically.

Jeremiah growled. "You don't deserve it. You treated *mamm* bad, too. Made her cry and cry, while she kept saying you never loved her."

Malachi's composure crumbled and tears sprang to his eyes. "I always loved your *mamm*. Anything your Uncle John had, I wanted to ruin it. When he courted his wife, I tried to interfere, not even realizing why. Hatred and bitterness can blind you, but I-I, well, I've given my heart to Jesus and He's changing it from stone to clay."

Jacob crossed his arms. "*Daed*, you read your Bible before, beating us over the head with scripture. If I hadn't seen Jane being helped by the Bible, I'd be leaving the Amish."

Luke pulled Jane tighter. "She's been an example to us all, but I won't be having my bride to be skittish like a wounded cat with you around, Malachi. Over time, maybe, but like you said, you'll prove by your actions."

All this time, Jane noticed something in her uncle's countenance. It was like he was a real man and he was trying to share his real heart. Being under Luke's protection, she felt free to say, "Let he without sin cast the first stone." She rose and with legs that felt like Jell-O, she embraced her uncle. "I forgive you and I believe you're sincere."

He fell into Jane, sobbing, and Luke ran to help hold him up. Malachi got on his knees and cried out what seemed to be years of sorrow and regret. Miriam slowly went to him, kneeling beside him, whispering into his ear things no one else could hear. Aunt Miriam had grown a backbone when he was gone and Jane had a feeling that things would turn out right in time.

Today, as they celebrated the love of God who came to seek and save the lost, Jane caught a glimpse of the power of this love.

When Uncle Malachi regained his composure, he handed Jane an envelope. "Open it. An early wedding present."

Jane's shaking hands obeyed and a money order for forty-thousand dollars was made out to her. "I can't take this. My cousins and aunt need it."

"I sold my *mamm*'s quilts. Antique quilts in rare patterns fetch a *gut* price out in Ohio. Jane, the money from the farm was yours and I used it up. Please, accept it."

"For Pete's sake," Ruth crowed. "We thought they were stolen. Why didn't you say something?"

"Shame. Didn't think anyone would want to see me. I would have sent a check, but truth be told, when Christmas came closer and closer, I realized how much I needed my family. Snuck into the schoolhouse to see Sarah's program, but Jane saw me and chased me out."

Jane cocked her head. "It was you?" Nervous laughter escaped her. "I thought you were Jonas."

Rose raised a knitting needle. "My grandson," she informed.

Moses clapped his hands to get everyone's attention. "Now, Malachi plans to live with one of the elders and slowly work his way back into his family, if it's alright with you, Miriam. He wants to prove he's changed."

Miriam's face was pensive but hopeful. "I agree." She hugged Malachi and slowly Jeremiah and Jacob shook his hand and Clara hugged him.

Jane noticed they'd all changed. Not hovering under a rod of steel, but they seemed as equals. Jane Eyre's insistence that she be treated as an equal came to mind, and Jane wondered if she'd ever get that book out of her head.

Karen Anna Vogel

Epilogue

I've been married to Luke for two years now and I'm rocking our precious baby daughter, Johanna Grace, only six months old. As I nestle her in my arms this brisk January day, I reminisce. I was afraid when we first wed. I have to admit that I feared Luke would have a temper like my uncle, but as time passed and it was calm waters in our home, I realized just how much healing I needed. And the good part is that time and love do heal. Luke can get this pensive frown that scares me at times, but he makes sure I understand he's pondering before making a hard decision. For instance, building our house forced us to make many decisions. He looked at floor plans and he insisted that the foundation be built into the bank of the hill. Well, I wanted a basement with lots of windows. He said how a house keeps cooler if built into the bank and I understood. I don't know if that sounds revolutionary to many women, but it was for me. *Ach,* and when we spend so much money on food for wounded critters Luke still takes in, I go over our budget and I understand why we need it in the first place.

Ruth and I have coffee together every morning, rain, snow, sleet or hail. She's become my *mamm.* I've bonded tightly with all the Miller clan, some of Luke's female cousins are like sisters and we all go to work frolics of all sorts, but mostly canning bees. We celebrate birthdays once a month, and I don't see how Ruth has the energy for it all, but I see her deep satisfaction and Luke and I hope we're blessed with many *kinner* of our own.

Ach, I need to back up and tell you about my wedding day. Well, it was January 19th and it was no small affair. Ruth, Rose and my Aunt Miriam made such a fuss over me, and I was able to accept their love. It was a landmark for me, thinking I wasn't worth much. Three-hundred people attended, and to my utter shock, George Washington Kettle and his family came down with Bishop Byler and Martha. Not having much kin, it meant a lot to me. George said he wanted to wear traditional Seneca attire, wanting to see how the Amish would react, but said I was the bride and the center of attention. When he saw me in my new green dress with white apron and white *kapp,* he couldn't get over the fact that Amish do not wear wedding gowns and don't exchange wedding rings.

Emma and Clara were my attendants. Luke asked Freeman King to stand with him since Clara's still courting him. Luke had his cousin Allen be Emma's partner. They got married last month. *Praise be*! So, Emma comes to some of the Miller frolics, although she spends more time over at Allen's parents place in Smicksburg.

Rose made a three tiered gingerbread cake, like she promised, and on the top stood a 'gingerbread cookie couple' leaning towards each other. Lots of Christmas cookies were eaten and it gently snowed all day, making everything white. I felt it was the Lord's doing, a sign of a clean slate and new life. All the dark frozen ground was covered with sparkling white.

My cousins are doing well, along with my Aunt

Miriam. It was very hard on them the day of my wedding, since the love all around only accentuated all they didn't have in their home. Jeremiah and Jacob wanted to come live with Luke and me, but being in the *dawdyhaus,* we had to say no.

Here's what happened concerning my uncle. He lived with Senior Bishop Daniel Byler and was slowly reunited with his family. It took nearly eight months, until the boys felt like they could share the same home. They were ever so protective of their *mamm* and sisters, but when real change came to Uncle Malachi, they gave it a trial run. He's been home with them ever since.

I see a change in Uncle Malachi as well. Luke wants to be home when he visits me, but Peanut gives him peace of mind if he would just pop over without remembering the rule. For instance, he stopped by the other day to bring yet another toy for Johanna and then apologized since Luke wasn't home. I'm not afraid of him any longer and hold no unforgiveness in my heart, but I think since Luke is my husband, he has a harder time with him. Aunt Miriam comes over often and I look at her like a dear aunt. She looks younger by ten years as she vows it's easy to live with Malachi. Well, we still need some time to tell for sure and certain, in my opinion.

As for Rose, she's still on vacation, living in the *dawdyhaus,* writing often to her wayward grandson, Jonas, who is completely English now. I think her coming here for a 'spell' was good because I've seen Daniel Byler's buggy over at Rose's place and she keeps beating around the bush about marriage. I tell her to "Look to God" and she laughs in that knowing way, since Jane Eyre says it throughout the book. Rose has read it several times and I wonder if it's opened her heart up to a new adventure, like it did for me. "Independence always has fences though," Rose said. "There's no such thing as real freedom, as we all need to submit to each other in community." She's right.

Sometimes I get so overcome with love for Luke I say, "You're a consistent Christian and a kind gentleman" just what Charlotte Bronte heard people say of her husband. Luke feels my forehead, asking if I'm ill. We laugh often as I quote from that book that God used to change my life: *Jane Eyre*.

Discussion Guide

1. Jane was spunky, speaking her mind at fourteen, but over six years of neglect and abuse, she's 'a hollow tree, the wind being able to break her.' Colossians 3: 21says: *Fathers, do not aggravate your children, or they will become discouraged.* Jane read the Bible. Psalm 119 tells of the joy and strength the Word of God gives. Read it and discuss.

2. Jane grew up under too much control. Once free, she yearned for independence. Can too strict a rules cause us to swing to the other end of the pendulum? Do you think Jane's trip to New York was a wise choice or was she just looking for greener pastures?3,

3. Luke Miller has been a constant in Jane's life since fourteen. He loves Jane unconditionally, even though he flares up at times. How important is it to nurture those ever faithful friends who walk down hard roads with us?

4. What are some of the tell-tell signs that Jonas Hershberger is a charmer? Proverbs 31:30 says:

Charm is deceptive, and beauty does not last; but a woman who fears the Lord will be greatly praised. (This applies to men, too.)

5. Rose is honest with herself about her first marriage. Do you think it aided in her healing and ability to love someone again? ~*~Or, do you think Rose shouldn't have been so outspoken?6. The Seneca in Western New York kept to some of their heritage and culture. They have proverbs about forgiveness and Jane gets a bit

agitated by George. Why? Can the truth hurt, like the saying goes?

7. What do you think of Bishop Byler? Did his care and concern for Jane, and being like a father figure aid in her healing? Can listening and kindness really make that much of a difference in someone's life?

8. Jane is told to rest for a season. Resting to heal emotionally, not making any major decisions, is so foreign to many. Resting can make us restless, thinking of hard times, but 1 Peter 5:7 says to a persecuted church:

Casting all your cares [all your anxieties, all your worries, and all your concerns, once and for all] on Him, for He cares about you [with deepest affection, and watches over you very carefully]. (Amplified Bible)

Peter was a fisherman and knew casting was hard, repetitive task. When I cast my cares on God, sometimes I feel like it boomerangs right back to me for days. So, it takes time. Discuss a time when you've had a season to rest and cast cares and concerns on God.

9. When Jane returns to Punxsutawney, she is given something tangible, a little house, something sacrificial the Amish paid for and built to show Jane they were sorry for not intervening in her life. How important is sacrificial giving verses a simple "I'm sorry."?

10. When Jane sees Aunt Miriam, she darts away. Is she showing poor character or is this a normal reaction?

11. Being 'forced' to bake with Miriam is painful to Jane, but Rose thinks it's the first step in towards forgiveness. Can we start to forgive without being having the warm-fussy feelings towards someone who offended

us?

A mother of a victim of the Nickle Mine School Shooting said on the PBS documentary, 'The Amish', said something worth pondering.

To me, when I think of forgiving, it doesn't mean that you have forgotten what he's done. But it means that you have released unto God the one who has offended you. And you have given up your right to seek revenge. I place the situation in God's hands and just accept that this is the way it was. And I choose not to hold it against Charles because it really doesn't help me anyway.

12. We find at the end of the story the root of Uncle Malachi's bad behavior. Finding the root of the fruit is helpful for us to be empathetic. Jane should have spoken up and abuse is never right, but my mom always said, "You've never walked in his shoes." Do you agree with not judging other, not knowing their past circumstances? Should there be a proving time, like the Amish had for Malachi?

13. Charlotte Bronte, the author of Jane Eyre, was a devout Christian. She often had Jane Eyre say "Look to God" in her novel. After reading *The Life of Charlotte Bronte,* I discovered her life was very sad and she 'Looked to God' her whole life. If you had a motto, what would it be?

14. Jane reads a book about an ancient orthodox prayer, The Jesus Prayer. *'Lord Jesus Christ, Son of God, have mercy on me a sinner'*. I stumbled upon this prayer while writing this book, after finding out some tragic news. I had no words, so grieved. The Lord's Prayer, I prayed as

well as the Jesus Prayer. I don't believe it's 'vain repetition.' Vain means empty. I'm saying them with a full heart. Do you have a prayer or can you write one yourself to use when in a hard season of life?

15. Of all the characters in Plain Jane, who is your favorite and why? Did you learn something from this character or make a life decision? Books have a way of helping us see into human nature. I gleaned so much by reading *Jane Eyre*, I highly recommend reading it.

Rose's Cookie & Treat Recipes

Ginger Cookies—Gingerbread Men

⅔ cup shortening

½ cup brown sugar

2 tsp. ginger

1 tsp. cinnamon

¼ tsp. cloves or allspice

1½ tsp. salt

1 egg

¾ cup molasses

3 cups flour, sifted

1 tsp. soda

½ tsp. baking powder

Cream together shortening, brown sugar, spices and salt. Add the egg, mix thoroughly. Add molasses and blend. Sift together twice the flour, soda, baking powder and add to the molasses mixture. Stir well and chill. Roll out a fourth of the dough at a time, on floured board to a little more than ⅛ inch thick. Cut with gingerbread man cutters or other shapes. Bake on greased cookie sheets in moderately hot (375-f) oven, 8 to 10 minutes. Cool before decorating.

Christmas Butter Cookies

1 cup soft butter

½ cup brown sugar, packed

2¼ cups flour, sifted

Cream butter until it resembles whipped cream and slowly add the sugar, beating well. Add flour gradually and blend thoroughly. Wrap in waxed paper and chill for several hours. Knead dough slightly on floured board, form into a smooth ball. Roll to about ⅛ inch thick and cut to desired shapes. Place on ungreased cookie sheets and bake in moderate oven (350-f) about 12 minutes. When cold decorate with butter icing, candied fruit, etc.

Anise Cookies

6 eggs, separated
1 cup powdered sugar
1 cup flour, sifted
3 tsps. anise seed

Beat egg yolks until thick and foamy. Beat egg whites stiff and combine with egg yolks. Gradually add the powdered sugar and mix lightly. Sift flour and add to the egg mixture together with the anise seed. Drop from teaspoon on greased cookie sheet, spacing about 1 inch apart. Chill in refrigerator overnight. Bake in slow oven (300-f) for about 12 minutes.

Snow Ice Cream

10 cups of fresh, white snow
10 ounce can sweetened condensed milk
1 tsp vanilla extract

Three ingredients, a large bowl and wooden spoons is all that's required. The sweetened milk actually freezes, which makes the ice cream, so if it gets soupy, add more snow.

In the bowel of snow, pour condensed milk and vanilla. (You can substitute other flavors. With wooden spoons fold over mixture until it looks like yummy ice cream and dig in. Very simple.

Maple Syrup Snow Taffy

Nothing is easier and fun to make when the snow piles up than taffy. It's really a candy. Laura Ingalls Wilder made it, so it goes back decades, a fun winter activity passed on and not unique only to the Amish. All you do is get white packed snow and pour maple syrup over it. When we lived around Cherry Creek, it froze instantly, but for those outside the Snow Belt, you may want to put in the freezer until you can pull up the stiff new candy you've just made. Yum! And pure maple syrup is healthy, so it's a guilt-free treat.

Karen Anna Vogel

About The Author

Karen Anna Vogel writes stories that take readers into a real life situation where they can learn to solve their problems in a Biblical manner or by the Amish philosophy of life.

Karen has worn many 'bonnets': stay-at-home mom to four kids, home school vet, substitute teacher, wife to Tim for 35 years, Christian counselor. Writing has always been a constant passion, so Karen was thrilled to meet her literary agent, Joyce Hart, in a bookstore...gabbing about Amish fiction.

After her kids flew the coop, she delved into writing, and ten books later, she's passionate about portraying the Amish and small town life in a realistic way, many of her novels based on true stories. Living in rural, PA, she writes about all the beauty around her: rolling hills, farmland, the sound of buggy wheels.

She's a graduate from Seton Hill University (Psychology & Elementary Education) and Andersonville Theological Seminary (Masters in Biblical Counseling). In her spare time she enjoys knitting, photography, homesteading, and sitting around bonfires with family and friends.

The best place to chat and connect with Karen is at her author page on Facebook at:
www.facebook.com/VogelReaders.

Karen Anna Vogel

Plain Jane

Printed in Great Britain
by Amazon